SUMMER LIGHTNING

SUMMER LIGHTNING

MAGIC AT MYERS BEACH™ BOOK THREE

ALAN B. GIBSON

Published by Florid Romance
an imprint of LMBPN Publishing
PMB 196, 2540 South Maryland Pkwy
Las Vegas, NV 89109

Version 1.00, June 2023
eBook ISBN: 979-8-88541-754-9
Print ISBN: 979-8-88878-428-0

THE SUMMER LIGHTNING TEAM

Thanks to the JIT Readers

Jan Hunnicutt
Karla Hull
Lex Robertson

Editor
The SkyFyre Editing Team

To Robert Scott Beard, my real-life heat lightning for thirty-one years.

CHAPTER ONE

Theos

Clipping the wings of my fairy subjects will no doubt make me the most hated king in the history of fairy kings. I take that back. Grounding is a better choice of words, since my measure has nothing to do with the unspeakable act of removing a fairy's wings. It's only a prohibition on flying. But, regardless of what they call it, they'll hate me.

Taking away such a treasured pillar of the fairy lifestyle is unfortunate, especially following the unpopular round of fairy dust rationing I had to impose a short time earlier. Everyone has been on edge for a long time. But due to the invasion of the Third Kingdom next door, even fairies can understand that we can't have everyone flitting around and getting caught in the mayhem.

The ban is also a temporary safety measure. Without the restriction, fairies might accidentally fly off too far and discover that they don't have enough juice to return. And while nobody likes the cutbacks, my experts tell me that for the time being, the clampdown on flying will cut our outlay of dust in half.

These efforts will also free up precious supplies for what fairies need it for most: their regular dustings. Granting wishes and sweeping away people's bad dreams consumes a lot of energy, and routine maintenance infuses them with magic and keeps fairies robust and sharp. The dusting also ensures strong, healthy wings and keeps them lubricated so they can pop out and retract smoothly—not that they'll need to worry about that for now.

These drastic measures remind us every day that the heartless individual who caused this pandemic is still at large and very dangerous. Responding with violence has always been our kingdom's last resort, but Zsombor, the Third King, and I will be putting our heads together to work out a strategy to take them out. Of course, we need to identify and then find them first.

Ever since we learned about the contamination, my genius brother, Alias, has been working like mad to make us new dust. Considering that he's working with only five of the nine ingredients that he needs to produce the good stuff, we're all amazed at what he's come up with already. His latest formulation has actually restored life to our weakest fairies. And while it's giving a modicum of vitality to the others, until we find the rest of the ingredients, it will lack the power to accomplish much more.

Never before have fairies faced such a challenge, but I can think of no one more prepared to tackle it than he. He's a perfectionist, though, and needs constant reminding that despite a few hiccups, what he's created so far has been nothing short of a miracle.

In the meantime, the other two kingdoms have begun pooling their reserves, which we've all started sharing. Our father had always been generous when their supplies ran low, and their returning the favor is so gratifying.

I was born with a charmed life, of course, but I'm still dumbfounded when extra good luck comes my way. Call it a coincidence if you like that the Cavalcade of Champions kite-surfing exhibition took me to Myers Beach in the first place. Or kismet that I happened to see Lily throw her homemade fairy dust in the air during her skit on the boardwalk and fell in love with her.

I have no doubt that when the local Chamber of Commerce started calling their town "Magical Myers Beach" for its perfect and enviable combination of sand, surf, and summer breezes, they had no clue of its double meaning, and certainly couldn't have guessed that the same air and water they touted held vast quantities of fairy dust elements.

As soon as Lily put that good luck pendant around my neck, the beach's magic became obvious. Hard to believe that I found the things I was looking for in the same beautiful place where I found Lily, the woman I didn't realize I was looking for. She's already making an amazing queen, and everyone here in the kingdom loves her.

So far, the gradual move to Myers Beach has been going well, in part due to the other aspect of the beach's magic: the town is small and sleepy enough that we can live and move around undetected.

Despite these bright spots and Alias' progress, one of these days we will have to level with our subjects. Our situation is dire. Even at the reduced level of usage, I'm told we'll run out of fairy dust in two months. And unless Alias can produce more in time, we all will die.

CHAPTER TWO

Alias could have used magic to conjure up the coffee he planned to bring Greta. As prince, he was technically exempt from the Fairy Dust Austerity Program, not that he would've had to waste dust on something as simple as making a cup of to-go coffee. A snap of the fingers would have sufficed.

After the three kings, he was the most powerful fairy, and apart from being responsible for the fate of three fairy kingdoms, he had also been entrusted with the increasingly complicated ground operations at Myers Beach.

He needed dusting to give him energy, too, though not as much or as often as regular fairies. As the kingdom's public-facing royal, he wanted to demonstrate solidarity with his subjects, and so he tried to modify his outward-facing lifestyle whenever possible to economize on his usage. And that was why he opted to pick up coffee the old-fashioned way, from Joe's Java Joint.

Like most fairies, he'd been a tea drinker. It wasn't until he began hanging around with Greta, and she'd introduced him to the wonders of coffee, that he'd gotten hooked. And, whether people liked the man or not, Joe made the best on the boardwalk.

Stepping through the coffee shop door set off a witch's cackle, and Alias burst out laughing at the familiar sound. Greta's former store, The Witch's Cauldron, had triggered the same kind of alert, and Alias wondered if Joe was branching out and selling witch stuff now that Greta's store was out of business.

Joe was on a step stool changing the lettering on the menu board, and he turned around to see who found his new gadget so funny. Breaking from his normal crotchety persona, he lit up at the sight of a familiar face.

"What's with that cackle?" asked Alias. "Sounds a lot like the doorbell gizmo that Greta had."

"That's because it's the same one. Oddly enough it was one of the few things that survived the fire. She gave it to me, because she knew that I got a kick out of it whenever I walked in her store." He turned around to punch in the final letter on the board. "The thing still cracks me up every time."

"Speaking of Greta, I came in for two of her famous coffees. I'm on my way to The Fairy Kingdom and wanted to take her one for old time's sake."

"Sorry, buddy. No can do." He got down from the stool and pointed up at his revised menu. "Since she decided not to be a witch anymore, for some reason that I'll never understand, and she rebranded herself as a fairy queen or whatever, she asked me to change the name." He shook his head. "I don't understand that woman anymore. Her new drink doesn't even have coffee in it."

Alias looked up at the revision. Gone was *Greta the Witch's Brew* and in the place of honor at the top of the specialty drink list was *Queen Greta's Fairy (chai) Frappuccino.*

"I see you raised your prices, too."

"Yeah, well I had to. These drinks use a ton of ingredients and take forever to make. Besides, that Zsa Zsa fortune teller woman who rented the second floor ghosted me. Here one day and gone the next. Stiffed me on two months' rent. Then those damn Hollywood folks promised they'd shoot their reality show here, and I had to make improvements that cost me an arm and a leg. When Zsa Zsa left, I guess the show fizzled, and they skipped town without paying, too." He swiveled his iPad to take Alias' order.

"Then, I guess I'll contribute to your desperate situation by having two of your expensive fairy frappuccinos. And I'm guessing by the wonderful aroma that you just made croissants." Joe nodded, and Alias held up two fingers.

"Okay. Two fairy frappuccinos and two croissants coming right up," said Joe. He scrunched his nose. "Where's your sidekick?"

"Christophe? He's been out of the country for a while."

"Funny. I don't think I've ever seen you two apart." He chuckled. "The way you guys order the same things all the time, if I didn't know better, I'd guess you were…you know —" He made an exaggerated limp wrist gesture. "A couple."

"A couple of what?" Alias asked, forcing a grin.

Joe laughed and slapped his thigh. "That's a good one. Speaking of fairies––" He slid the latest copy of the *Myers Beach Tattler* across the counter. "This happened."

Girl Finds Creature on Boardwalk! UFO, or Tinkerbell?

Hearing Joe's fairy slur annoyed Alias, but not as much as seeing the girl in the photo pinching one of his beautiful six-inch green fairy subjects by its pink, translucent wings. He turned away so Joe didn't see him gulp. He'd known that particular fairy since he was in school.

"At first, I figured it was one of those doctored photographs that everybody and their brother seems to be doing these days. I mean, what the hell do you think it is?" Joe tapped at the masthead. "The damn *Tattler* has been getting more and more like a grocery store tabloid, but the reporter who wrote the story came in this morning before you and swears the picture is real. He was walking by when the kid found it. Right there out in front under one of my tables. The story even mentions my store. See?"

While Alias was devouring the article and one of the fresh croissants, Joe poured espresso into the cups of crushed ice. "It's got to be some kind of bird, right?" he asked. "Except that the wings are all wrong. And without a beak the head looks almost human, and an old one at that. Look at those wrinkles!" He drizzled on the caramel sauce. "On the other hand, the darned thing does kind of look like one of those fairies from the cartoons. But Tinkerbell? Come on."

Alias faked a chuckle. "Yeah. Ridiculous. A fairy in Myers Beach? What next?"

"Exactly." Joe pointed to the headline again and lowered his voice. "But you know, as a store owner, I hope it turns out to be a cute fairy. Better than a little green man from Mars running around on our beach doing who knows what and scaring tourists away."

Alias looked up from the paper. "Did the reporter say what they did with her?"

"Oh, it's a female?" Joe put on his reading glasses and bent down for a closer look. "How can you tell?"

Alias caught himself and backtracked. "Gee, I don't know why I said that. I honestly don't have any idea. I guess I meant to ask what they did with *it.*"

"Well, *it's* with Detective Stetson, whatever *it* is, but not for long. Get this. The Pentagon is sending their people to pick it up. Imagine, our little sleepy town drawing attention from the Feds."

Alias wasn't worried about the Feds, or agents from anywhere. He would make sure that nobody got their hands on one of his fairies. Still, he fished around for more information.

"What's Mayor Jim think about all this?"

"He was in this morning, too, and while he didn't come right out and say it, I'm guessing he was the one who contacted the Defense Department. You know, to try to get them to nip this story in the bud and make it go away." He wiped down the counter. "I'd like to make Mayor Jim go away. In my opinion, we should be capitalizing on this UFO thing or whatever it is. The publicity could put our damn town on the map, and we could all use more business around here."

Alias shuddered. They'd chosen to relocate the fairies to Myers Beach because they'd found so many of the fairy dust elements there. Being a small, sleepy beach town was a plus, because it helped them remain under the radar.

Had the story focused on the Tinkerbell angle, he believed readers would respond with an eye roll and yawn.

But the word *UFO* in the headline never failed to get people's attention. For reasons he didn't understand but for which he was grateful, the world was always more prepared to accept the reality of aliens than the possibility of fairies. He held up the newspaper and looked around the coffee shop.

"Where can I get a copy? I'd like to show it to Greta, but your rack is empty."

"Sold out. See? I told you this thing would be good for business. Give her this one. I've got another one in the back."

"So, how is Greta?" asked Alias, wanting to change the subject. "I've been busy and out of the loop."

"Beats the heck out of me. She stopped jogging in the mornings, if you can believe that, so she doesn't come by regularly anymore. I only see her once in a while, when she sneaks out of her tea house, or whatever the heck that place is, and pops in here for a real caffeine fix."

He continued rambling as he stirred the frappuccinos. "And don't ask me why she's even staying in town, since her brand-new Spanish-sounding husband left to go home to wherever he was from. You'd think newlyweds would want to be together and be all lovey-dovey, but what do I know?"

"Well, you know, her husband is taking over his family business," said Alias. "So they've both got a lot on their plates." He could hardly tell Joe that Greta had married a fairy king. "And since she gave her building to The Fairy Kingdom next door, the place is twice as big, and she's helping with the remodeling."

Joe popped on the lids. "Yeah, well, giving away one of

the best buildings on the boardwalk is another thing I don't understand. Her new hubby must be rolling in the dough, for her to do something that stupid." Alias pulled out his credit card. "You don't have cash?" asked Joe.

"Never."

He frowned. "Every time I run one of these charges, the damn credit card companies take me to the cleaners." He sighed as he swiped it. "Especially this one." His eyes popped when he read the front of the card. "Holy crap! How the hell do you get a credit card with only your first name on it?"

Alias laughed. "Let's just keep that a mystery. I've got to leave now. Greta is expecting me."

"Speaking of mysteries. I have to hand it to the new owners of that tea house, whoever they are now. They must be doing a bang-up business because the place is always crowded. But I sure as hell don't know who their customers are. I pass by every day and never recognize a soul." Joe walked him to the door and put his hand on Alias' shoulder. "Hey, I want you to know that I'm thinking about running for mayor, and I could use your support."

meant making an effort at least to take on the appearance of a native Californian. Should their relocation end up being long-term, they would all undergo further and more extensive training to learn strategies for not only how to blend in visually with humans, but to act like them as well.

"So, what do you think happened?" Greta asked.

"It appears she violated both of our house rules. I have to assume that for whatever reason, she ventured out before she had regained all her strength. My guess is that she ran out of steam before she could get back."

Her rebellious temperament had often landed her in the hot seat with the headmaster, so Alias wasn't at all surprised to learn that she'd bucked The Fairy Kingdom's system, too. He remembered plenty of improv sessions getting out of hand, like the time she'd encouraged her class to stage a food fight under the guise of creative improvisation.

For their foolish behavior, the headmaster sent everyone home for the rest of the day, and she had gotten a lecture. But this time, Gabor's irresponsibility put their entire Myers Beach operation at risk, and her drumming down would come from Alias. Furthermore, to set an example, he would have to figure out an appropriate way to punish her, a task he was not eager to perform.

"She sounds like someone I would like to have known," said Greta. "I was close to my drama teachers, too, and I'm so sorry you lost her."

Alias thought back at how much Miss Gabor meant to him growing up and how she'd helped him through more than one tough time. Like drama coaches around the world, she'd always had a sympathetic ear to give students with their personal problems. And while they had never discussed his biggest issue with her outright, by her winks and nods, he was convinced she'd had him pegged as gay all along.

"Let's not jump to conclusions," he said. When a fairy from his kingdom died, a distinct rose-colored ring appeared around the crown of the head, and since he'd seen no sign of it in the photograph, he was confident in his prediction. "She's always been a tough cookie, and I'm not ready to write her off. I'll even go out on a limb and suggest that you two will become friends. Why not? You're both so verbal and quick-witted."

"I'm glad to hear that," said Greta. "We can take steps to make sure nobody leaves the building alone from now on. In the meantime, I hope you won't be too hard on her for not going out as a human. I mean, she's at that forgetful stage."

Putting the blame for going out alone on her chronic inability to toe the line was a no-brainer, but he wasn't comfortable ascribing the other violation to forgetfulness, because he knew her too well. Even in her retirement, Dame Gabor was still a drama queen, and it didn't seem like her to miss out on the opportunity to dress up in a costume and take on a new role. Besides, he'd spoken to her a few days earlier, and he'd found her sharp as a tack.

"Can you talk the police into letting us in for a quick look?" he asked. "I only need a minute."

"Barbara Stetson owes me a big favor after she humiliated me with that false arrest," said Greta. "Now that she's the big cheese, I'm sure I could convince her to let at least one of us in for a couple minutes."

Stetson deserved the promotion and the commendation from the governor. She'd been pressured to arrest Greta by an incompetent higher-up who'd been so eager to close the high-profile murder case of Rona Divine that he took the easy way and put the finger on the wrong person. When Alias showed her footage of the real killer, she arrested him. She then investigated further and connected him to a string of other murders in Southern California.

"My plan is to let Dame Gabor handle most of the escape by herself," said Alias. "I just need a minute to explain to her what she needs to do." He sucked on his drink through the straw. "I like your new Fairy Frappuccino, by the way. Dee-licious!"

Greta led the way to her office to discuss the details in private. She shared the office with the fairy who had saved her life, which she admitted to Alias was ironic considering how at odds she and Stefán had been for so long over the Witch's Cauldron's fog machine.

On the way, she gave him a tour of the most recent renovations of the spa and treatment center. Thanks to the efficacy of Alias' new dust which made the convalescence period shorter than they'd expected, they were able to treat and turn over the new waves of incoming fairies smoothly every week. As they minimized the space needed for intensive care, they expanded the rooftop pool deck and added a small theater and a second dance floor.

It helped that the fairies fell in love with Greta. Whether they'd suffered from the poisoning, or from the stress of relocating to an unfamiliar world, no one was better suited to shower them with kindness and support than the woman who had devoted her entire human life-time to making people feel better.

Greta had expected to leave Myers Beach immediately after her wedding to assume her new role as Zsombor's queen. The contaminated dust hadn't reached their kingdom yet, but she and Zsombor knew they would need to implement immediate conservation measures to stretch out their supply. When they learned how little remained, they decided to begin sending their fairies to the beach as well, as a precaution. To coordinate that effort, Greta volunteered to remain in California.

But as hundreds of less sick ones arrived, a different challenge arose, and their assimilation required a different set of logistics. Though they didn't need as much serious medical treatment, they did need to be housed. Money was not an issue. Neither was space. With no further purpose for the building that housed her once famous boardwalk shop, she had signed the deed to Theos and Lily to expand The Fairy Kingdom.

While the fairies recuperated in Lily's original building, the next-door addition was ideal to house the incoming population, provided the fairies agreed to remain at their normal six-inch size while they were indoors.

Greta was a whiz at organization. She'd written her MBA thesis on innovative organizational models for small businesses, and she credited the success of her own store to systems she put in place from the beginning. She also designed the floor plan.

To accommodate them all, the two original fourteen-foot stories above the main floor were replaced with twenty-four twelve-inch floors. That allowed them to build plenty of apartments situated on tree-lined paths and multiple playgrounds and social areas. They even included a park and a swimming pool on every floor.

Using this model, they were able to keep the living quarters of the two kingdom populations separate yet allow them to share the spa and medical facility, where fairies received treatments as well as regular dustings.

To create the appearance of business as usual, the main floor remained open to the public, at the human scale. Greta's old store was transformed into a comfortable lounge that opened into the original tea house dining room, and the combination of the two spaces was spacious enough to serve as the common room for the fairies of both kingdoms.

New fairies arrived every week, and while the influx created challenges, she and Alias were pleased with how smoothly her system operated.

When Stefán came into the office, arms loaded with paperwork and glasses perched halfway down his nose, Greta and Alias filled him in on the plan in case things went awry. He reminded Alias that Stetson had met him before and that he would need a new identity.

He joined them for tea. "You could always transform yourself into a short, plump man with thinning hair. They'd never suspect a thing."

They gave him Christophe's surname and made up a bunch of credentials so that Greta could pawn off their new creation as acclaimed ornithologist, Professor DuBois.

Along with passing on their plan to Dame Gabor, the sting operation had a second goal: to convince Stetson that the unidentified object she was holding in her office for safekeeping was neither a Martian nor a Tinkerbell looka-like, as the newspaper suggested, but a bird.

"Sounds good. Let's go," said Greta. "We won't call her first. It'll be harder for her to say no if we show up at the station together."

"Good idea, but we'll have to hold off for a little while. I have an appointment in the Third Kingdom."

She chuckled. "Appointment, Alias? Sounds like you miss Christophe. Is that why you're going?"

He looked at the floor. "You got me. I've never been able to lie very well. But don't worry, I'll make the trip quick. All we need to do is slow down the agents a bit, so they don't arrive here before I get back. I suggest we get them stuck in traffic and make them miss their flight. The traffic in DC is horrendous already, so pulling that off will be simple." He snapped his fingers. "If we need more time, I can always conjure up an electrical storm and ground their next plane."

"You can do all that from here?"

He winked. "Yeah. Being a fairy prince has its perks. It's a cool trick, and as queen, you're able to do it too. I can show you how."

"But what about Dame Gabor? Do you think she'll be hungry?"

"I realize you're new at being a fairy, Greta, but you must have figured out that while eating and drinking is fun, we don't need to. So don't give her another thought. I suspect she misses her vodka, but she's probably sacked out and loving the vacation."

CHAPTER FOUR

Alias hadn't set foot in the palace of the Third King for a couple hundred fairy years, not since he was a teenager. He had wanted very much to return to the beautiful place that he once considered his second home, but bad memories had kept him away. At least the two responsible for his trauma weren't there any longer. There was a new king on the throne since he'd left.

Ordinarily, a visit by a royal highness would involve an audience with the king, but he'd grown up with the new Third King and knew he didn't need one. He'd told Theos he feared that a visit to the throne room might trigger his past trauma. His brother agreed and arranged for a change in protocol that allowed Alias to make his stay brief.

He hadn't gone to the palace to chit-chat, anyway. While the attack on the kingdom had been thwarted, the attempt to kidnap the Third King rattled fairies everywhere. One of the reasons he traveled there was to see for himself that security had been restored and there was no further threat.

Verification meant not relying on the king's version of events. The new king was young and green, and neither Theos nor Zsombor felt confident that the kingdom was being run by a strong or steady enough hand.

When they learned that a gang of humans had breached the palace walls, he and Christophe had been at dinner in Myers Beach to celebrate the wedding of Zsombor and Greta. Theos had wanted to assist, but the pandemic had stretched his resources thin, and with so much else on his plate as a new sovereign, he didn't want to be seen devoting time and energy elsewhere. Zsombor had his hands full, too. His subjects were already on edge, and they looked to him to protect them from a possible invasion of their own country.

After consulting with Theos and the Third King, Christophe offered to spearhead the investigation into the ringleader behind the attack on the dust. While they all agreed that no one fit the profile better than Györfi, since the man logically couldn't have been alive, Zsombor had his hands full finding the real culprit.

Being of the Third Kingdom, Christophe knew his way around, and he dropped everything and left immediately to defend his king and protect a kingdom that insiders considered fragile.

There had been a second cause for celebration that night: the defeat of Zsa Zsa Hajdu. They still hadn't understood who she was, other than that she'd taken the name of a long-dead lounge singer. They didn't know where the evil witch came from, either, or her motivation to siphon away Zsombor's spirit. In a gruesome battle atop the

Hersey Lighthouse, Alias, Greta, and Zsombor combined their magic and wits to overpower her.

In the end, it was Greta who hurled the witch off the lookout and into the dangerous waters of Retribution Shoals. Alias and Christophe dove to the bottom to verify that she was dead. They never found the body, but as they picked through the bones of the pirates and other hapless individuals who'd fallen victim to the shoals before her, they came upon a vein of a fifth fairy dust element. That major discovery had been a third cause for that same celebration dinner.

The uncharacteristic quiet in the palace resulting from the lockdown, together with the beefed-up security along the perimeter of the grounds, made for an unorthodox arrival for Alias. But since he was acting quietly on his own, he didn't expect the princely fanfare they'd always given him.

All the kingdoms were cutting back non-essential activities, and he understood that the paring down of the staff to a skeleton crew wouldn't have permitted it, anyway. Moreover, given the circumstances of his abrupt departure from the palace, he had no idea how he would be received. Apart from the silence, though, nothing on the inside of the palace appeared to have changed.

As he walked the main hallway toward the solarium where he knew his friend would be waiting, he slowed to peek into one of the familiar and opulent reception rooms. Those rooms and the never-ending corridors reminded him of the games of tag hide-and-seek he'd played with the young king.

Though the population of that kingdom was the

smallest of the three, the palace was by far the grandest. The residence was not unlike other massive estates in the area with vast surrounding property, but it was unique to the fairy world. For reasons no one could remember, the fairies of the Third Kingdom presented in human form all the time. Their homes, furnishings, and all the other trappings, were built to human scale.

As prince, Alias had already received intensive training in advanced fairy magic, and even though he was half-human, he was born the next most powerful fairy behind the three kings. Because blending in with the human world was increasingly crucial for their survival, his parents sent him to the palace to become accustomed to living in that simulated physical human environment and learn to pass as human without the use of magic.

The boys were nearly the same age, and it was decided that they would benefit the most by receiving a classical education together. By learning from each other's strengths, the hope was that Alias could become more proficient at human activities, and the Third King might pick up tips on how to harness human emotions.

His brother Theos and cousin Zsombor attended a special academy. Because they were next in line, their school prepared them for leadership and facilitated making connections with fairy royals outside their kingdoms. Because the king had assumed the throne at such an early age, albeit with his aunt as regent, he'd already been given an immersive, though modified course in that unique schooling.

The double doors of the library were open as he passed, and a roaring fire warmed the room and invited him in. Of all the rooms in the palace, the library occupied a special place in his heart, because it was there that he'd spent the most time alone with the Third King.

The same comfortable dark leather chairs he remembered flanked the fireplace. They'd sat there when their tutor taught them philosophy. He ran his hands across the arm of the one that always had been his, and the familiar earthy smell brought back memories of inspiring lectures and lively discussions about the great thinkers.

On this visit, he chose to sit on the sofa. Nearly every afternoon, he and the king would dig deep into its sumptuous softness and read aloud to each other in Latin or Greek. He kicked off his shoes and stretched out lengthwise across the cushions, like he used to do, remembering how the king would do the same from the other side. And how after reading the classics, they'd lie there together like that for hours as they practiced their foreign accents.

The ornate clock tucked into a shelf to the left of the fireplace chimed the quarter hour, and a chill ran through his body. It wasn't that the sound reminded him of the ticking clock of his own fairy dust project. The bookcase itself gave him the creeps.

Rich floor-to-ceiling shelves filled with books lined all the library walls, but that one section was different. Unlike the many passageways in the palace that were truly secret, everyone knew that steps behind that particular bookshelf led to the chambers of their tutor. Thoughts of the eccentric human made him queasy, and he stood up to shake away the thoughts of the petty man.

He made one last tour past the rest of the palace's impressive collection of books and gradually replaced the negative thoughts with happier memories. He'd meant to go straight on to the solarium, but his mind wandered. Without realizing it, his body automatically turned at the next hallway, and he caught himself standing before the gold-encrusted door of his old rooms. He took a breath and pushed open the door. The vast living room was just as he remembered. Something about its vibe, though, seemed off.

He grinned when he saw the basketball hoop. In college, he'd enjoyed playing pickup games, but nobody ever believed his claim that he learned his skills from growing up with a full court in his living room.

Spying a ball on the floor where he'd left it centuries ago, he dribbled to the free-throw line to make his signature jump shot. The ball hit the rim and bounced back. He took another shot, and that one hit the rim as well. Missing both was surprising and depressing. Still, the last thing he would do was quit.

He'd learned about quitting when he was young. He and Theos had grown up riding horses, and one day, when he was training, his horse had shied in front of a jump, and Alias went over its head. It happened again. And then again. Discouraged, he started to walk away, but his coach grabbed him by the shoulders and lifted him back up onto the saddle.

"Don't let me ever catch you quitting like that again," he yelled. "That's what losers do. Winners get back up there and keep at it until they succeed." The coach left the indoor arena and shouted from the tack room. "When you make it over one more time, I'll let you stop for the rest of the day."

Alias took another shot, and when he missed the mark

again, he took a breath to consider what might be causing his anxiety. In the meantime, he wasn't about to leave on a downer and disappoint his old trainer, so he used magic and sank three in a row.

He caught the lavender fragrance from across the room. While the power structure of the Third Kingdom had changed since he was there last, he felt the choice of the scent had not been coincidental. He'd watched the staff sprinkle lavender on his sheets and pillowcases back then during the daily ironing. They knew he was hooked on the fragrance. Even as an adult he continued the ritual with his own linens.

His mother had imparted to him the importance of treating palace staff as real people, rather than servants. As a former literature professor who'd never had much money, she'd felt that both he and Theos should never take their positions for granted.

She and the king insisted both boys spend at least part of their time helping the staff make up rooms to learn from them how to handle a hard day's work. During Alias' stay in the Third Kingdom, he'd naturally befriended many of their servants, and he suspected that at least one of them from the old days was still on staff and had been the one to make up his old bed.

Smoothing his hand over the thick duvet, his eyes misted as he recalled the riotous slumber parties and pillow fights, and how on some nights the young king would sneak down from his room with a plate of cookies, and they'd lie there and giggle and tell stories late into the night.

When he entered the solarium, Christophe was

lounging sideways across the arms of the king's throne, which had been moved from the actual throne room during Alias' time away.

"The king likes it better in here," he explained. "Because the room is so much brighter."

Alias gave an exaggerated bow, one appropriate for a king, but he snickered. "Your Highness. Where is the king?" Christophe laughed back and pointed to the garden with his thumb. "How did you manage to get a run of this place?" Alias asked. "You'd never get away with it in our kingdom."

"Well, I guess since I quashed three invasions and saved the king's life, they consider me somewhat of a hero."

"We all do." Alias walked closer. "But you don't look the least bit battle-scarred."

Christophe smirked and waved his hand over his face. "You thought I'd let anyone mar this masterpiece? Anyway, like they say, you should see the other guys." Though they shared a laugh at the cliché, Alias was relieved to see his friend unharmed.

Christophe motioned for him to come closer so he could whisper. "Actually, I snuck in." He pointed to an inlaid wall. "There's a secret panel over there. The servants don't even know about it. I found out because the thugs tried to get through the tunnel that leads up to it."

"My, my. Such palace intrigue." He touched Christophe's arm. "You were gone a long time."

"Yeah. They tried to get in twice more, which is why I stuck around, but those human thugs were no match for this fairy."

"We were all rooting for you."

Christophe inclined his head. "I was able to send some of them over to Zsombor for questioning, so I'm hoping he'll be able to figure out who's behind all this." He flicked his bangs out of his eyes. "What's happening back home at Myers Beach?"

"Gosh. The Fairy Kingdom is filling up with more fairies than Theos ever imagined when we started this adventure, and faster."

"You haven't seen anything yet," said Christophe. "I've heard that lots of fairies from here are leaving to go there, too, so we'll need even more space."

"So, if you think that the threat has passed, can you come back with me? An incident came up that has the potential to grow into a real PR nightmare. I could really use your help to straighten it out."

"Of course, but I may need a couple days." He rolled his eyes. "The king wants to see me."

"That makes two of us. I mostly came to see you." Alias walked closer. "I wish you could see yourself. The way you're lounging on that throne gives the impression you belong on it."

Christophe sat up straight and struck a few kingly poses. "What do you think?"

Alias smiled and bowed again. "Sex on a stick, Your Royal Highness."

Christophe stood and gave him a hug. "Thanks. I'm proud of you for coming. From the few stories you've told me, I know that being back in this palace was difficult."

"I'm not staying long, anyway. I have to get back soon. I'm meeting with an agent from the Pentagon, and I have to pretend to be an ornithologist." Christophe raised an eyebrow. "Don't ask!" said Alias. "It's a long story."

"Well, they made up a bed for you down the hall, in case you wanted to stay over."

"Yeah. I smelled the lavender when I checked it out earlier. Thanks." He swallowed the lump in his throat. "But, if it's all the same, I'd rather sleep somewhere else. And let's go back home tomorrow."

"You can sleep with me if you want. I doubt they'd mind, as long as we don't make a big deal about it." He rolled his eyes. "The king, you know."

CHAPTER FIVE

Greta and Captain Stetson hadn't seen each other since the attempted arrest, and not surprisingly there was an awkwardness in the air when the three of them met at the police station. Skipping the small talk, Stetson rubbed her hands.

"Let me guess. You're here about the article in today's paper?"

Greta nodded and got right to the point. She introduced Alias in his disguise as Doctor DuBois and rattled off a list of his impressive but fake credentials.

"Doctor DuBois has graciously offered to provide his expert analysis of your UFO prisoner. It is indeed fortuitous that he happened to be in town today of all days. And how fortunate too, that he was able to take time away from his research with The Endowment for Oceanic Solutions to do us this favor."

"Look, Greta. Everyone and their brother is asking to do the same thing, and I've had to say no to them all." She took Greta's hands. "But we both know I owe you one for that unfortunate episode in our recent past."

"Yes, well, I'm hoping we can put the incident behind us, Barbara."

Stetson turned to DuBois. "We are grateful, sir. Approximately how much time do you need?"

Doctor DuBois took off his glasses and rubbed his temples. "To simply make an identification? Hmm. If, in fact, the specimen is true to the photograph in the newspaper, which of course I've already studied, I should say no more than a few minutes."

"All right, Greta. On your personal recommendation, and being that he's affiliated with the Endowment, I'll allow him a quick peek. But you must promise not to tell anyone that I let you in." She looked up at the wall clock. "And please make it fast. An agent from the Pentagon will be here soon."

"The Pentagon? Why on earth would they be interested in this sweet thing?" asked DuBois.

"I've been asking myself the same question. But, in any event if they see you leaving the station, they'll stop you. Then they'll want to question all of us. And knowing how they work, an interrogation like that could tie everyone up for days."

She unlocked a door to the glorified walk-in closet lined with metal shelves that served as the evidence room. She handed him a shoebox, and Alias gulped when he pictured his former teacher and a Dame of the Kingdom lying inside.

"I'm pretty sure it's dead, whatever it was, but I'm a softie, so I made it a little bed with a towel."

DuBois adjusted his fake wire-rimmed glasses and pulled out a pair of surgical gloves that he snapped like a professional before he slipped them on. "That was very considerate of you, Captain." He pointed to the fairy. "May I?"

She nodded, and he lifted the fairy's head. "Hmm. Aah. Yes. Interesting."

"So, do you know what it is?"

He thickened his French accent and laughed. "Oh, my, yes. And rest assured, Madam, that what you have here is not a Martian, so you can tell everyone in Myers Beach to breathe easy."

"So, it's a bird, after all?"

He coughed. "I suppose you could say that, but I'd prefer to use more specific terminology. This adorable beauty in my hand is of the highly intelligent *viridi aliquid minima* family." He rolled the tiny thing on its back and rubbed its tummy. "More frequently referred to as, *puella viventem.*" Then he gave the fairy a light jab. "Without examining her further, I'd say this little rascal is of the variety, *incorrigibilis.*"

Stetson let out a breath. "That's certainly a mouthful of names for such a tiny thing. Do you mind repeating them so I can write them down?"

Alias obliged and then continued. "They're not always this small, of course. I've seen adults of this particular species as tall as six feet two."

She waved away the image. "Gosh! Can you imagine the chaos, if one of them that size showed up here?"

"Their flitting around can sometimes be annoying," he said. "They have minds of their own, and so are nearly impossible to train." He bopped the fairy's head. "But they're generally quite peaceful little creatures, and they hardly ever stray very far from their nests. And they're more common than you think. Believe it or not, there have been many recent sightings of these little rascals in the Myers Beach area."

"If it was so easy to identify, I still wonder why they're bothering to send their people all the way out here." Stetson tapped her watch dial and gestured to the closet.

DuBois sighed and waved his hand. "Yes, well, governments, you know. If they'd only listen to us experts."

Before he put the top back on the box, he sprinkled some dust on the fairy's head. When she blinked back, he mumbled something.

"Were you talking to me?" asked Stetson. "I didn't recognize the language."

"Oh. Sorry. I didn't mean to be rude. It's just a phrase we say in my country when one is in the presence of death." He bowed his head in a fake solemn salute and walked the box back to the captain, who returned it to the closet.

"Thank you for the professional opinion." Stetson pointed to the back door. "Now, let's get you out of here, so I can deal with the Feds."

The bench across from the police station gave them an unobstructed view of the front door, and as they settled in to wait for the agents to arrive, Greta laughed and gave him a poke.

"You were hysterical. *Little green something? Live female? Incorrigible?* All I can say is that it's a good thing Stetson didn't take Latin."

"I took a chance," he said, "and I'm pleased that you picked up on the humor. I was always pretty good at it, and I hope I got my declensions right."

"I'm sure it wouldn't have mattered. By the way, what did you really say to Dame Gabor? I'm guessing that it wasn't what you told Stetson. I was standing next to her on the other side of the room, and she was nervous and grinding her teeth so hard, I couldn't hear."

"I clued Dame Gabor in on her role in the rescue plan and suggested that it may take some improvisation on both our parts. You'll see."

Soon a black SUV pulled into the No Parking slot directly in front of the building, and they watched a man in a dark suit and a shiny metal case walk into the station. Ten minutes later, the door opened again, and he walked out. Stetson shook hands with him, and when he started down the steps, Alias flicked a finger.

Suddenly, the man stumbled. He fell against the handrail and dropped the case, which clattered on the concrete sidewalk. As he sat rubbing his ankle, Alias flicked again and the locks on the case clicked. The top sprung open, the shoebox lid burst off, and Dame Gabor flew out.

All eyes followed her as she zigzagged overhead and then crashed into a streetlamp. She dropped to the ground, where she flitted about in a momentary daze. The agent grabbed the shoe box and rushed over. Just as he was about to scoop her up, she rolled a few feet away.

He nearly caught her a second time, but she flipped away again, and for the next few minutes, the frustrated and out-of-shape man chased her around the grounds of the police station.

At the top of a retaining wall, the three-time award-winning fairy actress bent over and panted. Then, she raised herself up on one wing, staggered, and collapsed to the ground. Then she gagged and dragged herself a couple more inches. As she lay on her back, she let her mouth fall open, gasped again, and let out a slow gurgle, before rolling her head to one side. She produced one final faint chirp and then stopped moving completely.

"Got the damned thing now!" said the agent, reaching toward her with his shoebox. His hand was an inch away when she squawked and bit his thumb. He winced in pain and toppled backward over the wall, and as he lay on the ground massaging his shoulder and sucking his bloody thumb, she flapped her wings and made a beeline to the roof of the police station.

"Cock-a-doodle-doo," she cried, striking a pose to resemble a weathervane. Convinced she'd milked her audience for as long as she could, she took a bow and then flew out of sight.

"I'm sorry you had to make the trip," said Stetson to the agent, who was still rubbing his ankle. "I told you it was only a bird. A famous scientist gave me the name of the species, and I can give it to you if you need to know. It turns out they're more common around here than you would think. At least, that's what he told me."

"Brava, Miss Gabor!" Alias cheered as they relaxed at his swimming pool later that afternoon. "You still know how to bring down the house."

"Yes, well, Your Royal Highness, it's hard to top a good death scene." She smiled and took another sip of her Cosmo, to brace herself for the lecture that would undoubtedly come from her prince.

Alias knew his manners, one of which was to show respect to his elders. But while his father had made Miss Gabor a Dame of the Kingdom, his title outranked hers, which was how he got away with giving her the scolding when she lay in the shoebox and the lecture to her at the pool that afternoon.

Just as he opened his mouth, she held up her hand to stop him. "Not so fast!"

Greta gulped at the irreverence. Then she looked further confused when Alias and his former teacher burst into laughter.

"It's a running in-joke," said Dame Gabor between guffaws. "The great actress Elizabeth Taylor delivered that infamous line in a television commercial for one of her awful perfumes. Little did she know the line was originally mine, but Alias did. I'd shout it out when the curtain began to fall at the end of every show, and they'd raise it back up each time. It was always good for another round of applause."

"Yes, and I can see that commercial now," said Alias. "Wasn't she coming out of fog or mist or something?"

"No. That was the Vaseline she demanded they smear on the camera lens to disguise her aging face." She let out a belly laugh and took another gulp. "Some people just can't handle the truth."

He sat up straight. "Okay. It's time to get serious." He asked her to explain what she was thinking by walking around as a fairy plain as day on the boardwalk all by herself.

She stood and threw back her shoulders. Then she bowed her head and made the sign of the cross. Alias grinned and turned to Greta. "I've seen this act before. I think it's from when she played Joan of Arc."

Gabor looked back up with tears in her eyes. "Guilty. Yes, I left the premises on my own, so I'm guilty as charged." She stretched out her arms as though pleading to a jury. "But I'm innocent of the other charge." She hiccuped and began to teeter, and Greta helped her back down to the chaise.

"How so?" He asked.

"I had an outstanding human disguise." She stood again to pantomime her story. "I'd swished out of the tea house in a long sweeping summer dress, dark glasses, picture hat and all. I looked every bit the California lady of leisure. I even affected an authentic valley girl accent.

"I noticed that I'd caught the attention of a lovely older gentleman. Naturally, I played the coquette, and he followed me around as I pretended to window shop. Occasionally, I'd even slip into one of the more upscale boutiques. Finally, when I was ready to let him win, I reclined on that nice new boardwalk bench in front of our building and gazed out at the horizon.

"At last, the gentleman summoned the courage to approach me, and since I'd made him work hard enough already, when he invited me for a coffee, I let him take me to the joint a couple doors down.

"We had a delightful time. He let me do most of the talking, and I regaled him with stories of my most acclaimed performances on the stage. Then, as I was bringing a paper cup of the most delicious Fairy Frappuccino to my lips for a second sip, the weirdest thing happened. My hand froze in place. Even my pinkie finger, which I'd extended to add that touch of gentility.

"The muscles in my mouth stopped working too, so instead of going down my throat, that lovely drink spilled out over my lips like a fountain and ran over the front of my fabulous dress. And since I'd ordered the sixteen-ounce size, the liquid kept flowing. Regrettably, I couldn't speak either, so I wasn't even able to ad-lib an explanation.

"Imagine my panic when my bare arms started turning green in front of my eyes? By his horrified expression, I could tell that he noticed it too. He pretended not to know me and stood to leave without offering any assistance. Men. What good are they?

"I had to think fast. These days we don't carry fairy dust. Of course, even if I'd had some, I wouldn't have been able to toss it around, since I couldn't use my hands or arms. I was never so humiliated.

"I know it was against kingdom policy, but I couldn't let him or the rest of the Myers Beach coffee crowd see me complete my transformation in front of them. So, I used what little magic I could muster, and I improvised. As it turned out, I had enough to make everyone around me, including my date, forget what they saw.

"Unfortunately, though, it didn't leave me enough to get

me back to The Fairy Kingdom intact. So, I shrunk myself down to my normal stunning six-inch self, jumped off the chair, and landed under the table right there at Joe's Java Joint. Not my best exit.

"All I can say is that it was a good thing that girl saw me lying on my back and picked me up before some uncouth person stepped on me with their flip-flops."

"You poor dear," said Greta. "How awful!"

Gabor threw her head back and clutched her chest. "Yes, it was, but for his sake, I hope I never run into him again."

"Don't worry," said Alias. "You won't. I'm grounding you."

CHAPTER SIX

Notwithstanding the dramatic and humorous interpretation of Dame Gabor's misadventure, Alias did not consider paralysis of the limbs and turning green against one's will a laughing matter. Especially if they were adverse side effects from a treatment that was intended to restore health.

As the newest iteration, Dust Number Three had been surprisingly effective. So named from the addition of the third element, *danog*, that Theos had discovered in the Myers Beach air, Alias called it his workhorse dust. He'd been using it to stabilize and maintain the fairies' health with excellent results and no side effects.

He'd examined her recently and was impressed with her vitality. The principal drawback of the dust they called D3 was that it lacked staying power, and he likened it to a battery that didn't hold its charge long. So, without any facts suggesting the contrary, he believed that Dame Gabor had simply run out of power, an explanation that he was comfortable with.

He was hopeful that *redach*, the element that he and Christophe found at Retribution Shoals, would provide the extra oomph D4 needed. They'd almost missed the *redach*. During the first few passes, they were positive that what they were seeing along the shoals in such huge quantities were oysters. They looked just like one called Aunt Betty's that Alias remembered from a restaurant in Massachusetts.

Like shucking an oyster, that fifth element had been stubborn to open and refine. Unlike the *danog* that required an entirely different system to capture, *redach* and the other three were more like ores and needed an extraction process akin to smelting.

Fortunately, there had been ample space on the levels below the compound's lab to set up such a facility. Pushing the rock beyond its melting temperature had been the easy part. Figuring out how to do it without releasing toxins into the atmosphere or water had taken a long process of trial and error. All five needed different methods of handling and storing, too. They learned that the *sudf* they'd discovered under The Fairy Kingdom was extremely delicate and required strict temperature control, unlike the *igdia* and *tepa* Theos had found underwater, which were hardy.

Convinced that his team had finally figured out a viable and suitable way to extract the *redach*, Alias was eager to begin incorporating it immediately and make D5 a reality.

Until it was ready and to prevent another close call like Gabor's, Greta had given their staff instructions to monitor the fairies' behavior more closely, especially those who left the building. But, unless and until another serious event arose which would give him a reason to change his mind, Alias planned to refer to Gabor's situation as a mishap, not a side effect.

Apart from still lacking a few ingredients, the effectiveness of his dust was impressive, given his other handicap—he was working without a recipe. He knew what went into it, of course. Every fairy of every kingdom could recite the names of the nine elements of fairy dust from an early age. There was even a schoolyard song.

Yano, Danog, Arbara, Urst–
Redach, Igdia, Tepa, Sudf.
Fstl Fstl!

Since he didn't have all nine on hand, and he was racing against the clock, he'd simply added each new ingredient as it was discovered to the previous iteration. Only one fairy per kingdom had access to the full ancient code. The document specified the exact quantities of each and the order in which they were to be added together. That one fairy had also been expected to commit the recipe to memory.

Entrusting such priceless intellectual property to the care of only one individual might seem irresponsible to humans, but not so in the fairy world. Fairies routinely lived to an average age of twelve hundred years, and they never got sick. At least, not until the deliberate tragedy.

The formula did exist elsewhere. Each kingdom had its own leather-bound copy. At the time of the contamination, Theos' Keeper of the Dust had been a strapping five-hundred-year-old with more than half of his life ahead of him. His premature death complicated things, because he'd kept their book in a secret place for safekeeping. Since neither he nor Theos could put their hands on it, Alias found himself without the recipe.

The other two kingdoms were of no help. They had both run out of their own dust centuries ago and acquired what they needed from Theos' kingdom. With no ongoing manufacturing systems, over time the locations of their fairy dust manuals were also forgotten.

Two years before the contamination, humans on the other side of the northernmost boundary had been using a system of hydraulic fracturing to extract oil and natural gas from beneath their own land. On a routine inspection at the border one day, the Keeper of the Dust had noticed that the company's operations had been edging dangerously close not only to their border, but to the tip of the kingdom's underground vein of elements, and he'd alerted the king to the encroachment.

The initial fracking process had not posed a problem. Aside from a few other chemicals that were harmless to fairies, water made up most of the liquid they injected at high pressure to shatter the rock formations. Small amounts of the liquid had seeped across the border before without causing any negative ramifications. The bigger threat to the kingdom's most valuable asset was not toxicity, but rather the massive and constant vibrations from the process, and twice the king lodged formal complaints through the proper human political channels.

When the king heard of the humans' most recent intrusion, though, he lost his patience and authorized a large-scale mischief campaign to scare them away for good. He rallied his naughtiest fairies to cause equipment failures so serious, so costly to repair, and so frequent that the company left the area and went belly up. The abandoned site eventually fell into ruin from inactivity.

With the business a thing of the past, no one in the kingdom paid attention when the property changed hands. The Keeper of the Dust no longer made checkups of that end of the kingdom as frequently, and he wasn't present in the mine the day the water laced with iron ore blasted through cracks in the rusted-out fracking tubes and seeped into the nine elements.

Many months had passed before the Keeper and his workers came to scrape the elements to make the next batch of fairy dust, and any of the polluted water had long since evaporated and left no visible trace of the sabotage. But the damage was done.

Fairies dropped dead by the thousands from iron poisoning. Many more got violently ill, and by the time they discovered what had happened, they'd already made new dust from the contaminated elements and shipped it to the four corners of the kingdom, inadvertently dusting fairies everywhere with the lethal iron and initiating a true pandemic.

The king convinced his advisers that the perpetrator had been a human. Even the most disgruntled fairy wouldn't destroy the one thing that supported their life. The person would have had to be in a position to know the location of the vein and possibly even the Keeper's schedule. They would also have known that iron was poisonous to fairies. Finally, they would have to know how to adapt the fracking infrastructure to deliver lethal iron to the most fairies in the quickest time.

He told them to make a list of potential suspects, which they would discuss and narrow down later that day. When they returned, the task was simple, because there was nothing to narrow down. They each brought a list with the same name: Györfi.

Since he had spent enough time in the palace of the Third King dining with the other servants to have heard someone mention their vulnerability to iron and the location of the vein, or even the Keeper's schedule of visits. He might have just as easily heard about the fracking operation. Being a well-educated and imaginative man, he could easily have figured out how to use those mechanisms.

Györfi was the perfect suspect in every way. Except one. He was almost certainly dead.

CHAPTER SEVEN

When the man the boys would call Uncle Györfi had first stepped out of the modest vehicle that dropped him off at the front door, he didn't seem evil. And he wasn't wearing the gigantic chip on his shoulder that would later define his personality.

Instead, his wide eyes sparkled like a child's at the imposing facade of the magnificent palace he would be calling home. Servants appeared instantly to unload his shabby suitcases and cardboard boxes of books, and while others fussed over him on the way in, his heart raced at the instant improvement of his lifestyle. His face was frozen in a grin at his good luck when he walked through the immense doorway.

While his fawning and gaping at the opulence continued for days, he was understandably awed. Few buildings were as magnificent as the palace of the Third King. And though his new personal living quarters were modest compared to the luxurious furnishings in the rest of the palace, they represented a significant upgrade to his former digs.

His father had been a milliner in Budapest, and as a young boy, he'd watched him develop tremors in the very fingers he'd relied on to pay the family's bills. Soon came the memory loss, and then hearing and speech problems. Finally, madness. They later learned that mercury, the chemical he'd used to cure the felt for some of the hats, had been responsible.

His mother left Budapest and took her son to London where she worked as a charwoman to pay the bills. Sometimes, she'd take him to the houses she cleaned, and while she'd make him hide in the kitchen, he would occasionally slip out and into the living quarters, which was where he got his first taste of opulence.

He'd also discovered books, which he'd sneak from their libraries. For reasons his mother couldn't fathom, her son was a voracious reader. One day he was caught in the library by the lady of the house, and though he explained that he'd been reading and not stealing anything, she tested him. When she asked what book he'd read, he pointed to a large bookcase.

"All of them," he said.

She pulled one from the shelf and asked him to tell her what it was about.

He threw back his shoulders and gave her a thorough review, even quoting a few passages. She chose another, and when she found that he was able not only to describe the storyline but analyze its structures and character arc development, she sent for his mother.

Convinced the boy was a true savant, Mrs. Birnam

offered to be his patron, and with his mother's permission, she made arrangements to send the nine-year-old to a special school, where he became exposed to the best and brightest minds in England. By the age of eighteen, he'd finished his doctoral degree and fallen into a career as a tutor for the wealthy, which had been enough to set him up in a nice part of town.

It was through his Hungarian background and connections in London through the Birnam family that he'd been approached by the Third Kingdom.

He wasn't anyone's real uncle. That name change was his idea and for his benefit. He'd always been proud of his earned title, Doctor, but given the grandeur of his new dwelling and considering that court protocols required him to address the two young men as *highnesses*, hearing the boys call him *Doctor* Györfi sounded inadequate. So, to level the playing ground a bit, he gave himself a title of his own. Uncle. His new name gave him the illusion at least that he belonged.

Before he accepted the position, he'd been told that the young boys had received the finest instruction available and were well positioned for him to accelerate their education. He'd heard that before. His experience taught him that rich people often exaggerated the capacity of their children to learn.

After an initial session, though, he was relieved to discover that the ones who'd interviewed him hadn't misrepresented the boys. He could tell that they were bright and eager to learn, but he was appalled at their lack of core knowledge. He wondered how it was possible that as teenagers who'd allegedly received the finest education, they knew little more than how to read, write, and count.

He could never appreciate how prepared they were in the ancient and complex history of the fairy world, nor the skills in advanced magic both royals received. Since the Third King had ascended the throne as a youngster, he'd already been required at that early age to undergo the extra and extensive training required to rule.

Alias' parents and the Third King's aunt were smart enough to predict that knowledge about the fairy world, however complete, would not be sufficient to prepare them to thrive in an environment that increasingly over-lapped with humans. Alias' mother had been a full human before she married his father, and so she understood more than the others what was at stake and that the time was precisely right to accelerate his education.

They hired Doctor Györfi for a specific job: to teach the boys all the sciences, history, philosophy, art, and world literature. Also, instruct them how to dress, act, excel at sports, order food and wine, play games and musical instruments, and otherwise fit in seamlessly with human culture. Their boys' education was at stake, the aunt had stressed, and they wanted him to take his time to do it right.

He'd never been asked to give such extensive tutelage, but he rose to the challenge with passion. And he'd finally get to experience the finer things in life that he'd only observed before now.

With the job description as tutor to a king and a neigh-boring prince, he would have been the envy of his colleagues, had they let him brag about it. A non-disclosure provision, however, stipulated that he cease communication with anyone outside the kingdom until all the terms of his contract were satisfied. Keeping mum seemed an easy tradeoff for the invaluable access to a king and a prince.

Within minutes after inking his contract, Györfi learned the reason for the gag order. The members of the two royal families and the others with whom he'd be rubbing elbows were part of another far more interesting and influential network. Though to all outside appearances they looked like normal rich people, they were fairies, with magical powers beyond his wildest imagination.

He was confident of his credentials, and he felt up to the task. Furthermore, if he played his cards right and took his time as the boy's aunt suggested, he envisioned stretching out his new life of luxury for a dozen years. But his face contorted when she announced that they were giving him only three.

His assignment was a heavy lift, and even with boys of superior intellect, such a time constraint couldn't possibly allow him to do much more than cover the basics. He was sputtering out a catalog of concerns and caveats when the Third King's aunt interrupted him.

"Overruled!" she decreed.

Hoping she wasn't serious, he rubbed his hands nervously as he waited for her to break into a smile and tell him she was kidding. Instead, she snapped her fingers, and the boys shared a giggle as their tutor's troubled face relaxed in front of them. Making worries disappear was a trademarked fairy forte.

She added one private rule for the boys which didn't sit well with them. Doing it right meant that they were to learn from him the old-fashioned way—through books, lectures, and homework, and she forbade them to use magic during their sessions with him.

Alias was used to restrictions on using magic because his human mother was still extremely close to her relatives, and it sometimes irked him to have to keep a low profile when they visited. The Third King had never been restricted, and they bonded immediately over the unfair ban and their mutual irritation.

Outside of class, Györfi witnessed the boys conjure up magic all around him. With flicks of their royal fingers, doors opened and closed behind them, and objects materialized or disappeared as they were needed. Even the lowest member of the palace staff could complete their simple tasks the same way.

The phenomenon wasn't confined to the palace. Later, whenever he ventured out with the boys anywhere in the kingdom, he learned that the story was the same. Every inhabitant of the Third Kingdom possessed some level of magic power.

They all had wings, too, which they could call forth from between their shoulders at any time. The boys' royal translucent ones were more magnificent, and the young king's were larger than Alias', but regardless of the size, everyone flew everywhere.

Györfi had brains, but he longed for the money, luxury, and easy existence of the fairies. Growing up, other kids always had stuff he didn't have, and because of the notoriety of their last names, they were given opportunities to thrive that he hadn't been given until Mrs. Birnam discovered him.

But the lifestyle living with the fairy royals taunted him with wealth that far exceeded that of Mrs. Birnam, and with unimaginable magic that came from just the flick of their little finger. They all had those powers. Everyone, except him.

From the moment he stepped into their world, he craved what they had.

CHAPTER EIGHT

Alias wondered how quickly the article in their local paper with a circulation of under ten thousand would appear outside Myers Beach. Given the agent's stunning failure at capturing Dame Gabor, he hoped that the Department of Defense would seal the report and sweep it away, putting an end to the entire debacle. Through The Endowment for Oceanic Solutions, Theos had influential connections at the top who agreed, and within the hour, the right person at the right level put the kibosh on the story.

But a blogger named Pat—who used they/them pronouns—had seen the original article in the *Tattler* and recognized that the photo of the adorable girl was the ticket to making their blog go viral. The result was an overnight bonanza. Dozens of people with no firsthand knowledge of the incident or Myers Beach weighed in on the blog with their opinions.

Pulling snippets from the testimony of a Doctor DuBois about the creature's size and from nonsense people commented on the blog, Pat put forth the preposterous new theory: what the girl had found was only an infant, but something far more sinister was about to threaten the town.

Pat attached an artist's rendering that someone had sent them. The sketch depicted the adult form as a super-intelligent, giant, jagged-toothed, man-eating freak.

The big question people are asking me right now is how quickly these creatures reproduce. I'm guessing at the speed of light, because a Doctor DuBois asserted that Myers Beach is already crawling with them. Please hit the Subscribe button below to stay abreast of minute-by-minute updates.

While lawyers for the girl's parents were seeking injunctions against using the image of their underage daughter, a second, uncredited, photo was making the rounds. No one anticipated that a picture of a Department of Defense agent sucking his thumb on the police station lawn would run the next day in the *Tattler* above the fold.

Tiny Creature Outwits Pentagon! Still at Large!

A Defense Department spokesperson denied the existence of a mission to Myers Beach, and beyond admitting that the man in the photo had once been a low-level messenger, refused to comment further. Humiliated by the photograph and frustrated that his higher-ups would not back him up, the agent organized a press event of his own to set the record straight, where he released a personal statement.

He maintained that officials had indeed briefed him at some length on the sensitive mission they'd assigned him: the retrieval of a small comatose unidentified flying object being held for him at the Myers Beach police station.

He said that what he found waiting for him, however, had been anything but comatose, and he went on to describe the savage beast, and the hair-raising chase that put him in harm's way multiple times as it tried to kill him at every turn.

His voice broke as he spoke of the courage that brought him so close to the fiend that it bit him. The battery of doctors and forensic specialists standing behind him at the press conference agreed. From the teeth marks and the large chunk of flesh missing from his thumb, the agent couldn't have been nipped by a six-inch bird. Instead, he'd been chomped on by something far more fierce.

He described the Myers Beach police captain as so incompetent and bumbling that she had secured perhaps the most malevolent threat to modern society in a flimsy shoebox. And that, because the Pentagon chose to ignore his story rather than take action, the beast was currently at large on the California coast. He ended his statement with a warning that the creature possessed a super-advanced intellect. The fact that it had eluded a senior field asset packing the most sophisticated tools and equipment was proof.

The wire services distributed his statement, but a story about a bird biting a man and something about a shoebox didn't gain much traction. The outlets that did pick it up didn't treat the sensational story seriously, and that evening only a few local news anchors ran it as a fun and quirky end piece to their broadcasts.

Under pressure from the police department to rebut the accusation of an incompetent police department, the *Tattler* agreed to run a follow-up story. Stetson hoped such an editorial would convince the public that not only had they followed strict safety protocols, but that the girl actually found a bird, not a UFO, and certainly not a blood-thirsty creature. They had plenty of proof. A renowned ornithologist had said so, and the department supplied the paper with specifics and quotes from Doctor DuBois.

In a rare concession to unity, Mayor Jim added his own pressure to run the article, suggesting it could be crucial to defusing the public's tension and could go a long way to return calm to the town.

Thanks to Pat and other bloggers, though, the online story had grown much more interesting legs of its own. The editors relegated DuBois' statements to a small stand-alone paragraph on the cartoon page and chose to put the artist's rendering from Pat's blog on the front page. They also took a different approach with their headline.

Seven-Foot Monsters Run Rampant in Myers Beach. Locals Terrified!

The media soon gave a name to the phenomenon which promised to be on the scale of the Loch Ness Monster, and Myers Beach's new celebrity, Big Tiny, became the impetus for a new cottage industry.

The story that had begun on the front page of a small local newspaper now dominated social media around the world. Within twenty-four hours, every hotel and spare room in Myers Beach was booked by network stringers and ordinary gawkers, all hoping to catch the sighting of a lifetime.

Beach ne'er-do-wells rebranded themselves as guides who, for a substantial fee, would take people to where the giant winged creatures roamed. For the budget-minded, they offered maps and self-guided tours. And to assist folks in actually catching the beasts, Joe removed a few tables from inside his café and repurposed the space to sell nets, stun guns, and extra-large leg cuffs.

The established souvenir stores were quick to stock Big Tiny t-shirts and coffee mugs as fast as they could be produced, but the frenzy was not limited to the Myers Beach boardwalk. A crafter in New England was cranking out homemade Myrna, the Myers Beach Mermaid dolls, and was allegedly making a killing, even though with a clear set of wings and a lack of a fin, Big Tiny looked nothing like a mermaid.

CHAPTER NINE

Alias was speaking at a staff meeting. They'd just finished discussing the new protocol since the fairies had been coming to town, and he wasn't sure he was that comfortable with it. The idea that he was suddenly forced to act demur in his role as prince rubbed him the wrong way. He was not used to being treated within his station and it felt stifling just thinking about all the "Your Highnesses" he would receive in the near future. But he couldn't let his own issues with it show. He had to be their unflappable prince.

"I hate what's happening, but let's try to be positive. Think about it. As long as people keep searching for huge monsters and not fairies, maybe they won't notice the hundreds of real fairies who are actually living here. Still, until they go away for good, we must be extra vigilant to remain under the radar."

"But you're the prince, with more power than the rest of us combined," said Stefán. "Couldn't you use your magic to make them all disappear?"

"Yes, of course," Alias answered. "In two seconds. But I'd like that to remain a last resort, because it would only draw a different kind of attention to our town and encourage more lunatics to come. We must find a way for them to leave on their own."

The circus atmosphere thrilled one fairy in particular: retired actress Dame Gabor, the center of the media frenzy.

"This may have been my greatest role," she mused. "The world is celebrating my comeback." Her eyes lit up. "I've got an idea, Your Highness. Since my performance was what brought them here, why not use me to send them away?"

"I'm listening," said Alias.

"I could be your eyes and ears on the outside. Think about this. If you let me take the sun and swim in the ocean every day, which I hope you realize is my true passion, I'd be in an excellent position to hear the latest scuttlebutt. I could report to you every day on anything I pick up that might impact the mission."

At first blush, he thought her suggestion had merit, and he needed some time to consider what to do next. But granting her permission to leave the confines of the teahouse would require him to reverse his punishment.

"I know what you're thinking, Your Highness, but I'm sure you realize that I've learned my lesson. Besides, I've never felt better."

That he believed. After the incident, he'd treated her with high-test fairy dust from his personal stash. Having made a one-hundred-percent recovery, he doubted she would run out of steam again. Because she'd only broken one of the rules and given lifelong service to the kingdom, never mind the soft spot he had for her, he agreed to the exemption.

She nodded enthusiastically as he spelled out the terms of their new arrangement, whereby she could spend the daytime outside at the beach as long as another fairy in good standing accompanied her. She also had to promise not to stray from the immediate area in front of the board-walk, but when he reminded her not to forget to blend in with the beach community, she stopped nodding and rolled her eyes, instead.

He tapped his temple, which was the sign that he'd given her permission to connect with him telepathically. " You know how to reach me."

"Yes, of course. By the way, acting the spy will be simple. You may recall that I once starred in the title role of Mata Hari, so I'm already familiar with the part."

A few years earlier, a couple had co-written and self-published a paperback novel titled *Interview with a Fairy,* a fictionalized version of an actual encounter they claimed to have experienced. The catchy title helped bring the novel to the number one spot for part of a day within its very small and niche sub-genre, but the milestone provided them with newfound credentials as "best-selling authors."

They started an online group called Friends of the Fairies, which they advertised as a safe place for people who would like to share stories of their actual experiences with fairies. Fans of the book and curious visitors dropped in, but despite the growing membership of enthusiasts, no one joined who could verify a meeting with an actual fairy.

What they preferred to share were drawings, pictures, books, poems, and music. Discussions of face-to-face meetings with fairies devolved into members hijacking the forum with their personal fantasies.

The membership soon tired of the rehash of the couple's anecdotal encounter, and several suggested that without supporting photographs or anything else tangible, they had been exaggerating all along. With nothing new to add, the topic and the group became stale. Some complained that their intentions in starting the group had been fraudulent and that they'd only done it to broaden the market for their book and increase sales.

Thanks to the power of hashtags, one of the Friends of the Fairies got wind of Pat's blog. Enlarging and circulating the photo of the girl invigorated the members, and when someone else added a link to the *Myers Beach Tattler*, suddenly the group found a real focus.

For the next day and night, they pored over the fairy's features and discussed the details at length. Even the quietest members felt free to express their opinions about the brand-new revelation. After much study, they reached a consensus and issued a press release that MorningDew, one of the co-founders of the Friends of the Fairies, read on her podcast.

"Once again, the government and big corporations are keeping the real truth from us," she insisted. "They want everyone to believe that Big Tiny is an overgrown bird. But the collective minds of the Friends of the Fairies have put in the time to study the wings, the tiny legs, the authentic specific green cast, and a dozen other features. And we can hereby state without hesitation that the object in the photograph is a perfect specimen of a young male fairy. Furthermore, there is likely an entire coven in Myers Beach." She signed off as she always did. "We're the Friends of the Fairies, and we should know."

One of them did a quick search on Myers Beach, and upon learning that there was a tea house named The Fairy Kingdom, they posted a follow-up. "Coincidence? We think not!" After issuing a second press release, they began their plea for money. "Please help us travel to Myers Beach to uncover the truth that the mainstream media is afraid to report."

Via the Big Tiny hashtag, the *Myers Beach Tattler* picked up their press release. Falling for their expertise on the subject and with an eye toward reinvigorating the Tinker-bell/fairy angle and their circulation, they ran with the Friends of the Fairies finding. A new headline added to the chaos in a town already overrun with crazies.

It's a Fairy After All!

Panel of Experts Confirm Coven at MB.

When Alias arrived at Joe's to meet Dame Gabor for what she referred to as their intelligence briefings, he had to squeeze between pop-up tents on both sides of the door to get through.

The sign on the tent to the right read, "Locked and Loaded," where Joe was selling stun guns and other weapons for those who still believed the creature was a giant monster. For the followers of the revised fairy theory, the "Catch and Carry" tent on the left displayed his new offerings––butterfly nets and waxed canvas bird bags.

Dame Gabor was reading the latest issue of the *Tattler*, pretending to smoke from a long cigarette holder. Joe came out from the kitchen about the same time, and Alias burst out laughing when he saw him dressed head to toe in camo.

"What's so funny?" asked Joe.

"You." Alias waved his hands at all the merchandise. "And how far you're taking this."

"Look. Our paper of record says it was a fairy after all. Apparently, we've got a whole coven, so somebody's got to sell people this stuff."

Dame Gabor tossed her head and affected her best Bette Davis accent. "But a coven, Joe? You said a coven. That's a group of witches, not fairies." She tossed the newspaper aside and took a long drag.

"Hey, don't blame me. I don't work for that rag." He stared at her. "And put that out. There's no smoking allowed in here." She shoved her cigarette holder in his face, and his eyes lit up when he saw there was no cigarette in it. "Hey, that's neat. Where can I get one of those?"

She held up her hand. "Sorry, trade secret." Then she blew a series of perfect smoke rings in his face.

"Okay, Missus Smartypants. Then what do you call a group of fairies?"

Without thinking, she and Alias responded at the same time. "A finagle! A finagle of fairies."

Joe raised an eyebrow. "How the hell did you both know that?"

"I knew this because I wrote a paper on collective nouns for a Linguistics class in grad school," said Alias. He forced a laugh.

Joe shook his head. "They give you credit for that? No wonder schools are turning out weirdos."

When Joe was out of earshot, Dame Gabor lowered her voice. "Speaking of weirdos, a whole new group passed by me this morning. They were headed to the beach with their fairy-themed beach towels and ridiculous strap-on wings."

"And?"

She tapped on the headline. "Turns out they're this panel of experts the paper talks about."

"Aah, the Friends of the Fairies I read about."

"Yes. And despite calling themselves friends, I fear that they are going to create headaches for us. For one thing, I overheard them planning to take tea at The Fairy Kingdom. Can you imagine them snooping around inside?"

Alias wasn't concerned about humans wanting to enter The Fairy Kingdom. The bigger problem was keeping the fairies from going out.

"I spoke to one of the group who said the girl who found the fairy on the boardwalk created the opportunity of a lifetime, and that they were in town to get to the bottom of the story."

Alias groaned.

"It gets worse. Apparently, none of them are going to leave until all of them encounter a real honest-to-goodness fairy. Of course, I didn't have the heart to tell them that they were speaking with one and that it was I in the photo."

"I'm proud of you for resisting. It couldn't have been easy."

"Seriously, Your Highness, we need to think of a way to get rid of them before they complicate things. There are enough kooks running around the beach already."

CHAPTER TEN

Alias woke the next morning with a yawn and a large stretch to ease the ache his back had developed the night before, poring over the social media nightmare that his sleepy little town had become. With a gentle kiss to Christophe's forehead, he slipped out of bed and padded barefoot down the tower steps to the kitchen of the main house in search of caffeine. As he set the black tea on to boil, he decided that both he and Christophe could use a relaxing day to unwind from the stress of the media storm.

As the tea was steeping, he flicked at the pot, sending it to a table beside the pool. Then he grabbed the paper his staff collected for him every morning and he read up on the latest Myers Beach news.

"I heard you laughing. What's so funny?" asked the hoarse voice from behind him. Alias turned to see a sleep-rumpled Christophe shuffling onto the deck. "Did I smell tea?"

"In the pot," Alias sipped his and nodded to the pink pot

and the second cup and saucer. He held up the *Tattler*. "I was laughing about that gay pride festival Myers Beach is hosting that we read about in the flyer. They apparently want to celebrate the real fairies among us, not the fake magic kind."

Christophe raised a brow. He scanned the tiny descriptions of each event outlined in the article that Alias had spread on the table. "Actually, this is pretty great news, because it gives us a perfect out. And it's going to give us some fun things to do. How do you feel about the open mic night planned for the Tiki Hut?"

Alias grimaced at the idea of bad karaoke but knew Christophe got a kick out of the whole thing. He shrugged. "But only if we agree that I can use magic. I can't stand the sound of my human singing voice."

Christophe gave him a sly look. "Deal, if you'll agree to hold hands with me in public again."

Alias shivered at the idea. A short time ago, he'd thought nothing of small displays of affection with Christophe, but the times had changed in Myers Beach, along with the local demographics.

While he'd been clear about his sexuality and lived openly for years in the human world, he'd chosen a different approach in his fairy world. Subterfuge had never really been his forte, and he always felt a little sick to have to hide away pieces of himself from his subjects, but with so many of his countrymen now living as locals, his home turf seemed less safe from exposure.

Keeping that aspect private had been an old choice, and he vowed to become more open. It helped that the political winds had shifted in his favor. Two of the three kingdoms had changed rulers, and with Theos and Zsombor in his corner, he felt free to take steps to come out, even baby ones. Still, even during a weekend when everyone would be in costume and acting a bit crazy, holding hands with his lover seemed like it might be taking things too far.

While they finished their tea, they argued playfully over which other events they might attend. Then Alias happened to look out over the infinity pool at the white-caps in the ocean below.

"Surf's up!" he said, relieved at the lucky turn of events and knowing that Christophe would agree that surfing would take precedence.

He set aside the schedule, and they were about to leave their house when they heard a bump against the front door. When they opened it they found Dame Gabor helping Stefán get to his feet. He was sweating and his skin was pallid. He'd obviously been too weak to stand, and his fall had made the thump.

"I, I, we...." Stefán gave up and closed his eyes without finishing the sentence.

Dame Gabor pulled his head to her shoulder and stroked his hair. Then, not missing a beat, she picked up his lines.

"What he was going to say was--" She lowered her head and swallowed. "What he was going to say, was, was...."

Alias had never known her to falter with words. Witnessing her struggle to spit out whatever was so important that she and Stefán had to make a personal visit to tell him set off alarm bells in his head.

She turned to the side and then swept her hand over

her face. He recognized the theatrical gesture as what actors did when they wanted to compose themselves and change to a new character. She took a deep breath, and while he could see that she was trying to appear strong, he saw the wetness in her eyes and the fear behind them.

"We have a crisis at The Fairy Kingdom," she said at last. "Every fairy has fallen horribly ill. Every last one of them, except Stefán and me." She patted his damp head of hair. "And apparently now he has, too. We can't call what's happened a relapse, because even the fairies who weren't ill before now are sick as dogs. No one can get out of bed, let alone walk around. It's quite the situation."

Alias acted fast. With the flick of a finger, Stefán disappeared from the steps and reappeared under the rich duvet of one of his guest room beds. He and Dame Gabor stood at his bedside.

"You wouldn't happen to have some of your old classic dust lying around, would you?" she asked. "As you can see, I'm the only fairy still standing, and I'm positive it's because you used it on me. If you could spare some for Stefán, I'd consider it a great favor. This sudden bleak turn of events has everyone on edge back there, and we really need all hands on deck."

She was right. Stefán was in charge of The Fairy Kingdom and crucial to their operations. Reviving him immediately called for classic fairy dust. Fortunately, Stefán had kept himself in shape and had youth on his side, so Alias only needed to use a light sprinkle. After a few moments, Stefán sat up in the bed and was ready to talk.

"What happened?" Alias asked. "You and the others

should be full of pep. Didn't you give everybody a dose of my brand-new dust just yesterday?"

The day before, a dozen or so fairies had reported flu-like symptoms, and Stefán asked Alias to stop by to give them a quick check. The conditions Stefán described sounded like a perfect use for his new formulation, dust Number Five. He had been confident that D5 with the addition of *redach* would not only refresh the fairies but keep them that way. He took an extra bag immediately and gave Stefán instructions on how to administer the booster to all the fairies.

"Yes. I gave it to everyone exactly like you showed me." Stefán looked at the floor and shifted his weight. "And I hate to say this, Alias, because nobody wants to hear it, especially you. But D5 has to be the problem." He pointed at Dame Gabor. "She was at the beach when I dusted everyone else, so she didn't get the booster. Look at her. She's strong as an ox."

Alias didn't need to hear another word. He grabbed a bag of his previous formula, D4, and they hightailed it to The Fairy Kingdom. The mood inside was dark, and his eyes welled with tears when he walked down the endless rows of tiny beds filled with fairies he'd made sick.

Dame Gabor held his pouch of dust as they made their rounds. She'd transformed herself into a nurse, complete with a starched hat and white shoes, not as comic relief this time, but rather to add an atmosphere of solemnity and comfort to the care they were giving. Alias personally dotted each head of the thousands of desperately ill fellow fairies with the exact same amount of dust using the utmost care. And when Dame Gabor dabbed at her eyes and periodically choked back tears at the heartbreaking scene, she was not playing a role.

"I want to go home," yelled an older fairy. "You're killing us here!"

Alias took the man's hand and stroked his head. Then after he explained how everyone had been doing their best, he sang the man a familiar fairy lullaby.

"You amaze me," said Dame Gabor. "And now I understand why you're the prince. Nobody else could possibly be as strong as you. Except, of course, your brother, Theos the King." She genuflected according to protocol.

Alias shied away from the compliment. She'd called him strong, and while he appreciated the sentiment, he didn't feel that way. Not since he knew it was his fault that they'd suffered. He shut his eyes against the memories of that morning, when he'd spent time worrying about what they'd think of him because of his sexuality. His integrity as a scientist had never been at stake.

He'd thought taking a relaxing day with Christophe would be good for him, but now he realized that he should've been in the lab, researching more, looking at the dust more, doing something else *more*.

Their healthy green coloring and clear eyes returned to the fairies throughout the evening, and while there didn't appear to be any rhyme or reason for the differences in recovery times, they made a note of each one, and he didn't leave the building until the last fairy was on their feet.

Back at home, the hard truth of D5's tragic failure stared him down. Until that setback, he'd been feeling optimistic about both the project and his life. With only four more elements left to find, he saw the light at the end of that tunnel getting brighter. By revisiting the palace of the Third King, he'd taken the first step toward confronting a childhood nightmare. Finally, his deepening relationship with Christophe gave him great joy.

Like his half-human brother, Alias was grateful for his brains and good looks. Though the fairy half of their genetic makeup dominated in most ways, the mishmash of genes was complicated, and one human trait that he could live without reared its head too often: stress. He was already shouldering the fate of three fairy kingdoms and didn't need the glitch with D5.

He tossed and turned all night and woke up in a sweat, an uncommon condition for a fairy. Without a recipe, he was essentially working blindfolded. Using D4 had been the best option for emergency treatment, but not for the long-term, and D5 had been obviously leading them in the wrong direction.

He remembered Dame Gabor's heartfelt compliment the night before about how strong he'd been. Under the weight of his growing responsibilities, he didn't feel particularly strong, and he was glad he wasn't the king. But he was the prince, and in charge of the Myers Beach operation. So, until he got a better grip on his next steps, to prevent any further accidents, he called for an immediate lockdown of The Fairy Kingdom.

From the outset, he'd taken the approach that the more

ingredients, the better the dust. That the addition of each new element would improve the power and efficacy of the previous formulation, not make it worse. But since the fifth didn't work the same way, he knew that his hypothesis was wrong.

He'd never been one to make sloppy mistakes, and so he figured the correction would have to come from fixing a flaw in his logic. He decided to go back to basics and reread the writings of the Greek logicians he had studied long ago to see if that could shed any light on his dilemma. He'd begin with Galen and then move to Aristotle, Socrates, and Plato. He read at super speed, so it wouldn't take him long.

He knew where to find those books. On his recent visit to the palace library in the Third Kingdom, he'd seen them in the same places on the same shelves where they'd always been. But to read them, he wouldn't have to travel there. Manifesting a bunch of books right where he was sitting in his living room would be easy enough.

The one thing that was impossible to recreate was his class notes. When he fled the palace, he had been in such a hurry that he left all his personal things behind. He'd always been able to manifest anything he needed with a snap of his fingers, but he'd have to pick those up by hand.

Györfi may have had his faults, but during his time as their tutor he'd fulfilled his contractual duty. He'd introduced the boys to the wonders and complexities of the human world they would never have seen without him, and he turned the boys into scholars.

Thanks to their ability to write fast in fairy script, he

and the Third King captured practically every word out of the man's mouth, and by the time Alias left, he'd had binders full of notes, hundreds of them. Eager to reread one particular lecture, he made plans to go to the palace and to his old room again, where he'd left them.

CHAPTER ELEVEN

Alias stood in his old room gazing at the shelves full of his notes, and with a wave of his hand, he sent them to a long table in the library so he could study them in comfort. Instead of beginning with Galen as he'd intended, he pawed through the binders to search for Uncle Györfi's first lecture, on the subject of luck.

He laughed when he recalled how their tutor bragged that the lecture would be the most important one they'd hear, and how Györfi flailed his arms around to ensure that they gave him their full attention. When he caught them snickering at his theatrics, he chided them and warned them that one day they'd realize how lucky they were to receive such valuable wisdom.

"Luck favors the prepared mind."

He explained that the great chemist and microbiologist Louis Pasteur spoke those words in 1854. During that famous talk, he suggested that people who have prepared themselves with knowledge are better positioned to make the most of chance events.

Though modern history had attributed those words to Pasteur ever since, the concept wasn't entirely original to him. Centuries earlier, the Roman philosopher Seneca had structured the same principle somewhat differently, when he said that "luck is what happens when preparation meets opportunity."

Györfi gave examples of the many ways that scientific smarts combined with serendipity had led to brilliant innovations from the cavemen to the present, and he cited both quotations to remind them that it was up to them to make their own luck. He also used the lecture to elaborate on what it meant to have a prepared mind. The steps he outlined to achieve that weren't original, either. Dozens of other scholars before him and self-help gurus after him used more or less the same list.

That list was what Alias wanted to review. He found the binder he was looking for right away. Györfi delivered the lecture first in Latin, and Alias had written the title on the binder cover: *Fors favet animo paratis.* Since Györfi claimed it bore repeating, he presented it another day in French, and then again in English, each time with the same enthusiasm.

Alias credited Uncle Györfi for his love of Latin. He especially enjoyed those days when they were required to speak it exclusively. When they noticed that Györfi was presenting his lectures in Latin more frequently, the Third King joked that Alias had become the teacher's pet. He was just as good in Latin as Alias, but French was his favorite language. While Györfi was aware of that, he never seemed to afford the king the same kind of special treatment.

The Third King brought it up again later the next day.

Györfi had delivered *Fors favet animo paratis* in Latin, and when he happened to look up from taking notes, he swore that he saw the man wink at Alias, which he cited as another manifestation of Györfi's obvious favoritism. Alias thought he'd seen it too and had dismissed the gesture as a friendly acknowledgment that he was giving the class in Alias' favorite language.

Later, the Third King wouldn't let the wink go without a discussion. "Will you finally admit that Uncle Györfi was flirting with you? We both saw him do it."

"Please, drop it. He was just being friendly. Anyway, why me?"

"Come on, Alias. Everybody says you're gorgeous, you and your brother. Why would you think Györfi would be any different?"

Alias swallowed. It wasn't the first time he'd been told that both he and his brother were the most handsome fairies on the planet and had amazing bodies to match. Unlike Theos, who was more muscular, Alias was one of those slender guys who didn't have to work out. The skinny jeans type, but with abs of steel.

"Um, what about you?" His throat was dry, and the question got caught on the way out. "Do you think I am?"

The Third King pulled his knees to his chest and sat up. "Well, duh, yeah! Have you looked at yourself in the mirror?" Alias blushed. "Look, I'm not saying you did anything to egg him on or anything, but didn't you notice how he kept rubbing his eye afterward like he had something in it? I say he was faking it. He got caught flirting with you, and he knows that we both know."

"Okay, maybe you're right, but can we pretend we

never saw it? I don't want to jeopardize our relationship with him."

From the beginning, the rapport between the boys and their tutor had been professional, even amicable, though not always rosy. Like so many other brilliant men and women throughout history, Uncle Györfi's personality was complicated by an ego that often went unchecked. Over time, too, the enormous differences in their social standings frequently resulted in miscommunications.

Alias felt no emotional attachment either to the man or toward his role as their tutor, and he never gave those missteps a second thought. He assumed the Third King felt the same way. But those same missteps seemed to plague Györfi. Alias could tell by the man's expression and slumped shoulders that every misinterpreted remark or gesture reminded him of his inferior social status. His red face showed his embarrassment, too.

Both boys had always cut him slack. The tutor was carrying a heavy assignment, a burden made worse by the intense pressure of their parents' expectations. Still, Alias appreciated his friend's observations and he vowed to be more vigilant.

As he pored over the lecture notes, he heard the clock chime. That time, rather than reminding him of the book-case door, the striking of the lone bell drew his attention to how quiet it was in the room. Quiet was how he remembered it too, except for those times when Györfi would forget to close the bookcase door shut.

The dark and mournful tune they'd hear coming down from his upstairs chambers was nearly always the same, a cut from a vinyl recording by a female lounge singer named Zsa Zsa Hajdu, famous for her crooning style that had been the rage in the 1940s. Considering that the style put an emphasis on singing softly, the boys found it odd that he turned up the volume so loud. Sometimes late at night, Alias could hear the music all the way in his bedroom and Györfi singing along.

Despite his boast that he owned all of the dead woman's recordings, the boys got a private laugh over the fact that he only played one cut, *Are You Lonesome Tonight?*

Alias brought his notes to the sofa and read for a while, but the song kept playing in his head and vied for his focus. Finally, he gave in. He set his notebook on the floor, kicked off his shoes, and laid his head back on the soft armrest. He closed his eyes and thought back to that one summer afternoon that, in most respects, had been like any other.

The Third King had been lying opposite him and Zsa Zsa Hajdu's voice was streaming through Györfi's open door. They'd been declining Latin nouns together when he felt his friend's bare toe graze against the instep of his foot. Not bump into. Almost lingering.

He didn't snap his foot away immediately. If he'd listened to his heart pounding wildly at the delicious sensation, he would have let his friend's toe touch him forever. The details were foggy, and he squinted to remember them.

Human boys weren't supposed to touch each other. Neither were fairy boys, the green kind. After a few moments, he had forced his foot away. Then again, it may have been the other way around. The Third King may have pulled his foot away first. It's what should have happened. The person who accidentally bumped against someone was always the one who was supposed to make the course correction. He thought hard. Perhaps they yanked their feet away at the same time.

Alias stretched out his long legs along the cushions and pointed his toes to find the exact spot where the union occurred. Whether exploratory or accidental, he remembered how the touch had thrilled him and racked his body, and that his heart had thumped against his ribcage, and his brain had turned to mush.

He'd always been a whiz at those declension drills, but he was having enough trouble breathing to concentrate on anything else. The Third King must have noticed that he was making terrible mistakes, and to get him back on track, he banged his whole foot against Alias.' Alias remembered how futile those efforts had been, because the more contact he felt, the more discombobulated his brain.

Their toes touched several times again the next afternoon. But unlike the first time, which might have been dismissed as accidental, the ones the next day were deliberate, at least the ones Alias initiated.

Over the next few days, the innocent tapping morphed into full-on crazy toe wrestling. While they'd kept their eyes either closed or buried in books before, this new game was playful, and they could actually look the other one in the eye while their toes poked and circled around each other. With its combative elements, he could dismiss it as a guy thing, almost a sporting event. And though there were no rules or points, the matches were definitely competitive.

Alias took a breath as his mind recreated the exact day the toe wrestling stopped, and how the warm bottoms of their feet found each other and pressed together instead. And how they kept them that way for hours every day from then on.

One afternoon, as Györfi's favorite tune was blasting down at full volume, he remembered them putting down their books at the same time and snickering. The Third King jiggled his throat to mimic the woman's vibrato, and he was rolling his eyes at the bookcase door when suddenly it swung open and Uncle Györfi burst in.

The boys quickly pulled their feet apart and pretended nothing had been going on. Their eyes darted back and forth in nervous exchanges, but they soon relaxed when their tutor ignored them, took a seat on one of the leather chairs, and started to read.

The next morning the boys discussed the incident over breakfast. The Third King insisted that Uncle Györfi had been spying on them and knew exactly what they'd been doing all along. That he'd turned up the music extra loud so they wouldn't hear him coming down his steps and he could catch them in the act.

He had wanted to report the incident to his aunt, but Alias talked him out of it. She would want to ask questions and know what they were afraid he'd see. While touching their feet together shouldn't have been a big deal, he suggested that she might turn it into one. And since neither boy could verify that Györfi had even glanced their way, they let the incident pass. So did Györfi. And the boys resumed their foot cuddling when they knew they were alone.

Months later, Alias found himself struggling to solve a logic equation, and he asked Uncle Györfi for help. His tutor had been happy to assist but explained that he'd been extremely occupied with a project, and hoped Alias wouldn't mind meeting in his private chambers.

When he heard what Alias planned to do, the Third King grabbed his wrist. "I get the feeling that you've made up your mind, but I'm telling you. Nothing would get me to go up there alone. He's a great teacher and all, but there's something about him that creeps me out. If I were you, I'd ask him to come down to the library. Don't forget, he works for us."

Alias went up anyway. Györfi found the flaw in Alias' logic instantly, but he explained that he wouldn't be doing a very good job as his tutor if he simply identified the mistake. He insisted that working it out together would be more productive, and he moved from his chair and sat beside Alias on his loveseat.

In short order, Györfi helped Alias discover where he'd made the omission when he'd assigned values in his truth tables. He then showed him how to use a system of lexico-graphic ordering to avoid making omissions like that in the future, and Alias' eyes lit up at the breakthrough.

Györfi congratulated him with a pat on the back for figuring it out so fast. Then Alias started to snicker at his mistake. Györfi joined in the laughter, and soon they were giving each other friendly elbow jabs. Györfi made eye contact and followed his last jab with a light squeeze of the boy's thigh.

Alias stood to gather his things. He held up his hand for a high five, and Györfi returned the gesture. Alias was still laughing when he left the room.

"The guy's all right," he told the Third King the next day

as they lay on the library sofa in their usual position. "I was really stumped, and he showed me a trick I can use on truth tables for the rest of my life. If you're interested, I'll show you how." He dug his toes into the bottom of the king's foot. "And he didn't say anything about this. So see? You and I have nothing to worry about."

Shortly after midnight, Alias was back in Myers Beach speeding across a monster wave. Any time he got to surf was his favorite time, but surfing at that hour was special. At that time of night, the water always looked black, like fresh ink on paper, and instead of instilling him with the fear of the unknown, it always helped him wipe the anxiety of the day, clearing the slate clean for the next project.

For him, surfing was a rejuvenating nightly ritual, to steer his favorite board over the waves washed with silver fire from the moonlight. At night, he would likely be the only one out there.

It wasn't that humans didn't ever surf at night. It was that the darkness presented challenges to them that he didn't have to face. The trick to surfing in the dark was to decrease the number of unknowns. Opting for a familiar location was one way to make it easier, and it helped if the spot had a history of calm waves. And of course, for humans, the absence of rain or fog was a plus.

The memory of that one-on-one session with Györfi was still fresh in his mind as he leaned into the waves, and he snickered at the realization that he'd been applying a truth table to night surfing. But it was hard not to feel

Györfi's presence daily. The man had not only taught him how to think, but he'd also taught him almost everything he knew.

He missed surfing with his team during the day when he'd go out to help mine the *tepa* and *igdia*. Since most of his kingdom had relocated to Myers Beach, he hadn't had enough time to enjoy the ocean or science, two of his favorite things. He'd been more focused on appearing as a strong and steady prince.

A flash of pink lit the sky ahead of him and he paddled out past the breaking waves so he could sit on his board and watch the magical phenomena. He couldn't blame Greta for wanting it to be hers, but he knew it couldn't be. Heat lightning was his.

He reversed the direction of the small path of ocean beneath him so that the waves took him out, rather than to shore. Surfing or flying inside the band of heat lightning energized him and helped clear his mind. Eyes facing straight ahead, his board gripped the waves and he let his mind fly as he sped across the water into the pink light.

CHAPTER TWELVE

Theos

My heart truly aches for my brother. He's been the golden child of the family all his life, so the failure of his formula must be killing him. Dame Gabor told me how broken he was at having to start over from scratch.

He told me he's worried about the amount of classic fairy dust left in stock at the compound. What he'd originally brought was meant to be his personal stash, but more than half our population lives in Myers Beach these days, and he needs to dip into it frequently to fix the normal problems associated with that many fairies. I wish I could help him, but of course we barely have enough for ourselves.

I know he blames himself for much of the town's chaos, too. He said it was his own fault for a couple of comments he made when he was pretending to be Doctor DuBois in the police station. Greta told me that she could hardly keep a straight face because he'd been so funny, especially when he put on the glasses and surgical gloves. I wish I could have been there to see him.

But he said he was having too much fun and got carried away. Instead of leaving well enough alone, he went off script. Like mentioning that he'd seen his so-called viridi aliquid minima *as tall as six feet two. He was referring to his own size, of course, and he admitted the in-joke was only for his and Greta's benefit.*

As it turned out, that throwaway line was the one that the idiot press glommed onto. Not surprisingly the media apparently didn't find a six-foot-two measurement sensational enough, because by the time the story made the headlines, they'd added another foot, which stretched the fabled monster to over seven. He swears he never said that the town was 'crawling with them,' either. He distinctly remembered telling the captain that there had been more and more sightings, and he'd only added that to make the 'bird' sound not so rare.

It's too bad he didn't tell me at the time that he'd wanted to take those comments back. I probably could have made that happen.

Greta said he was a natural actor, and she wasn't surprised when I told her that he'd studied acting under the great Miss Gabor. She wondered why he hadn't gotten into the business, since he was obviously such a natural. I didn't answer, of course, but being so smart and naturally talented at so many things has kind of been my brother's curse. He's never known where to put his focus.

And I fear that not so far beneath his happy-go-lucky personality, he's really not very happy. I know he struggles to remember what happened that last day in the Third Kingdom, too. My father gave me the broad strokes, but he suggested I keep it to myself for fear of embarrassing Alias.

When we find those last few ingredients and things return to normal, I'll have a sit-down with the new Third King and see what we can do to unravel the story and make things better for my brother.

86

CHAPTER THIRTEEN

To accommodate the hordes of newcomers to town, Joe had added more tables and crammed them so close to each other that Alias and Dame Gabor had to practically whisper to keep their conversation private.

"I may have inadvertently set a bit of mischief in motion." She arched her brow. "Possibly a way to get rid of some of the nut jobs running around here. I hope you won't mind."

"That will depend," said Alias. "Tell me more, Dame Gabor."

"I will, but first, you've got to stop calling me Dame Gabor. I know I'm more than three times your age, but now that we're friends, it's time you called me Rita."

He laughed at the preposterous suggestion of calling his former teacher by her first name, and a mouthful of Frappuccino went down the wrong way. "Not a chance. I would never feel comfortable doing that. You earned your title, so I'm sticking with Dame Gabor. You use mine, after all."

She rested her elbow on the table and waved her cigarette holder again. "As you wish, Your Royal Highness."

He leaned in and cupped his hand. "But you should probably start calling me Alias, like everyone else around this town, at least in front of other people when we're outside The Fairy Kingdom. And definitely promise to stop using the term *Highness* around Joe. He's the town blabbermouth, and if he hears you calling me that, everyone will know by dinner."

She blinked. "Oh, my gosh. You gave me a great idea. He'll be just the ticket to make my little scenario work."

"Something tells me that your scenario won't be little, but please, go on."

"So, I was lying on the beach this morning when I overheard the people next to me mention my name. Well, kind of. They were talking about Big Tiny. Someone had read a blog post about how Big Tiny reproduces. I wanted to cover my ears, until I heard one of them asking if fairies laid eggs. After the shock of their ignorance wore off, I got this idea."

Alias covered his mouth to keep from laughing. "This is already pretty stupid, so I can't wait to hear where you're going."

"I'll tell you what I said and then explain why. I managed to casually mention that I was in the media and that I'd heard from a very reliable source that before the girl caught her, the fairy had in fact, been laying eggs all over town."

She threw her head back again and let out a practiced stage laugh. "I may have gone overboard with how I said the eggs got fertilized, but from the looks on their faces, I could tell they were eating it up. I wasn't at all surprised though, considering how gullible humans can be. Let's not forget that the panel of experts stated that we lived in covens.

"Apparently my voice carried to a couple of kids under an umbrella next to me on the other side. They got wind of it and started pestering their dad to find them fairy eggs.

"The father was a big guy with a gravelly voice, not exactly the type you'd expect to be interested in fairies. He definitely loved spoiling his girls, though, and after putting up with the whining for several minutes, he got exasperated. He told me that he would find them one if he had to turn Myers Beach inside out."

"Hmm. I hope you're not suggesting an egg hunt. Since they won't find any, they could end up sticking around until they do. That could be ages."

"Yes, unless we tell them where to find them. So, I casually mentioned that fairies bury their eggs deep in the ground, like those giant turtles. I said that a bunch of us were going to dig around the skatepark, because a worker reported finding an egg there." She wiggled her eyebrows. "So, what if while they're digging, I don't know, they get arrested for defacing public property? Do you see where I'm going with this, Your H, and how Joe might make this happen?"

Alias nodded. Even if their scheme only got rid of a couple dozen, the prank would be fun. When Joe walked past their table within earshot, she took Alias' hand and pretended to speak privately.

"Please keep this *entre nous*," she said in a voice loud enough to reach Joe's ears. "You know the fairy the girl found under this table? Well, this morning I heard that she'd been laying eggs all over town before she got caught."

Alias whispered back. "I heard the same story, something about a workman finding a couple in the ground by the skatepark. Go on."

"Yes. And here's the real secret about fairy eggs, that nobody around here seems to know." She looked to both sides before continuing. "Turns out that they're not just normal eggs. They're aphrodisiacs." She sat back and winked. "Like, really incredibly powerful ones. The guy who found the one says he thinks there are probably hundreds of them."

Alias slapped his cheek and whispered back. "Oh my gosh! Then if you could get your hands on one, a fairy egg would be worth a fortune."

Joe broke into the conversation. "What's this about fairy eggs? I promise I wasn't listening to your conversation, but I believe I heard the lady mention something about an aphrodisiac."

Dame Gabor repeated her story to Joe. Then she put her finger to her lips. "Now listen. I only told you because he said you could be trusted. But mum's the word, okay? Can you imagine the stampede if the word got out? People would be digging holes all over Myers Beach."

CHAPTER FOURTEEN

Christophe was a champion. Alias was not. At least not on a skateboard. As a surfer and a natural athlete, he could ride a board well enough, but he'd never bothered to go much beyond the basics.

Because of the gap in their skills, there was no expectation to compete, and their times together at the skateboard park tended to be fun and lighthearted. He mostly enjoyed watching Christophe whiz along and demonstrate his latest routines and the advanced tricks that had surprised judges and won him trophies.

Christophe had planned to give Alias some pointers on mastering the Gazelle flip, but skateboarding wasn't the main reason for visiting the park that day. They were there to check up on their fairy egg-digging mischief campaign. Skateboarding wasn't the reason Greta showed up, either.

She'd finished her part in overseeing the transition at The Fairy Kingdom and had turned over the operation to Stefán's capable hands. In a day or two she was leaving

Myers Beach to join Zsombor in her new home, and she wanted to visit with her friends one more time.

The skate park was mobbed when she got there, but not the pump track. She could see that Alias and Christophe had that part to themselves. It was the ground around the track that was so crowded with people. At first, she assumed they were spectators thrilled to watch a professional skateboarder in person, but when she got closer, her jaw dropped.

It wasn't just the garish fairy costumes that many of the otherwise normal men and women were wearing, or the pointy pixie ears and strap-on plastic wings that gave her a giggle. What made her eyes grow wide was seeing them digging huge holes all over the park with pickaxes and shovels. Alias and Christophe rushed over to join her, and when they saw the confusion on her face, Alias passed her a flyer that he found on the bench next to them.

WE PAY UP TO $500 CASH FOR FAIRY EGGS.
　　NO LIMIT.
　　See map on reverse side for location.
　　Shovels and pickaxes for rent or purchase.
　　Ask for Joe, at Joe's Java Joint.

"What's going on here is a little mischief that Dame Gabor and I cooked up the other day," Alias explained.

"Fairies laying eggs! How does anyone keep a straight face?"

"It's got to be hard. But what you're witnessing here isn't only Joe's doing. He's just taking advantage of a bunch of gullible people, which is what we hoped would happen."

Greta cracked up when he filled her in on the rumor they started. He pointed to the flyer and then to the group of people. "Thanks to your friend Joe and his big mouth, our scheme is unfolding faster than we imagined."

"You're a devil for not telling me, but I'm glad I'm here to see it play out."

Christophe hooked his thumb at the people in costume. "Speaking of being gullible, do humans really think that fairies look like that?"

"As a former human, I am sorry to say that they do," said Greta.

Christophe snickered. "It's not completely their fault. It's Joe's aesthetic. When I went by his place today, I noticed that he's renting fairy costumes now, along with the weapons. I saw the shovels, too, and since he's gotten so crazy himself, I didn't bother to ask what they were for." He looked over the park. "Now I know."

"As a businesswoman, I know how tempting it can be to cash in on events like this," said Greta. "Joe has a good head for business, so I'm not surprised. But I'm beginning to think his moral compass is on the fritz."

Heat lightning flashed on the horizon and the light flickered against her pendant. "We haven't seen heat lightning for a while," said Alias. He slid an arm around her shoulders. "It reminds me of the night we met, and I remember how much we both said we liked it."

They gazed at the lightning for a moment as it washed everything in the park in dazzling pink before Greta shook herself and looked down at her pendant. She unhooked it from her neck and handed it to him.

"Before I leave, I want to give you this. I clearly don't

need it anymore, since it brought me a husband and many other fantastic things. Plus, since you did such a great job of polishing it for me all those times, I think you should have it. I checked with Theos, and he agreed."

Alias beamed as he placed it around his neck. "Aww. I'm not much of a pendant guy, but this is so cool, getting to wear the one that belonged to my big brother and best friend."

"Well, I'm sure it will bring you a ton of luck."

"Yeah, the good kind, right?"

"Of course. Not that you need it."

"Thanks. But I feel like I could really use some about now."

"Nonsense. You're the luckiest man I know…next to Zsombor, of course, who was so lucky, he got me." She looked at his skateboard. "I see you finally nailed your flip. You're not giving up surfing, are you?"

"Not a chance, but yeah, it fell together a few minutes ago," he said. "And I owe it all to this guy." He pulled Christophe over and gave him a big hug. They separated, but their faces were only an inch apart when he added his next compliment. "You were right, honey. Doing a Big Flip first helped me do the Gazelle."

"Why don't you two fairies just kiss and be done with it," boomed a gravelly voice. "Everyone can see that you want to." The large, sweaty man was leaning against his shovel at the edge of a huge pit. "I came out here to find fairy *eggs*, not effing fairy faggots."

Faggot was a trigger word for Alias, though he never understood why, and when Christophe saw his discomfort, he stepped between them before Alias used his magic and did something he'd regret. "Um, you're the one wearing ridiculous fairy wings," said Christophe. "Not us."

The man unbuckled the harness and tossed the costume wings on the ground. "Let's be clear. I'm not like you. My kids made me wear those." He glared at them again before turning around and digging again.

Greta frowned at the man's insult to her friends. "I still don't get it. Why is digging up the skate park such a good idea?"

"Look, any of us could make these idiots disappear with a wave of our hand," said Alias. "And believe me, that's what I wanted to do a minute ago. We all know they're not going to find eggs of any kind. The hope is that when they finally realize that they'd been duped about the fairy egg bit, they might feel stupid for believing in the whole story. And then maybe they'll leave."

"Yeah," said Christophe. "And at the very least we're planning to leak what they're doing to the cops. Hopefully, they'll arrest the goons for defacing public property. I'm surprised they're not here already."

"Well, even without this fairy egg thing, the town has become a joke. You should know that some group called the Friends of the Fairies has been driving everyone crazy at The Fairy Kingdom wanting to know what's going on inside."

Greta paused to think for a moment, and then her eyes lit up. "Hey. I've got an idea to add a twist to your project and scare the pants off them. Since they're looking for eggs, let's let them find some. Just not the kind they're looking for." She told them what she was thinking, and the guys laughed. "Ready? First, I'll need a little distraction. Alias, will you do the honors?"

He waved a hand at the hundred or so flyers that littered the ground. Instantly, the pieces of paper folded themselves into origami birds. They lined up facing him, and when he gave the signal they flapped their paper wings and took off from the ground. They fluttered overhead and let out shrieks so deafening that the humans had to drop their tools and cover their ears. Then the birds dive-bombed into their heads and faces. Anyone in a fairy costume was a target. While the humans were swatting away the birds, Greta held out her open palm and screamed.

"Look! I found one!"

Suddenly, the birds flew to a nearby tree branch. Freed from their pestering, the humans rushed to examine the perfectly shaped five-inch oblong egg Greta was holding. They raced back and used their flashlights to see if they would be as lucky as she was. Cheers rang out over the park when they discovered shiny eggs at the bottoms of every pit.

Except in the one dug by the burly man who had called Alias and Christophe fairies. Flushed with anger that everyone had found one but him, he grabbed Greta's egg and pointed his finger.

"That's mine," he growled. "You stole it from one of the holes I dug."

Greta sneered back. "That's ridiculous!" She flicked her finger, and one of the origami birds darted down from the tree and pecked at the man's nose. He winced, and as he swatted the bird away, he lost his balance and toppled backward into the hole he'd dug.

"What do you think, boys? Is it time?" she asked. Alias and Christophe nodded, and when she snapped her fingers, every egg in every hole in the skatepark hatched at the same time. The origami birds were the first to notice the thick, long snakes that had broken through their eggshells and slithered out of their freshly dug nests, and they squawked like crazy. Men and women scrambled to their feet and abandoned their tools as swarms of angry snakes hissed and chased them around the park.

Alias laughed. "To be fair, you never said that the egg you found was from a fairy." As Greta and Christophe shared in the laugh, heat lightning flickered again behind them. He turned and took a deep breath. As his chest expanded, his new pendant pulsated, and the stone became less green and more blue. They were examining the stone's new color when they heard stuttering from the man who'd fallen into his pit.

"S-something's very wrong," he stammered. "P-please help me."

The three of them looked at each other, wondering which one would step in to help, but when they saw him flutter up out of the pit powered by his own set of real lavender wings growing from between his shoulders, they backed away. Greta manifested a floor-length mirror, and the man shrieked when he saw his reflection.

"Hey, tough guy. Now, who's the fairy?" she asked.

The man reached around to rip away his new growth, and he yelped when they didn't come off.

Alias walked behind him to get a better look. "Hey.

Better stop doing that, or you'll hurt yourself. These things look permanent." He grinned at Christophe and Greta. "Okay. Whoever had the idea to do this gets a prize. This was genius."

Christophe laughed at the man. "Welcome to the fairy club. Want to see what real fairies can do? Watch this." He clapped his hands, and the snakes and the humans they were chasing froze in mid-action. "Not a bad trick for a fairy faggot, is it?"

"Who are you people?" said the man. By then, he was sitting on the ground rocking in place with his arms around his knees. When Christophe heard him sob, he clapped again and froze him in place, too.

Christophe jumped down into the man's pit.

"Hey!" he called from the bottom. "There's a box of some kind down here. I can't tell what it is, but I'll bring it up." In a split second, a large mound of mud appeared at Alias' feet.

"Greta, look. My pendant is glowing. Do you know why it would?"

"It's hard to tell," she said. "When it glowed for me, though, it was generally a good sign."

He waved at the mound, and the dirt fell away to reveal an ornate wooden chest.

Greta stooped to finger the carving on the top and whistled when she recognized the initials. "CHG! You know, I'll bet this is the buried treasure historians have been talking about for eons. I'd guess the H in the center stands for Hersey, as in the Hersey Lighthouse."

"I remember your little lecture," said Alias. "You said Hersey posed as a man and became a famous pirate captain. That's probably where the 'C' comes from, captain, wouldn't you think?"

"Yes, yes," shouted Greta. "And the G, for Gabby, though her real name may have been Gabriella. Captain Gabrielle Hersey. Man, the story really was true! A part of me always believed it was a myth."

The rusty lock fell to the ground at Alias' touch, and when they pulled back the heavy top, gold coins spilled out over the sides. "Spanish Doubloons," she said, "like the one in the Myers Beach Museum." She held one closer. "No, wait. This isn't Spanish. It's the other kind. A Brasher Doubloon, and worth a lot more. There's a fortune in that chest."

"Help yourself. We don't need it," said Alias. He turned to Christophe. "I'm sorry. We don't, do we?"

Christophe shrugged his shoulders and laughed. "I really appreciate it when Alias includes me in decisions about money. He forgets sometimes that I'm just his lowly fairy boyfriend who is still insecure about his financial relationship with a prince."

"Yeah. A lowly fairy with great connections. Greta, you should have seen him lolling on the Third King's throne when I went there the other day. That behavior would never fly in our court."

Christophe smiled. "What can I say? The king took a shine to me. Frankly, I've always gotten along well with the palace staff, and I think I got away with it because they looked the other way."

Greta closed the lid on the box. "Look. I don't need the money either, so if it's cool, I'll cash in this loot, and we can divvy it up between my foundation and The Endowment for Oceanic Solutions. I'll toss some to a couple retirement homes I used to visit, too."

Christophe hopped back down into the hole. "Actually, there are quite a few more of those chests down there. Now that we know what's in them, I'll just send them up to the house, and we can sort out the loot, as you call it, later."

"Fine with me." Greta gestured to the man with the wings. "So, what are we going to do with him? Do you think he's learned his lesson?"

Alias snapped his fingers, which set the park in motion and unfroze the man. He trembled when he saw the snakes chasing humans again, and he bellowed when a large one coiled around his foot. When it curled up his leg, he jumped up and stomped and kicked to shake it off. His panicked eyes begged Alias for help.

Alias nodded. "Yeah, yeah. We'll get to you. What's your name, by the way?"

"Bruce," he said. The three of them covered their mouths and snickered, and when he asked what was so funny, Alias ignored him and gazed at the pockmarked skatepark. "Bruce, you and your dopey friends made quite a mess of our park, and we've got some major cleanup to do. Do you want to do it, or would you rather a couple of faggots showed you how?" He didn't wait for an answer. "I'll start."

He clapped his hands, and the snake retreated from Bruce's leg. Bruce dropped his head in relief when he saw the reptile slither across the park and down into one of the holes. Greta clapped her hands and the rest of the snakes raced across the park and slipped into the same hole. She clapped again and the entire flock of origami birds flew off down from the tree and dove in after the snakes.

With the snakes safely away, the humans fled the park. Christophe pointed at the shovel on the ground next to him and it sprang to life. Then it and all the other shovels refilled the holes with dirt. When they finished, he clapped and commanded the grass to regrow. Then he pointed to the shovels and pickaxes, and they spun around in the air and landed one by one with a clatter in a nearby dumpster. In less than a minute, the humans had escaped, the tools had vanished, and everything in the skatepark had returned to normal, except Bruce and his wings.

"I'd say at least fifteen or twenty folks will leave town and never come back. Are you pleased?" asked Greta.

"Absolutely, and it was a great stress reliever. We should do something like this every day."

"Look. I don't know who you are," said the man on the ground. "but you guys can obviously do anything. Please, make these go away."

"I don't know, Bruce, are you sure?" asked Christophe. "When you know how to work them, wings don't have to just be for flying. They can be quite useful in lots of other ways." He winked at Alias and Greta. They popped out their wings and turned so their backs faced Bruce and they flapped them at his face, tickling him with their silky lightness.

"Come on. Please. I'm serious. What am I going to tell my family?"

"We don't care, Bruce. You have a big mouth. You'll think of something," said Alias.

Greta jumped in. "I think we should let him keep them.

It seems a shame to waste magic just to make his perfectly good set of wings disappear when most people would die for them. Let's not forget what a jerk he was and the hateful things he said to you guys."

The man's hands shook. "Okay. Okay. Look. I'm sorry. The words just came out. I didn't think about what I was saying."

Alias made a big production about putting his arm around Christophe in front of the guy. "My friend is right, Bruce. You're a bully. But I'm not, so I'm going to give you a little extra time to consider not being one, either." He flicked a finger. "Okay. Your wings should fall off on their own...eventually. What do you think, guys, two or three days at the latest?"

"Yeah. Not long," said Christophe. He gave Alias a peck on the cheek. "They're going to leave pretty nasty scars, though. Probably for life."

CHAPTER FIFTEEN

Mayor Jim had expected his reelection for another four years to be a slam dunk. While there were those in the community who wished he'd been more progressive, most people were pleased with his steady, trustworthy, and non-controversial leadership. But Big Tiny's arrival closely coincided with his announcement to run again and threw a monkey wrench into the race.

The town's opinions about dealing with the phenomenon were deeply divided, and Mayor Jim ended up with a challenger: Big Joe.

Jim's message was clear. He and approximately fifty percent of the town had become distressed by the unwanted tabloid sensationalism and disliked the riffraff that came with it. Though he couldn't prove it, he'd heard that many of the regular tourists were not returning because of the tawdriness that people had begun to associate with their once-charming town. Most of all, they complained that there was no longer enough parking for locals.

He railed against the unlicensed vendors who kept popping up on the town's beloved boardwalk selling Big Tiny trinkets and competing with the established merchants. Chasing them away every day, he maintained, was putting stress on the police department's assets and budget.

His reelection campaign slogan was simple and predictable, like his tenure as mayor.

Just say NO to fairies...and to Joe!

Joe's campaign, on the other hand, referred to Big Tiny as a miracle, their lucky break. He said that business had never been better for the shopkeepers and hoteliers and cited the massive infusion of dollars into the community since the phenomenon began. Provided that they were all making more money, Big Joe, as he'd rebranded himself, encouraged the townspeople to not only accept the Big Tiny myth but embrace it.

His public relations instincts went to work, and within a few days, yard signs and posters popped up everywhere. He even made an exception to his long-standing objection to sandwich board signs, and when Alias and Christophe were walking by, Joe was standing back to admire his latest.

Official Meeting Place of the Friends of the Fairies - MWF - 10 am

Paid for by Big Joe for Mayor.

"Joe, does this mean you rented your second floor?" Alias asked. He tried not to gawk at Joe's new bleached blond hair and gold hoop earrings.

"Not yet. But between us, I plan to offer this group a

pretty deep discount if they make it their headquarters. I figured it would be worth it for the prestige, and all."

Alias pointed to the board. "Looks like you got them meeting here on a regular basis already. How did you pull that off?"

"I stole the idea from the Sea Catch restaurant. You know how the Rotary Club meets there every week? Same thing."

Alias rolled his eyes and avoided disputing the comparison. "Well, you certainly have a lot going on," he said. "Lucky you."

"Listen, guys. I know you're nuts about my new frappuccino, so today they're on the house."

Christophe elbowed Alias. "Should we tell him we can't vote?"

Joe ushered them in and asked for their honest opinion on what he'd done to the place. As soon as he opened the door, their hands immediately went to cover their ears against the disco music that blasted from a new set of surround sound speakers.

"Too much?" asked Joe.

Alias nodded and pointed at the cups and saucers that were rattling on the glass shelf behind the bar from the vibrations of the oversized subwoofer. They waited for him to turn down the volume before deciding to stay, and on the way to a table, they took in the redecoration. Gone from the walls were the worn-out posters of NASCAR drivers. In their spots, he'd plastered giant glossies of Judy Garland and a shirtless Cristiano Ronaldo.

Their frappuccinos came with a flyer.

"I'm assuming you know about the Alphabet Mafia?" Joe said with a question in his voice that implied he was about to give them the answer. Alias shrugged his shoulders and gave the flyer a read. Many of the local businesses were participating in a series of events called the *Alphabet Mafia Fairy Extravaganza*, and the flyer promised full days of parades and partying from Friday evening into Sunday afternoon.

The organization behind the weekend called themselves the Queer Collective, a group of LGBT+ artists, influencers, and socialites. The theme was *Fairies, Out and Proud*, which played into one of the stated goals of the group: "to take back the name *fairy* for gays." They'd picked Myers Beach to host the event for obvious reasons.

"I don't get it," said Alias.

"Well, well, mister linguist, I'm surprised you don't know, so let me enlighten you." He put a hand on Alias' shoulder and recited an explanation that sounded scripted and rehearsed. "The Alphabet Mafia refers to the ever-increasing addition of letters to the LGBTQ+ acronym. It's urban slang." He squeezed Alias' shoulder and walked toward the bar.

"Correction," said Christophe. "Alphabet Mafia is not urban slang. It's an urban *slur*. Some bigot started it a while ago."

Joe came back and this time patted Christophe's shoulder. "That may be true, my friend, but it's my understanding that the gays have claimed it now."

"They have?" asked Alias.

"Yes. So, that makes it cool for everyone to use. Do you get it now?" He smiled, and this time he made it all the way to the bar.

Alias scratched his head. "That's not the part I didn't get. What I don't understand is why people need another term to refer to gays. And by the way, I hate hearing straight people use the word *fairy*. Like that's supposed to connote something pejorative. And gays want to bring that back?"

"I know," said Christophe. "But I'm confused for a different reason. Why the hell is Joe's Java Joint sponsoring a gay-themed weekend?"

"Sponsoring? What did I miss?"

Christophe pointed to the box of type at the bottom of the flyer. "Sponsored in part by Joe's Java Joint and the Big Joe for Mayor campaign committee."

The flyer boasted discounts to anyone who showed up in a fairy costume, which you could rent at Joe's Java Joint, and the *Extravaganza* would culminate in a massive costume contest with the winner getting dinner for two at the Sea Catch.

Alias stuffed the flyer into the pocket of his blue and green board shorts to reread later, and he took another sip of Queen Greta's Fairy Frappuccino. Despite Joe's political ambitions and any other motivation behind it, the weekend's theme did sound like fun.

The boardwalk crowded with people running around in costume could provide the cover that he and Christophe needed to let their real wings out and have fun. Going to a few events would go along with his new determination to work toward being himself, especially around his subjects.

The costume angle gave him another idea—the event could serve as a much-needed reprieve for the fairies who he'd kept in lockdown. Letting them out to stretch their legs and wings for a few days without the fear of standing out seemed worth consideration. He decided to run the idea past Theos and Zsombor to get their approval. He'd also send a message to the Third King, since some of their fairies had moved to Myers Beach, as well.

He had to hand it to Joe. Appealing to gays by organizing a whole weekend for them was a good move. It made him appear progressive and hip to the liberals while standing up for business. With the interest in politics by the local youth on the rise, he covered all the demographics. The incumbent mayor wouldn't stand a chance.

"So, now do you still think Joe is a horrible person?" asked Christophe. "I mean, would he put up money for something like this if he hated gays?"

Alias didn't have to think. "Yes. He's disgusting. He doesn't give a damn if Big Tiny is a monster or a fairy. Or, whether it even exists. It's all about him. Big Joe for Mayor."

When Joe passed by again, Alias pointed to the large group of men and women eating at the long center table. They all wore fairy wings.

"Yeah. That's the group I was telling you about. Nice, huh?"

"Brilliant!" Alias wondered if Joe caught his sarcasm. "I got that. But what are they eating? Looks like something new."

"Brunch. I'm letting them test it out."

"Another home run," said Alias. "Gosh, all this special treatment makes me guess you're running for office."

He laughed and gave them a wink. "Ha! That's a good

one. Well, I do have to think about my base. And I got a twofer with this group. Gays and fairy lovers."

Christophe reached to touch his wrist. "Joe, you do know that the Friends of the Fairies aren't locals, don't you?" Joe jerked his head around. Christophe continued, "They came here from all over the country hoping to see an actual fairy." When he saw Joe gulp, Christophe added another nail to the coffin. "And um, I hate to burst another bubble, but most of them probably aren't gay either, at least not the women."

The color drained from Joe's face. "So. Not gay and can't vote."

"Probably not. But when you run for national office, I'll bet they'll back you one hundred percent."

Joe dragged himself over to the bar, and two minutes later he plopped the group's check down in front of one of the members, informing them that another party had reserved the table and that they'd have to finish up.

Dame Gabor slipped into the booth with Alias and Christophe. "I'm glad I caught you," she said. "The natives are restless."

Many of the fairies had moved past grumbling and were entering the militant stage. She heard them argue that they'd be better off back in their homelands. Despite the hardship of the pandemic at least King Theos had lifted the quarantine, and fairies there had a modicum of freedom.

"I think they're getting tired of playing gin rummy and doing jigsaw puzzles all day. They want to do fairy things, you know, grant some wishes and create a little mischief. I've seen the more vocal ones making signs. Something about a picket line."

Alias sighed and pulled out the flyer. "Give me your opinion, will you? Christophe and I think letting them out for the weekend might be a solution, even if it's only temporary."

Dame Gabor loved to brag about her perfect vision. Nevertheless, she squinted and pretended to struggle to read which gave her the opportunity to pull out a gold filigree lorgnette. She held the flyer up to the light. "Well, I do love a parade, especially a gay one." She handed it back to Alias. "I hope they have a nun on roller-skates."

"A who on what?" asked Joe.

"My dear," she said. "It's not a gay parade unless you have at least a couple of nuns on skates. This time we may even see the lovely addition of a pair of wings."

When she was certain Joe was out of earshot, she spoke to the guys. "Your H, I think letting everyone out for the weekend is genius. You're going to make a lot of fairies very happy. If you like, I'd be happy to take charge of the outing for you."

"Gosh, I would love that. One less thing for me to worry about. You're a doll."

"What could be more fun than the boardwalk full of fairies disguised as humans wearing fairy costumes?" She thought for a moment. "You know, I might even throw a private gala of my own. I'll call it a 'Gay Nineties' party. All the men will be gay, and all the women will be over ninety." She threw her head back and laughed at her own joke. Suddenly, she got serious. "Why do we come here, anyway? Joe is obviously a bigot."

"I think you're probably right," Alias said. "But I confess. I'm addicted to his frappuccinos."

She held up her hand. "Then I'm ashamed of you, Your H, for not walking your talk. You remind me of the gays who can't quit that homophobic chicken restaurant." She yelled across the crowded room. "Hey, Joe! This table wants to know if you're a homophobe. Are you?"

He ran to shush her. "Come on, don't put me on the spot in front of my customers. I don't have anything against gay people. You guys know that."

"Liar, liar, liar!" she shouted. "I think you're a fake. You call yourself a sponsor for a gay parade, but you don't know the first thing about them." Alias started to reach for her arm to make her sit down, but Christophe caught his wrist. "And please don't bother telling me that you have friends who are gay," she continued. "I'm too old to listen to that crap."

He took her question literally. "Now, wait a minute. I'm sure I must have some." Then he leaned over and whispered. "Look. I just, you know, don't think being gay is natural."

"Like your hair color?" She stood up and slid her drink to the side. "Sorry, but I don't care how good these taste. I'm out of here, and I'm taking my two fairy friends with me."

Joe's jaw dropped and he sputtered. "Fairy friends? You guys are gay?"

Alias' face was still flushed from her outburst, and he was almost out the door when he turned around. "What do you think she meant?" He flapped his arms like they were wings. "Do we look like that kind of fairy to you?"

Dame Gabor walked them to her favorite boardwalk bench, and when Alias' breathing had returned to normal, she took his hand. "I'm sorry. I'd always wanted to be in a situation where I could use the *liar, liar, liar* line from the *Princess Bride*, and I got carried away. I didn't mean to out you."

He smiled. "Actually. It felt good. And your delivery was spot on."

"And I'm proud of you, Alias," Christophe said. He squeezed his thigh. When Alias jerked his head to look, Christophe withdrew his hand. "Did I do something wrong?"

"No." Alias placed his own hand on Christophe's and squeezed back. "You touching my thigh just reminded me of something from my past."

CHAPTER SIXTEEN

The Alphabet Mafia Extravaganza weekend opening parade didn't disappoint. Tourists, thrilled with the bonus of a colorful afternoon spectacle, flocked to the boardwalk. Both sides of the political spectrum turned out, too. Joe passed out coupons for twenty percent off a small, plain coffee (no refills, please). Mayor Jim lifted all parking restrictions, and the locals responded by lining the boardwalk.

The fairies at The Fairy Kingdom were ecstatic when Alias told them they were free to participate. They started planning their outfits immediately, and Alias was glad to see their dour expressions turn to ones of excitement and gratitude. He'd never liked keeping them cooped up, and he was thrilled to get Theos and Zsombor's support.

Not everyone came in costume, but it was mandatory for anyone that wanted to participate in the parade. That included the students in the Myers Beach High School Marching Band, whose uniforms for the event consisted of strap-on wings and pointy pixie ears. They kicked off the parade with a mournful rendition of "Somewhere Over the Rainbow," and then continued with a medley of show tunes.

Joe had appointed himself Honorary Parade Marshall and was surveying the spectacle from the special VIP reviewing stand he'd erected in front of his coffee house. When the band passed him, he shouted and pointed.

"Check out the piccolo player. That's my grandson! I can't believe he left his girlfriend long enough to do this. They're inseparable."

Alias and Christophe had an excellent vantage point for watching the parade, too, sitting on the railing of the boardwalk. Both were shirtless to show off their tans, and their wings were on full display. Alias kidded Christophe that his sparkly silver wings gleaming in the late morning sun looked very gay and were perfect for the event.

Christophe winked back. "They're also bigger than yours, in case you hadn't noticed."

When they heard Joe shout, they followed his finger to the band's winds section and were surprised that the only male piccolo player wore long, green bangs. When they caught the boy staring back at them, he and Christophe elbowed each other and had a laugh. "Gay," they mouthed together.

Several groups identified themselves with banners. *The Frisco Fairies, Bull Dykes from Long Beach, Pomona Poufs, Lipstick Lesbians from Laguna.* No matter the affiliation, everyone wore some type of fairy wings, and no one stood out.

Except, of course, the group of nine winged nuns on roller skates called The *Fairy Kingdom Sisters.* Alias did a double take when he saw that leading the pack and skating with backward crossovers was none other than Dame Gabor, dressed as Mother Superior.

He beamed with a different pride. Pride in the clever costumes and perfect behavior from all his fairies who turned out for a day of fun. Dame Gabor had stepped up to the plate, and he was grateful to have her back in his life. He pushed his bare leg against Christophe's, not worrying if anyone noticed. If they had, no one said anything. The day was perfect.

As they sat together watching the parade go by, he thought back at how far he'd come. For much of his life, his brain had desperately wanted to be sexually attracted to women, but his heart and the rest of his body preferred it the other way around.

He'd been the type that most people assumed was straight. Most of his acquaintances and teammates did. He was a prince, after all. In college, his friends were always trying to set him up on blind dates, and he'd tired of coming up with excuses for not going out. He broke a few hearts, too, when after building a relationship with a female, he wouldn't segue into the sexual phase.

He avoided hanging out with gays, too, for fear that people would think he was gay by association. He was born stuck. There was a lot in his closet, besides being gay. Being a fairy. Being a prince of a whole kingdom. He'd talked himself into believing that eventually the right pieces of his brain would somehow snap together, and he'd wake up one day a raging heterosexual.

But he knew that wasn't possible, because when he was a teenager, pieces had snapped together, just not the ones he imagined. After his feet touched the Third King's, he knew there was no turning back. From then on, his personality was formed in part by two fears: one, that his attraction to males wasn't a phase after all, and two, that someone might find out.

Christophe had always been comfortable in his own skin and insisted that he'd never been anything but himself. Besides, as he explained to Alias, his sexual identity was only one aspect of a much larger self. Alias envied that attitude and chalked it up to the advantage Christophe had by not being a royal.

But Alias did have that first love to hang on to and cherish. He'd admitted that to Christophe early on. The fling, as he referred to it, had been long ago, and while he fondly remembered the touch and certain other aspects about the time and place, the details remained foggy. He'd only been left with the feelings, which he was quick to admit, still gave him goosebumps.

"I know what you mean. I had one as a teenager, too, so I guess that's not unusual." Christophe had admitted to having a few additional dalliances.

"Do you mind if I ask where you guys got your wings?" Alias turned around to see the piccolo player. "I'm dying to get some just like them."

Alias caught the kid staring at his chest, and he stammered out a response. "Uh, yeah. Neat, aren't they? You know, I'm not sure." He turned to Christophe with a look that begged for help.

"No. Sorry, kid," said Christophe. "We've had them forever, so I don't remember."

"That's okay," said the kid. He shuffled his feet while he

continued to stare. "So, what's it like being gay...you know, at your age?"

Alias blushed. "Um. What makes you think we're--"

Christophe whacked his shoe into Alias' foot. "It's really great." He raised Alias' arm, to show they were holding hands. "Take your time to find the right guy, and you'll be fine."

The kid blushed. "I'm glad, because I think I already found him." He turned just as another kid jumped up behind him and hung on his shoulders. "This is Michael." He stuck out his hand to Alias and Christophe. "I'm Derek, by the way."

Michael kissed Derek on the neck. Then he put his arm around Derek's waist and they both leaned back against the railing.

"It's Derek's seventeenth birthday today, and to make it special I actually baked him a cake."

Derek poked him. "Yeah, and it should be interesting, too, since he's never cooked a thing in his life!" They laughed and Michael planted a big kiss on Derek's lips.

"Listen, guys," said Christophe. "Good luck, happy birthday, and all that, but I think it's time for us to leave." He and Alias hadn't taken two steps when they heard a man shout.

"Michael!" Michael spun away from Derek and acted as though nothing had happened, but he was too late, and his red face gave it away. The man who'd shouted was just as red, but from anger. "What the hell is this?"

"Listen, Dad, I can explain," Michael sputtered.

His father waved him away and pointed to Derek. "You! Aren't you Joe's grandkid? I better not ever catch you near my son again. He's not like you." He included Alias and Christophe when he pointed. Then he motioned for Derek to leave, but Michael threw his arms around his friend and held him tight.

"No! I love him."

The man screamed. "Get out of my sight, both of you! You make me sick!" His face flushed again, and his arms began to shake. Then his hand went to his chest, and he crumpled to the ground.

Michael cried and ran to him. "Dad, no!"

Christophe stepped forward. "Sorry, Alias, but I can't let this happen." He clapped his hands and froze the two boys and their father in place. Then he held up his index finger and made slow counterclockwise circles in the air. Alias' jaw dropped as he watched the scene reverse.

Michael's embrace was undone. The kiss, the shouting, all the action rewound to the point where Michael mentioned that he was baking Derek's birthday cake and that he'd never cooked before.

Christophe clapped and the action started again. This time Christophe intervened before the boys kissed.

"Listen, guys," he said. "Good luck, happy birthday, and all that. Oh, and Michael, isn't that your dad I see headed this way? Anyway, it's time for us to go." Michael's face looked like he'd seen a ghost, and he grabbed Derek's hand and slipped around the corner before he got caught.

Alias grabbed Christophe's bicep. "Um, I've got to know how you learned to do that. That's some pretty advanced magic."

"I have no idea. But I had to do something. I'd seen a

friend of mine go through the same kind of insanity with a parent, and the rewind thing just sort of came to me."

"Well, it was extremely cool. The boys are still together, Derek will get his birthday cake, and Michael's father won't have a heart attack. You've got to teach me how to do it. How much dust does it take?"

CHAPTER SEVENTEEN

Alias was in the lab explaining to Christophe that he was starting from scratch on a new hypothesis. He had sketched out a table and was filling in the rows and columns.

"Looks like a truth table," asked Christophe. "Want some help?"

"You know about them?"

"Yeah, a little. Why? You look surprised. Just because I was a fairy orphan, and not a prince, doesn't mean I'm not well-educated."

"You know I didn't mean anything by that. Your brain is one of your sexiest qualities and one of the things that attracted me to you in the first place. But truth tables? Come on. Hardly anyone knows about those."

Christophe grinned. "Well, I do, so move over and let me help you."

Alias handed Christophe his pencil and stepped aside. " And please, can you stop referring to your substandard background? That's never bothered me. In fact, I think we're very much alike."

He went over to the whiteboard where he'd been working on his formula. "Do you think anyone has any idea where this stuff comes from? Somehow fairies must have given the impression that we flit about doing magic and sprinkling dust all over everywhere like we had an endless supply. I doubt even most real fairies have any idea how it's made."

Christophe penciled in a line. "Come on. It's not their fault. Everything humans think they know is from television and movies. And as for our fairy brothers and sisters being clueless, well, don't get me started."

Alias leaned back against the lab table and chuckled. "I don't know what made me think of Joe just now, but I wonder what went through his head when he discovered that his customers had fled town without returning the costumes he rented them."

"Don't forget those pickaxes," said Christophe.

Alias laughed. "Yeah. I don't mind that he got stiffed."

"Me either. I could never figure out why you liked the place so much."

"I only went there because of Greta. And I think the reason she started going there in the first place was that he opened up early, and she would stop there after she went on her run. She told me it took a while, but she finally developed some sort of friendship with him. She liked chipping away at his crusty personality, and he enjoyed watching her try."

"It was a pretty weird relationship if you ask me," said Christophe. "From the few times I saw them together, I got the impression the two of them were putting on a show for our benefit."

"I noticed that, too," said Alias, "and frankly I found his schtick a bit tiresome. I wonder if she knew he was a bigot."

"He sure acted all buddy-buddy as long as we were buying his coffee, but then think about what else he does. He sells terrible weapons to horrible people. Things that are meant to hurt us."

"To be fair, if he knew we were real fairies he might not," Alias suggested.

"Baloney. But wouldn't it be funny if he found out?" Christophe laughed. "We'd be more of his two-fers."

"I think he's suspected us for a while. The other day I went there alone. You were still in the Third Kingdom. I stopped by to pick up a coffee for Greta, and he made a crack about how you and I always get the same things and even order for each other. He said that if he didn't know better, he'd guess we were a couple."

"Well, he was right. We did order the same things. But, duh, that's because we happen to like the same things." Christophe threw up his hands. "And that's the problem with homophobes. They make all these assumptions about what we do and don't do, and how we do it. They don't stop making lives miserable for gays until they find out their son or daughter is a homo."

"But it creeped me out. It's not like he caught us touching each other, or playing footsie, or anything. And if he guessed, I wonder how many other people suspect we're gay, too?"

Christophe stopped what he was doing. "What brought

this on all of a sudden? It's about that moron in the park calling us faggot fairies, isn't it? I saw your face."

"Yeah. I admit, his comment hurt."

"Come on. He wasn't the first jerk to call either one of us that. You used to let that stuff roll right off."

"That was when we had the beach to ourselves. And now that the gay weekend is over and I'm surrounded by my subjects again, I'm still worried what they'll think if they find out that their prince is gay."

"And why exactly does that bother you?"

"I don't know. It just does."

Christophe bopped him on his nose. "Aah. The great fairy conundrum. We can sweep away the nightmares of humans, but we can't make our own worries disappear. I wish I could. Believe me, you'd be the first one on my to-do list." He slapped his forehead. "See? Look at me. I fell into the same trap. Wishing for something I can't grant."

Alias poked him back. "Thanks. You always know just what to say. You always have." He put his arm around him.

Christophe laughed. "But getting back to that other jerk, the one in the park, I thought it was hysterical to give him a set of wings."

"Yeah, right? I wonder how he's doing. By the way, whose idea was that?"

"Come on," said Christophe. "Stop joking and take the credit. It was genius."

"Seriously, I didn't do it." He let the revelation sink in. "Wait! Then, if I didn't and you guys didn't do it either, how did he get them? I don't remember seeing anyone else around that could pull off that kind of magic, did you?"

Christophe stopped what he was doing. "No. But it had

to be someone. Standing on top of that chest of gold coins sure as heck didn't make him sprout wings."

Alias scratched his head, and then their eyes met. "But, what if the chest next to it has something in it that did?"

Christophe wiggled his eyebrows and raced to the other side of the lab where he'd lined up the chests from the park. He pointed at the first one, and the top blew open. "Rocks! It's just a chest full of rocks." He frowned when he opened the others. "The same kind in all of them. Bummer. Here, catch!"

Alias snatched the rock out of the air.

"Hey, your pendant is freaking out," Christophe said.

Alias looked down at his chest and noticed that the blue of the pendant was pulsating fast, like a light on a police car. "Now, what's it doing?" he muttered to himself. He brought the rock to the lab table, where he split it apart with a karate chop. When he pulled apart the halves, a red light filled the room and was so intense they had to shield their eyes.

"Amazing," said Christophe. "Your stone turned the same red, and so did your eyes. I hope that's not permanent. Your blue eyes were so sexy."

"Your eyes just turned red, too, by the way," said Alias. "But I'll bet it's temporary." He stretched out his arm, "Hey! Hold my other hand and tell me if you feel anything." As soon as Christophe made contact, his eyelids fluttered, and his head slammed back.

"Wow! What a rush!" He looked at the back of his hand and then pushed up his shirtsleeve. "And look at my skin!" His skin, normally a rich bronze, was overlaid with an intense cast of red. When Alias pulled off his shirt, his skin glowed the same way. "So, not just rocks, I guess."

"No." Alias grinned and put the halves back together again.

"What's so funny? This is creepy," said Christophe.

"Forgive the pun but I believe this is a red-letter day. What we have here is pure *arbara*. You do know that it's one of--"

"Yeah. I know. It's in the first verse. *Yano, Danog, Arbara, Urst*–blah, blah, blah."

Alias gazed at the long row of opened chests. "Yup." He noticed his pendant was getting brighter the closer he brought it to the rocks. Alias looked up at Christophe. "This find is going to bring us so much closer to the end. And thanks to you, we've got a ton."

Christophe picked up three more and started juggling. "That's great. But now I've got a ton of questions. Like, did this Hersey pirate woman realize what they were? Or do you think it was a coincidence? I read somewhere that pirates sometimes buried chests of rocks to make them heavy, and they used them as decoys to throw treasure hunters off track." He tossed another rock to Alias and they started to juggle the three together.

"Let's think about it," said Alias. To add to the degree of difficulty, he added a fourth. "If I was trying to trick people, I could see burying two or three. But why so many, unless she thought the rocks were valuable?"

"Good points," said Christophe. "But I guess we'll never know."

"Unless…" Alias winked. "We go back in time and watch her bury them."

They continued to juggle as he led Christophe to another section of the lab that housed the same technology that used to line the walls of The Fairy Kingdom, the system he'd invented to make it possible to visit the past.

The last time he'd used it was the evening that he and Greta watched Zsa Zsa siphoning the life force from Zsombor at the top of Hersey Lighthouse. Since then, he'd reconfigured it as a giant cube so that all four walls and the floor and ceiling acted like one gigantic video screen.

"To save time, we should do some research first," said Alias. "I have to ask you a question, and I hope you don't get offended. Do you know how to use Google?"

Christophe slapped his forehead, which ultimately put a stop to their juggling. Alias flicked his fingers at the rocks so that they gently landed in a pile on the floor. "Geez. Are you insulting me so I'll break up with you? Of course, I do. But if you need research done, I'd rather do it the old-fashioned way, using books. What do you need?"

Alias wanted everything they could find about pirates, their ships, the approximate time that they flourished, and how they handled their treasure. They didn't need to be movie buffs to know that piracy for the most part took place in the Caribbean, so what Alias specifically needed Christophe to research was pirates who might have existed in California.

Christophe disappeared. While he was gone, Alias pressed his palm against one of the cube's walls to activate the dashboard controls. He entered some coordinates and swiped with his finger until the location of the Myers Beach skatepark came into view.

Christophe was fast. He returned minutes later and

took a seat on one of the leather chairs in the center of the cube. He shared that the famous era began in the 1500s and ended sometime in the 1830s. He threw up holographic images of the most popular ships of the time and other relevant information Alias had requested.

Research on California pirates yielded disappointing results, though.

"California's only celebrated pirate was a Frenchman, natch." He thickened his French accent. "A guy named Hippolyte de Bouchard, who made a famous raid in Monterey in 1818. The only thing I could find about Captain Gabrielle Hersey was a reference to the lighthouse, which of course, we already knew about. There were no available details on her life or her pirate activity."

"Man, that was fast. Where did you find out all this?"

"The Library of Congress. Where else?"

"You never cease to amaze. I wish some of the other fairies around here were as fast as you were at getting things done." Alias sighed.

The lack of information didn't surprise him. Greta had suggested that the tale of the ship's grounding at Retribution Shoals had more than likely been fictionalized to add a touch of glamour and sizzle to the tourist attraction that again, supposedly bore her name.

But the lighthouse was real, and he remembered her also saying that it was one of the oldest on the California coast. Though the records relating to its construction didn't mention Hersey's name, historians estimated that the structure had been built in the late 1800s. To be sure they didn't miss the event, Alias made an adjustment, and he and Christophe began monitoring the location beginning on the first of January of 1800.

While humans could not perceive more than sixty frames per second, Alias and Christophe were capable of faster rates, because at those higher speeds, their brains did the watching, not their eyes. Even so, with an entire century to scan, they took turns to help speed through the nineteenth century.

They switched places at the ten-year marks. While Christophe worked the controls, Alias was sprawled out on the chair tossing a rock from hand to hand. When a two-masted sloop came into view, Christophe made a note of the date: August 24, 1816.

"Whoa! Look. Are you seeing this?"

A violent storm had taken over a wide swath of the ocean and the California coastline. Alias sat up, and together they watched the small ship struggle to keep from capsizing in the giant swells. Eventually, a bolt of lightning struck the sloop's foremast and when it snapped in two, it fell athwartship. The tangled lines and sails covered the helm.

They could see that the ship would have been impossible to steer, and having lost control the crew would have been powerless. Massive winds blew her toward shore. Despite her shallow draft, it was the heavy cargo that sealed its fate, and the ship ran aground on the jagged rocks near where the lighthouse would later be built.

The wooden hull was no match for the treacherous shoals, which tore into the bottom, but not before five launches laden with wooden chests had managed to leave the ship and row toward shore.

Once safely on land, five men dragged the chests about a thousand feet inland, where they began to dig a hole. When it was deep enough, the men lowered down thirteen chests one by one. When only four remained on the beach, the macho-looking captain raised his hand.

"It looks like Greta got the part about the buried treasure right," said Alias. "But I'm going to hate having to break it to her that Captain Hersey was a man, after all."

While the men were covering the holes with dirt and sweeping away all traces of their activity, the man in the captain's uniform counted out gold coins from one of the chests and put them in five pouches, presumably as payment for his crew. He set them aside and opened the second chest and selected a dozen or so rocks, which he dropped into a separate leather bag.

Christophe zoomed in on the second chest to verify that the rocks in the video were the same as those that were now sitting in their lab. "Did you see that?" he asked out loud. "The guy must have known they were special. Why else would he go out of his way to take them?"

They continued watching, and after the captain handed a pouch to each of the men, they saluted him and dispersed. Then the captain walked to the shore and sat on a large boulder and stared at the ocean. He'd brought one of the rocks with him and was tossing it from hand to hand as he watched the fierce wind and monster waves pummel the remains of his ship into splinters. Then the captain put down his rock and untied the bandanna from his forehead.

Christophe coughed. "Um, do you realize that you are playing with the rocks the same way?"

"I didn't, but I do now." Alias walked to the controls and

swiped left, and pointed to the readout on the screen that put the beach temperature at a blistering one hundred and two degrees. "Wow. I'm not surprised that he took off his bandanna."

It didn't surprise them either when the captain unbuttoned his tunic and tossed that to the side. Then he pulled off his wool hat, and when he shook his head, thick, luxurious curly black hair tumbled down past his shoulders.

"I hope you're not watching this," joked Christophe. " The guy is stripping."

"Who wouldn't in that heat? Anyway, nobody is around."

The captain reached around and untied his leather vest, which he let fall to the ground. When he ripped open the front of his pirate shirt, Christophe clicked his teeth. The captain was a woman.

"Wow!" he said. "I was wrong, and Greta was right about those initials. This woman really must be Captain Gabrielle Hersey. Look."

"Zoom in on her," shouted Alias. "This is getting good."

Christophe laughed and jerked his head around. "Sure, but why zoom in? Has my boyfriend taken a sudden interest in women's breasts?"

"No, but stop the frame," he said. "I just can't believe what I'm seeing. Captain Hersey, or whoever that is, looks exactly like Zsa Zsa Hajdu. And I mean *exactly* like her."

He gave the signal to start the action again. Soon, the same five pirates crept into view. Hersey must have heard them draw their swords, because she swiveled around on the rock to face them. But instead of drawing her own weapon, she crossed her long legs and picked at her fingernails.

"What the heck. Why isn't she going to defend herself?" Christophe asked.

They could see the men's lips moving and the tension on their faces. They were obviously shouting at her, but she didn't budge. Suddenly, someone must have given a signal, because they all charged at her at once. She barely looked up and flicked a finger at the closest one. The pirate stopped in his tracks. Then he clutched his chest and collapsed on the sand. The second, third, and fourth men met the same fate.

Seeing what happened to the men who'd gone before, the fifth man stopped where he was and laid down his sword in a sign of surrender. From the way he'd been giving orders to the other four, Alias and Christophe guessed that he may have been Hersey's first mate.

Nevertheless, his knees wobbled as he watched each of the other men follow her orders to sit up and hand back their pouches. After dumping their coins into her open treasure chest, she walked up to the first mate and stretched out her hand. He handed over his pouch without resisting, but Alias and Christophe could tell by wet eyes, facial expressions, and body language that he was probably pleading for his life.

The Zsa Zsa Hajdu lookalike waved her hand, and a cart and a mule appeared out of thin air. She nodded toward her four remaining chests, and the men obediently lifted them onto the cart. One of the men gave her a leg up, and she sat side saddle on the mule's back and trudged away down the beach.

The men looked relieved to see her leave, and they were still bent over struggling to catch their breaths when Captain Hersey turned around and smiled at them. They looked up and returned the smile. Then she shouted something and flicked a finger. Suddenly, the first mate's gleaming steel blade rose from the sand, and in one long clockwise swipe slit all five men's throats.

Christophe turned away and shook his head. "Gosh. I'm speechless. Hersey was a real badass."

"I can't disagree," said Alias. "But something tells me we should stop thinking of her as Captain Hersey."

"Why? Those guys saluted her. She must have been the captain."

"Again, I don't disagree. But I'm telling you, the way she knocked these men down so fast with a finger flick was exactly how Zsa Zsa did it to Greta."

"I hope you're not suggesting they're the same person. Hersey looked like she was in her mid to late twenties." He looked at the date on the screen again. "So, even if she lived to be a hundred, she'd be dead for I don't know, a hundred and twenty years."

"Maybe. Maybe not. She had some powerful magic. And she must have known that *arbara* was valuable. I wonder how it works?" He went back to his chair and picked up his rock. "Let's take turns following her and see where she takes us. Do you mind starting? I want to check on something. Heads up." He tossed the rock to Christophe and left the lab.

Christophe took over to document how the woman they still referred to as Hersey changed into a new outfit she pulled from her saddlebag and rode to the next town.

She went to a bank, where she must have cashed in at least part of the gold, because a carriage and driver appeared. After the driver loaded the two chests she dismissed him, took the reins, and headed inland.

Christophe heard a *pop*, and suddenly the entire cube went black. He raced back to the lab to tell Alias, who rushed in and banged his palm on every surface. "I don't know what the heck is wrong with it," he said when the cube remained dark. "It's nothing simple, that much I know."

"Well, I'm jazzed about this pirate lady, and I'm not ready to give up the hunt. Are you?" Christophe asked.

"No, but I'll need a bunch of fairy dust to fix this, the classic kind, and you know how I feel about dipping into that."

"Okay," said Christophe. "Look, I don't know how it is in your kingdom, but I had to learn how to do human things without using magic. I remember thinking how stupid it was at the time, but here we are, and I know just where to go."

While Christophe was gone, Alias called for his team. Discovering the *arbara* had been the lucky break they needed. The fact that a human grew wings in a matter of seconds simply by being in its presence was a testament to its power. So Alias felt optimistic that its addition to D5 might give his new dust the supercharge the previous one lacked.

He showed them how he split the next rock open, then he pointed to the glowing geode and watched it roll into a hopper for the first step in the processing.

CHAPTER EIGHTEEN

"All the paperwork relating to the establishment of the lighthouse is in this box," said the friendly docent at the Myers Beach Museum. "You're the first to ask to see them for as long as I can remember." She pointed to her gray hair and winked. "And as you can tell, I've been around a long time."

Christophe smiled politely at her exaggeration, and she directed him to a cubicle, where he sifted through decades-old utility bills and invoices for repairs and maintenance. Finally, he located a copy of the bank draft that funded the original project, which he brought to the docent for clari-fication.

"If I'm reading this correctly, it looks like someone not only paid to build the lighthouse, but their gift was substantial enough to fund it for perpetuity. Did I get that right?"

"Yes. Myers Beach was indeed lucky to have had such a generous donor. Money to maintain historical structures like this one is hard to come by these days, as you can imagine."

"The tale I heard was that the lighthouse was named Hersey after a pirate. Is that correct?"

"Yes. The donor specified that it be named for Captain Gabby Hersey, whom she maintained was a fierce and famous pirate. Honestly, nobody can find records of a pirate by that name, but then again, the donor was a bit of a mystery herself."

"How so?"

"We don't know why or how she recognized the need for the lighthouse in the first place. We doubt it was from a bad experience aboard ship. Back then, it would have been curtains for any vessel that got caught in those shoals. So, it's not likely that she would have survived, even if she'd been aboard."

"It's hard to make out the full name on the bank draft, though. It looks like Célia Giselle something, but the ink on the last name is worn. Can you help me?"

"Yes, absolutely. She made the gift in person at the local bank, and because she was illiterate, the banker did the paperwork. Her name is on the document, and his penmanship was excellent."

The docent went to the cubical and retrieved the paper on the bank's letterhead.

"Here it is. She could only write her initials, but the banker wrote out her full name. I probably won't pronounce it correctly, but I'll try. Célia Giselle Hajdu."

CHAPTER NINETEEN

Since he and Christophe had cut back on flying, and given that Mayor Jim had solved the parking problem for the weekend, they had taken Theos' Land Rover to town for the afternoon. On the way home, as they were bouncing over the bumpy road, Alias received unexpected news from his team. They had finished processing the *arbara* and were ready to assemble Dust Number 6 as soon as he got to the lab. He gave Christophe a high five.

"This is so effing exciting. I thought we were still a few days away. What do you think, should we floor it and see what this tin can has got?"

Christophe laughed. "We could, but I thought you were in a hurry."

"I am. What did you think I meant?"

"Let me." He twirled his index finger, and suddenly a little whirlwind surrounded the Land Rover. In a matter of seconds, the funnel cloud spun around the car until it dissolved and reappeared in its reserved parking spot in the garage of the compound.

Christophe saw Alias scrunch his face. "What's the matter? Didn't you think it was cool?"

"Of course, I did, but magic like that takes a lot of fairy dust, and what did the trick save us, fifteen minutes? Honestly, we both need to do a better job of conserving my stash."

"*Your* stash?" Christophe glared. "I suppose you're going to accuse me of using *your* dust when I did that bit with those boys at the parade, too, right?"

"Hey, don't get defensive," Alias reached for Christophe, but he backed away. "And please don't be mad at me either. I'm not upset. It really was a cool thing you did for the boys, too, and I'm sure it came from your heart—"

"But? I know a 'but' is coming. It sounds like you're suggesting that I've been irresponsible."

"Not, exactly. I was going to say that I hoped you'd noticed that we're running really low, and you know we're still a long way from having enough of the good stuff to throw around. Let me say it again. What you did at the parade was an excellent use of fairy dust, even if it took a lot, which I'm sure it did."

"I guess my approach to magic is just different from yours. And now it's time for me to add a *but* of my own. *But*, since we'll be one step closer to getting new dust by the end of the day, why can't you forget your uptight human side for a little while? Enjoy that milestone that's right around the corner with a little fun with me, okay? How about we celebrate all the successes you've already achieved."

Alias shook his head. "I agree. So why the heck do you suppose it's so hard for me to act like I believe it?"

"Duh. Your life lately has been one eternal stress test, that's why. Believe me, I'll be so glad when this is over and we can go back to being normal again."

"Weird that you're the one teaching me about human emotions, considering you're the one who's a full fairy."

"Yeah. And that's also the point. We can't forget we're fairies. Man, we should have it made."

Alias reached out his arms. "Point made. Now, will you give me a hug?"

CHAPTER TWENTY

Bruce landed hard when he fell face-first on the sand.

"Got 'em!" yelled MorningDew. She dug in her heels and pulled on her end of the rope. She and the others would claim later that they first saw the huge guy with the fairy wings when he emerged from beneath the boardwalk. It was dark, but as much as they could tell, he fit Big Tiny's description, and they followed him because they thought he was acting suspicious.

From the boardwalk, he had tiptoed a few steps across the beach and then crouched behind a palm tree. Staying in the shadows, he slunk thirty feet further and ducked behind the beach umbrella shed. They said he kept moving like that in the dark along the beach until they stretched the rope across his path and tripped him.

A bunch of them piled on, and while he shouted a string of expletives, someone slapped on leg cuffs. Another person complicated the capture by throwing a fishing net into the air, which missed the man but covered everyone else. While they were untangling themselves from the net and the large fairy wings, he managed to slug one of the men in the face. He kept swinging despite the leg irons until MorningDew disabled him with her stun gun.

It took most of the Friends of the Fairies to haul the heavy six-foot-three guy to their van, and he was still out cold when they dragged him to the door of one of their motel rooms. One more group effort lifted him over the threshold and pushed him through the door.

While the others took turns picking at his wings to see how they attached to his bare back, the man with the broken nose moved in to examine his teeth. Dr. Lawrence was a licensed dentist, and as the only one in the group, he insisted that he be the one to get the first look at the jagged incisors that had been so vividly detailed in the artist's conception of the adult fairy.

Though the doctor's nose was still dripping blood from getting punched the fairy was out cold, and he seized upon the once-in-a-lifetime moment to make dental history. He asked for a volunteer to take notes, as he explained there was data to collect and photos to take. He told them scholarly medical journals would fight over the papers he planned to write, and he needed to hurry before the monster woke up. Bruce had just smashed his face, so the dentist approached with caution. He peeled back the lips.

"Patient has no visible signs of swelling, lesions, or redness of the gums," he reported to the Friends of the Fairies volunteer. "Patient's lips are moist and not cracked, pink with generalized brown tones. Initial palpation shows no bleeding of the gums or loose teeth."

"We don't care about all that," yelled someone in the

back. "Can you move to the side so we can all get a look at the monster's mouth?"

"He does have one slightly chipped tooth," said the note-taker. "His left incisor." She consulted the napkin she used as note paper. "Dr. Lawrence said it was tooth number eight. Right, doctor?"

"Yes. Now let's see what's inside, shall we?" He pried open the man's mouth and poked around with his index finger. "Ah yes. A lovely crown with several restorations in an otherwise normal set of permanent teeth. Two loose amalgams that should be replaced as soon as possible."

Bruce regained consciousness and opened his eyes. When he saw the hand probing his mouth, he clamped down hard, and the sharp end of his chipped tooth stabbed the dentist. Dr. Lawrence yanked out his throbbing finger and fell backward, slamming into the group members who had crept closer to watch the proceedings.

When Bruce saw his legs chained together, he started yelling again. "Who the hell are you people, and why the fuck am I here?" Nobody had tied his arms, and when he started swinging he knocked over a lamp and swiped someone's open suitcase off the credenza. A man tased him, and he fell back and banged his head against the wall.

"I don't know how we forgot to secure his hands," shouted the same man. "But I saw handcuffs for sale at Joe's Java Joint. If you guys can hold him for a few minutes, I'll run and buy a pair. Hopefully, they're not sold out."

"Pick me up another stun gun, if he's got one, will you?" asked a woman who was already wearing a real gun in a holster across her chest. "I'll pay you when you get back."

Another woman crawled across the carpet and ran her

finger over Bruce's tattoo, *Bruce and Peg forever*, and she squeezed his beefy arms and legs. "I don't know. Now that I see him in the light and up close, he doesn't look fairy-like to me. When he's not growling at us, he even speaks English."

"Speaking English is no big deal. Fairies can speak all languages. Everybody knows that," chided MorningDew. "Can we please focus on his wings? We've all gotten up close and agree that by the way they are growing out of his back, they are definitely part of his anatomy. I say if Dr. Lawrence doesn't have anything else to add, we take a vote to get a consensus."

The dentist pulled his damaged finger out of his mouth. "Well, from the exterior, one could argue that his teeth resemble the standard human set." He wiped blood from his upper lip. "But as you know, I didn't have the opportunity to examine his oral cavity or much of his buccal mucosa, so–"

MorningDew interrupted. "Then those who agree that we've positively captured one of Big Tiny's adult male offspring, raise your hands." The tally was thirteen to zero, with one abstention, not including the man who'd dashed off for the handcuffs.

When he regained consciousness again, Bruce screamed and tugged against his new restraints.

"I have a question," said someone in the group. "What are we going to do with him?" It was the second time someone had asked, and Bruce roared back with threats to kill them all if they didn't let him go immediately.

MorningDew stepped forward and raised her hand in the sign of peace. "Fear not. You are among friends. We are the Friends of the Fairies, a group of human people who are sympathetic to you and your kind. We brought you here for your own protection. My name is MorningDew. Do you have a name?"

Bruce shook his head. "What the hell do you think, you morons. Of course, I have a name. Bruce." Someone in the back snickered, and Bruce glared at him. "Look at my ID if you don't believe me. It's in my wallet. Back pocket, left side...my left."

"It's a trick!" shouted the woman with the new stun gun. "Don't go near him. He might use magic on you. They're tricky. That's why they call a group of fairies a finagle, didn't you know?"

Instead of reaching for the wallet, the group backed away to confer again. The dentist was the first to voice his opinion. "Honestly, I think we've gotten in over our heads. We got what we came for. We've all seen a fairy up close, even if he's only a partial fairy. So, I say we let him go."

Bruce shouted from the floor. "Will you fools stop talking and listen for a minute? Look, I have a wife and two daughters, and we're staying at the Sandpiper Hotel on the boardwalk. I am sure they are worried out of their minds, and I promise you they've called the police by now."

MorningDew called them into a huddle, and after a brief conference they agreed that under the circumstances, they'd let him go. They stipulated that he could not use magic on them, and also that he would agree to pose for a selfie with each member.

Captain Stetson led the disheveled man into her office. "I'm the guy whose wife probably reported me as a missing person a couple of days ago."

"Nobody reported you as missing, but I know who you are."

"How? I haven't told you yet."

"You don't need to. Except for your name, it's all right here." She handed him the special edition of the *Tattler*. "That's you, isn't it?"

Captured! Fairy Bounty Hunters Nab Adult Male!

Except for the headline, Bruce's photo covered nearly the entire page. He was shirtless and sitting on the floor, with his bare legs flat in front of him to showcase how they'd shackled his ankles. He was handcuffed, too, and though his head was visible, they'd printed a narrow black bar across his eyes, the paper said, to keep his identity private.

But it was the wings that made the shot. Child-sized rose-colored wings that didn't look capable of lifting the large man sprouted from between his shoulders. Bruce gulped and scanned the story, which was short and sparse on details. The Friends of the Fairies, the group of experts and friends of the *Tattler* as well, took credit for the capture and the photograph.

The article outlined in broad strokes the extensive planning by the members and how they systematically staked out key areas in Myers Beach and set their trap. Their group's founder, who preferred to go by her single name, MorningDew, was short on details about how the actual capture went down.

"Our mission has always been to 'catch and release,'" she

was quoted to have said. "It's all in our name. We're Friends of the Fairies, not foes."

"That's me, all right," said Bruce. "But I have no idea who those lunatics were or who they thought I was, but the rest of the story is nonsense. They kept me chained up for hours, and when I tried to get up they tased me."

"So, you're not famous and you have no idea why they wanted you? Just where were you when the alleged kidnapping took place?"

"It's not alleged. I was hiding under the boardwalk, because I didn't want anyone to see my wings," he said.

"Wings?"

"Yes. The wings in the photo. They suddenly started growing out of my back while I was digging. I have no idea why or how."

"Digging?"

"I was digging a hole at the skatepark, minding my own business when–"

"Excuse me, but why were you digging a hole in the skatepark?"

"To look for fairy eggs. A bunch of us were. Anyway, I ended up with wings, because these two gay fairies and a woman used magic on me as a kind of punishment for something I supposedly said."

"I see." Stetson stopped writing as Bruce recounted the events.

"I tried to get away," he said, at the end of his story, "but I couldn't, what with the handcuffs and the leg irons and getting tased all the time."

"But you obviously did, because you're here."

"Yes. Finally, I persuaded them to let me work out a

deal. In exchange for my freedom, I promised to lead them to the spot where I ran into the other two fairies. Oh, and I had to pose for a selfie with each of them."

When Bruce finally got back to the hotel late and without a fairy egg to show for his time away, he found that his wife had not been worried at all. She'd been furious. So he could explain himself and because it would undoubtedly turn into a full-blown argument, she sent their daughters downstairs for ice cream.

"I actually did find an egg, but a woman stole it from me," he told her. Then he explained how the wings sprouted out of his back when he fell into a hole, and then how a group of lunatics kidnapped him.

His wife walked to the window. "This is the most ridiculous tale you've ever come up with as an excuse for your infidelity."

He stripped off his shirt. "No. No. You've got it all wrong. The wings evaporated a little while ago, but they were huge, I swear. You can see the scars on my back where they grew from." She glanced at his back and shook her head and pointed to the lacerations on his wrists and ankles and the red blotches on his chest.

She held up the newspaper and then threw it face down on the sofa table. "All I can say is thank goodness our children never read. Look. I'm not going to let you fool me again, Judge McPhee. By the way, I know about you and Mistress M," she said. "I found her business card in your jacket pocket. I thought we agreed that you were going to end that little S&M phase of yours." She swallowed the lump in her throat. "I also know about you and your fishing buddy, Frank."

Bruce blanched. "No, no. I'm telling you the truth. They really did chain my hands and feet, and the red marks are from the stun gun. I've just come from the police station." He unfolded the report he'd filed.

After much pleading and many tears, Bruce convinced her that he could show her proof. He said the group mentioned going to The Fairy Kingdom later, and he begged her to go there with him. On the way, they sent their girls to the hotel restaurant for dinner with instructions to start without them.

CHAPTER TWENTY-ONE

Dust Number Six, version one, was ready for prime time. Though he'd put it on the fast track, the team had conducted rigorous testing, which included experimenting on each other. Alias was pleased that there had been no adverse reactions, given that *arbara* seemed to be the most powerful ingredient of the six. The fact that a human grew wings merely by standing next to it was proof enough that the element by itself was magical.

What had taken them so long to figure out was how much to use. He was still gun shy from the debacle of D5, so to be safe, he opted to incorporate much less of this new ingredient than the others.

D6, though, contained a challenge of its own. Like the raw element itself, the dust left a distinct red stain on almost everything that came in contact with it. They'd tried dozens of ways to reduce or eliminate the residue, but nothing seemed to be effective.

The team knew that red stains or any other color for that matter on their hair, skin, or clothing would not cut it with their fairy population, so they went back to the drawing board. Alias pulled out the truth table he and Christophe had worked on earlier.

If *arbara* was essential to fairy dust, as it obviously was according to the rhyme, and no combination of other elements they had tried had been able to neutralize the color, then logically one or more of the three they had yet to find must hold the key to the solution. So, he altered the delivery system. Instead of sprinkling it in the traditional way, he instructed his team to package D6 as a powder that could be mixed with tea and taken internally.

He explained the rationale to Stefán when he brought him several jars of what he started calling his 'preparation.' The Fairy Kingdom served so much tea that they brewed it in gleaming elegant samovars. To make the mixing easy for the staff, Alias pre-packaged D6 in packets, one packet per full urn of tea.

After several days of dispensing the new dust in their tea, Alias stopped by The Fairy Kingdom to check on the status. In anticipation of his visit, Stefán had polled the fairies. Ninety-eight percent reported having more energy and feeling less depressed. He said that a couple of them even referred to an increase in their libido.

"So, all in all, it looks like you hit a home run with D6." He looked at Alias and pinched his face. "But there is one drawback."

Alias took a breath. "And?"

"It's that whoever does the mixing has to remember to wear gloves." He laughed and held up his hands that showed red fingertips. "We found that out the hard way."

"And that's all? Whew! You don't know how happy that

makes me. Finally, we're back on the right track. Oh, and speaking of hands. Christophe's and mine are still a little red from when we started messing with the *arbara*, too. Of course, we didn't know what it was then. But it wears off, as you can see."

"Then I should tell you about one other minor thing that I hope will wear off. A few of the same fairies who reported positive health outcomes from the tea said they felt on edge, and they haven't been able to sit still. Now remember, I'm talking about only a couple of them, so don't let it alarm you."

"Okay. That's good to know. Sounds a bit like being over-caffeinated, so yes, I suspect that will go away, too. To be safe, though, I'd like you to use only a half packet from now on. And then keep me posted."

"And I see that your pendant has finally gone back to a blue that matches your eyes."

CHAPTER TWENTY-TWO

Looking chic in a floor-length sequined sheath dress, Dame Gabor was in the middle of a set when Alias walked into The Fairy Kingdom lounge. She was filling in on vocals for the usual singer who'd had taken the night off, and she and her accompanist were performing pop songs from the seventies and eighties.

He plopped down to relax with a glass of prosecco in a comfortable chair in the atrium, and he was so into the music that he didn't hear the group of thirteen walk in and take over the long table in the front window. She elbowed him.

"Those are the nutjobs I was telling you about." Alias nodded to acknowledge that he'd seen them, but he leaned back and closed his eyes as she took to the microphone. "This next medley is from one of my favorite bands, Paul McCartney and Wings. Maybe you remember them." She lifted her microphone off the stand and worked the room during the set.

The Friends of the Fairies were loud, and as they

nibbled from the pupu platters and sipped their tea, Dame Gabor got close enough to see them airdropping photos to each other. She overheard how ecstatic they were to meet a real live fairy and how they had enough stories to keep their blogs and social media pages busy for a lifetime. When she'd heard enough, she wound her way back to the piano singing her own rendition of *Bad Company*.

During the next break she sat next to Alias. "I hate to disturb you, Your H, but I overheard a couple of those Friends of the Fairies talking about their travel plans. It seems we're finally going to be rid of them. They're all leaving tomorrow."

He answered without opening his eyes. "Good riddance, is all I can say."

"Incidentally, they must love our tea, so at least they have some good taste. They've been drinking so much, the new girl got tired of running back and forth with refills, and she brought out a samovar for the table. A gorgeous one from your palace, if I recall correctly. Austro-Hungarian Empire antique silver? Ring a bell?"

"Of course I know it. But the tea in those was meant for the fairies, and she shouldn't have served it to them, because I have no idea how humans will react to it." He pointed to their table, and when nobody was looking he snapped his fingers, and the samovar disappeared. "They seem a little drunk to me, but nothing more than that."

She heard the intro to her next song. "Listen. We'll talk in a bit. My gig is starting up again."

When Bruce and his wife got to the front of the teahouse, he peered through the window. "Look, those are the ones who chained me in the motel room!" he shouted, and he pulled his wife over. "I recognize all of them!" He burst through the door and stormed to their table. "This is my wife, and I demand that you tell her that you kidnapped me! She doesn't believe me."

Stefán heard someone shouting, and he rushed to the front to intervene in the contretemps, but by then, MorningDew was defusing the situation with her own surprise tactic.

"Hey everyone, look who's here. Brucie!" She turned to his wife. "Your husband has to be the funniest man I've met in years. He kept me and my friends in stitches all day." She poked him in the chest. "I'll admit that our little get-together may have started out on the wrong foot, but does this look like someone being held against his will?" She held up her phone and his wife gasped at the picture of them sitting next to him on the floor, with her head against his chest.

When the others held up their phones and showed similar selfies of him cozying up with them, Bruce's wife started pounding on him.

Suddenly, one of the members pointed to the man across the table. "Your skin is green. And look at your ears!"

The man looked bewildered and pawed at his ears to see what she meant. The woman who'd noticed took out a pocket mirror to check herself, and soon everyone at the table was rubbing their arms and screaming. They all had turned green, and their ears were large and pointy.

"You better wake up, Your H," Dame Gabor whispered to Alias. "I'm afraid we've got another situation."

When Bruce recognized Alias, his eyes lit up. "Hey

there, buddy! I know you. You're the one from the skatepark. This is my wife, Peggy. Would you please explain to her what happened?"

Dame Gabor grabbed Bruce's arm. "What do you mean by calling this man 'buddy?' I'll have you know that you are in the presence of His Royal Highness, the Fairy Prince." She genuflected.

While Bruce and his wife looked nonplussed, Alias took a breath and popped out his dress wings. He'd chosen his largest and most magnificent regal set, and their brilliant colors made everyone stop what they were doing to gawk.

Bruce's wife made an attempt at a curtsey. "Thanks, Bruce's Wife," said Alias, "but I'm sick of the two of you." He twirled his finger and they vanished instantly in a funnel cloud.

"We need some background music," said Dame Gabor to her accompanist. "Nobody will hear this, but I can't resist." She picked up the microphone. "My next song is *Broken Wings*, by Mr. Mister. I hope you like it."

Alias turned to the others. "And you! All of us around here have had enough of your nonsense! I'm sending you buffoons back to wherever you came from. You will never remember any of this, nor will you ever return to Myers Beach. Now, get out of my sight!"

He reached into his pouch and tossed a handful of fairy dust at the group, which reversed the effects of the tea. Then he went back to his chair and drank another glass of prosecco and watched as one by one, the Friends of the Fairies vanished from the room.

"I didn't want to have to get rid of them this way," he

said. "But those buffoons had gotten out of control. I know there's still a lot of chaos in town, but this is a start."

"It had to be done, Your H. Don't give it another thought." She took his hand. "But I do sense that something else is wrong."

He shook his head. "Yeah. I'm pissed at myself. I've been giving Christophe grief for the tiny bits of fairy dust he's been using, and look at me. I wasted half a bag on those nuts."

"Try to relax. I'll sing you a song." She returned to the microphone. "I'd like to dedicate this song by the Fifth Dimension to His Royal Highness, the Fairy Prince." She nodded to her accompanist, who started the intro to *Up, Up and Away.*

When she finished singing, Stefán tapped Alias on the shoulder and said he had something to show him in the dining room. Alias was not in the mood for another controversy, and though he begged not to go, Stefán insisted it was important. Alias finally left his soft sofa, if reluctantly.

Nearly every fairy in The Fairy Kingdom was standing in the dining room when Alias entered, and they took him by surprise with their cheers and applause. One of the older ones took the microphone.

"Your Royal Highness, we would all like to express our gratitude for getting rid of that group of morons tonight," he said. "They have been insulting, and disruptive, and to our minds had no place in our building. We are truly blessed to have you as our prince, because you recognize our problems and take care of our needs without our having to complain. Thank you for your service."

CHAPTER TWENTY-THREE

Since they were no longer patronizing Joe's, Dame Gabor stopped by the compound for their regular briefing. Alias was waiting for her in the living room, and he stood when she came in. She made a deep, dramatic curtsey.

"You know I don't want such formalities from you," he said, waving away her gesture. "I'm an informal kind of guy, and I only pull out the title thing when I need to project authority."

"I know," she said. "But I'm still an actress, and I love playing the part of the devoted subject." Dame Gabor waved away his concern. "So, have you been following the Friends of the Fairies scandal?" she asked.

"Don't tell me those crazies are back. I thought I got rid of them."

"Oh, no, you did. No question about that, but you'll want to see this." She dug into her Coach briefcase and pulled out the week's issues of the *Tattler*. "I know you've been busy all week, but I wanted to show you the series they started running. It's basically selfies those idiots took with Bruce. Some of them are pretty steamy." She pointed to the feature story that began on the front page: *Big Tiny's Kid: All Grown Up.*

The shots had been pulled from their social media posts, and while the background of each photo was the same motel room, and Bruce's bare torso and lavender wings were the focal point, the poses and captions reflected the personalities of the members.

In one, he had his arm around a woman who was aiming a stun gun at him. The caption read, *Big Tiny's kid better not try anything funny with me, ha-ha! No, really!* Another showed a dentist named Doctor Lawrence holding open the fairy's lips with one hand and pointing at its teeth. *I hope he flosses!* (Smiley face).

He brushed them aside. "I can't look at this anymore. These are absolutely ridiculous! How could anyone have ever believed that guy was a real fairy? You do know he's the same jerk who called Christophe and me faggots at the skatepark, don't you?"

"Yes, but I wish I had been there. A human growing wings off-script sounds like a fun scene. But I do remember his stupefied expression when you sent him and his wife away.."

Alias poured her a coffee. "Yeah, did you notice the way I did it?"

"Yeah, that neat funnel cloud thingy. It's way above my pay grade. Something only a royal could pull off."

"Yeah, but oddly enough Christophe showed me how."

"Hmm. Anyway, I want to get back to my briefing." She walked to the bar. "Before I do, would you mind if I put a little Irish whiskey in this? I find it gives my mornings a little extra kick. Besides, I don't have a full schedule today, and we're celebrating."

"We are? From what you showed me, it appears things are getting wound up again."

She slapped her thigh. "Oh, my golly. You are so out of the loop. Look. You know how guilty I've felt for being responsible for starting all this nonsense, right? Do you remember when I suggested that I should be the one to end it?" She wiggled her eyebrows.

Alias gulped. "I get the feeling I'd better add some whiskey to my coffee, too."

She laughed and did it for him. Then she pointed at their cups and topped them off with whipped cream. "Okay, don't ask me how, but I managed to take a peek at the police report that Bruce filed. I learned that he's from Dubuque, Iowa."

"And I care about that why, exactly?"

"Where he lives isn't half as interesting as who he is. Turns out he's the Honorable Judge Bruce McPhee."

Alias grinned. "Mmm. Maybe we should make sure that his voters find out what he does when he's not doling out punishment to them."

"You read my mind. I may have leaked his pictures to their local press." She giggled and wiped cream from her upper lip. "I heard people are calling for his recall already."

"Besides him and the Friends of the Fairies, a bunch of other people have been laughed out of existence, too. Like that blogger named Pat, who got everyone all riled up with their conspiracy theories. But Bruce isn't just sitting back and taking it. Apparently there are defamation lawsuits flying all over the place."

He raised his cup in a toast. "That's fantastic. And as far as I'm concerned, they couldn't be more deserving. You're a genius, so now maybe you could focus your talent on getting rid of the rest of the crazies here."

She looked down her nose. "I'm just going to pretend that you're not clueless. Do you think I only told Iowa about the judge? The chaos is over. Everyone's packing up, and we're getting the town back. It's in all the papers...at least in yesterday's *Tattler*. Look!"

Big Tiny. Big Hoax!

Alias fell back against the sofa. "You are the most amazing fairy I've ever known. What can I do for you? You're already a Dame, so I can't give you a better title."

"Hold that thought," she said. "I'll think of something. In the meantime, why don't you do yourself a favor. Fly to town with me and see what's happening for yourself."

The quiet and relatively empty boardwalk was the biggest indication of the overnight drastic changes to the town's complexion. With their gullible customers now gone, the pop-up food and souvenir vendors were nowhere to be seen, and the once omnipresent tour guides had disappeared, too, presumably to resume their full-time careers as surfers.

Alias peeked in a few shops and got a kick out of how the owners had already consolidated their fairy wares and memorabilia into *Collector's Edition* displays at triple the original prices. The media was gone, too, along with their miles of cables and sound trucks and satellite antennas. He was sure they hadn't left disappointed. They'd come to cover the madness, and it hadn't mattered whether it was Big Tiny, Big Tiny's Son, or a six-inch bird. They'd probably already moved on to the next sensation.

The cars that had made parking a challenge all those weeks were gone, too, which made the streets feel oddly spacious. He knew that by lunchtime everyone would have worked together to clean up the last few bits of confetti that hadn't been swept up after the parade. Until then, the remaining detritus from the weeks of chaos gave the town an almost abandoned feel.

Christophe was gone for the weekend on a skateboarding trip, and Alias already missed him. It reminded him of the time the Third King and his family left on a state visit and Alias spent a month alone in the palace.

He'd felt abandoned then, too.

Out of the blue one day, the Third King's aunt sent a runner with a message to Alias that she was taking the king and his sister away the following day. She knew he'd understand that he couldn't be included, and she hoped that while they were gone, he would agree to look after the palace. As the spare, Alias had been accustomed to the occasional exclusion, and as the highest-ranking fairy on the premises, her assignment didn't surprise him.

While he put up a good front, the news and the sudden departure devastated him. The foot incident had ignited a passion that neither of the young men had felt before, and since that day, not only had their feet stayed pressed together on the sofa every afternoon, the two of them became inseparable throughout the rest of the day.

They'd started eating breakfast together, generally in the king's chambers, though not always. Alias' suite came with its own dining room and staff, and sometimes he'd entertain there. Before classes, they'd often play a game or compare and review the previous day's class notes. And after classes and studying in the afternoon, they almost always played tennis, or basketball, or swam laps before dinner.

Since their friendship had blossomed, Alias had gotten in the habit of taking dinner in the evening with the Third King's aunt and sister, and being alone now meant eating by himself, which he found depressing. Without his beautiful soulmate, he spent the days wandering the palace and the grounds alone trying to fill the void. He found rooms he'd never known existed, and after a few days, he'd memorized every square foot.

He hung out in the kitchen and befriended the staff, who were always thrilled when a royal showed them attention. Though it took some convincing that they wouldn't get in trouble, he started showing up before meals to learn how to cook.

One afternoon, Alias was sunning himself at the pool. He'd shot enough free throws, and he was tired of studying. The pool was where he and the Third King had spent their last few hours together, and he sank into his lounge chair and tried to recall the feeling.

"Mind if I join you, Your Highness?" Györfi's voice was unmistakable but surprising to hear in a part of the palace that was off-limits to staff.

"Sure, why not?" he said without opening his eyes. "They're gone for another few days, but I don't see why they would mind just this once. Besides, I haven't had anyone to talk to for a while, and I'm bored."

Györfi pulled a lounge chair next to him and spread out his towel. "Man, this is the life, isn't it?" He lay back for a moment and then got up to adjust the back of the chair. Alias heard him struggling with the mechanism. It sounded as though the man had never used a chaise before, and Alias stood up to show him.

When he saw his heavy-set tutor bending over in too-tight bikini underwear, he covered his eyes. "Oh, man. You need to put something else on!"

"I didn't think I'd be needing a bathing suit, so I didn't pack one, and since it was only us two men out here at the pool, I figured–"

"No, no, no. I've got you covered," said Alias. He waved his hand, and suddenly Györfi was wearing a pair of pink gym shorts. "It's the house uniform. Keep them if you like."

Györfi leaned back again and sighed. "Ahh. You know the only thing that would make this day more perfect would be a martini. Your Royal Highness, do you suppose the Third King or his aunt would mind if I made myself a drink? It's been ages since I had one."

"Knock yourself out, Uncle Györfi." He pointed to the bar in the pool house, and he chuckled at how odd it was to see his tutor in shorts. He reminded himself that he was in charge, at least nominally, so he kept his eye on the man as he rummaged through the cabinets.

Györfi returned with two drinks. "I don't know what the legal drinking age is around here, but I made you one," he said. "I'm rather well known for my martinis, so today is your lucky day."

"That's nice. Thank you. I've never had one." He accepted the glass and took a sip. "Mmm. Dee-licious!"

"I should remind Your Highness that the Third King's aunt gave me the responsibility for teaching you boys about social drinking and eating and such, so I'm obligated to tell you that it's best to sip one of these. Any drink with alcohol, actually. Drinking too many of them or too fast can often lead to trouble."

"Really? That sounds like good advice. So, thank you for that, too." He tossed down the whole drink.

"Wow. Now see, that was what I was talking about. A little fast." He winked at Alias. "Since we're alone here, though, I suspect that we can ignore the rules. But if I'm going to keep up with you, I'd better hurry." He drained his in three gulps.

Alias closed his eyes and returned to thoughts of the Third King. He was enjoying the sun on his body. When he'd been a child, his parents took the family to beaches all over the world, which was where he and Theos developed the passion and the skills for surfing.

It was also when Alias had made up his mind to keep a tan throughout the year. Some color made him look good, and when he looked good, he felt good. He could change his skin color with the snap of his fingers, but he preferred tanning the old-fashioned way, on a chaise lounge.

He heard Györfi get up and walk to the bar again. "I made us another one," he said when he got back. Alias thanked him and tossed his right down.

"Can you feel it, yet?" Györfi asked.

"I feel warm, if that's what you mean."

"Yes. That's the martini settling in. I feel it too. Nice, eh?"

"No, I mean the sun feels warm." He turned on his chair to face the man. "Listen, Uncle Györfi. I just realized that I know nothing about you. They told us you were a genius, but I'd like to hear more."

"I'm happy to tell you my story, though my life certainly pales in comparison to the glamorous lives of you or the Third King. Maybe, after I tell you mine, you could tell me more about fairy things. About the three kingdoms, and your families, you know, so I can get some context for what I'm doing here. And, of course, I'd love you to tell me about fairy dust."

"Deal!" said Alias. "You start."

For the next hour and two more martinis, they swapped stories and shared family anecdotes. Györfi admitted that he'd been a bit of what they called a Whiz Kid. He'd graduated from college at age fifteen, and they both got a laugh when he claimed to be a nerd ever since. Alias also learned that while his tutor loved literature and philosophy, his real passion was for science, specifically chemistry.

Alias didn't reveal much that was personal. Exposing what made him tick was not in his nature, but he was happy to give him a thumbnail history of the three kingdoms. He explained that his father was king of the largest of the three and that his older brother, Theos, the champion kite-surfer, was next in line. Alias referred to himself as the spare.

Like most humans, Györfi was curious about fairy dust and asked if it was a myth, as he hadn't seen it used in the palace. Alias kept his response vague and suggested only that fairy dust was used for specific purposes.

"I notice that to use magic sometimes you wave your hands, and other times you snap or flick your fingers. I can't understand when you use one over the other."

"Yes, and I'm afraid we'll have to keep it that way. Fairies just know."

Györfi seemed satisfied at his answer and surprised Alias by rolling over on his side to face him. "I understand you like to play basketball."

Alias grinned. He couldn't imagine his out-of-shape tutor on the court, but he was tired of shooting baskets by himself. "I do. You play?"

"I used to throw a ball around back in the day, but I'm pretty rusty. You wouldn't want to reverse our roles and give your old tutor a few pointers, would you?"

"I suppose I could, but I need another half hour or so of sun, before I leave this chair, if you don't mind."

"Not at all. Why don't I mix us another drink in the meantime?"

Thirty minutes later, Alias put his shirt on and explained that the only basketball court was in his room, and he pointed the way. Györfi had not been in that section of the palace before, and as he staggered down the long private corridors, he would stop occasionally to lean against the wall to rest and gawk at the carved doors, the rich carpets, and the stunning artwork that covered the walls.

Watching him wobble alongside him filled Alias with regret. Györfi would be too drunk to handle a ball, if he ever knew how, and he didn't look forward to the waste of time.

"This room is all yours?" his tutor asked, as he pulled a t-shirt Alias had given him down around his belly.

"Yup," said Alias. "Neat, huh?" He found the ball and twirled it on his index finger while his tutor gaped at the vast room. Alias' plan was to get started strong right away. As drunk as the man was, he'd only need a few minutes to get him tired. Then he could escort him out. "Heads up!" he shouted, and he tossed Györfi the ball.

Györfi saw it coming, but he didn't seem to know how to catch it and he froze. The ball bounced on his hip and rolled across the court. He chased after it, but due to a combination of the man's natural lack of coordination and his current inebriation, the toe of his shoe knocked the ball forward a few times and made it roll farther away.

"Got it!" He shouted, finally, from the other side of the court. "Want to play a game?"

"You mean, one-on-one?" Giving him pointers, as he'd agreed to do was one thing, but playing a grossly unbalanced game was another and didn't sound like fun, especially just having witnessed the man's skills. Suddenly, he regretted even letting him join him at the pool. "Are you sure you're okay to play, Uncle Györfi?"

"Fit as a fiddle," he said. "Never felt better. What do you say, shirts versus skins?"

Alias clicked his teeth. "Gee. Since there's only the two of us, it's not really necessary to differentiate, do you think?"

"Probably not, but I remember it's what we used to play

when I was a kid. Well, I should say that I mostly watched the other kids play."

Alias humored him, and so that he wouldn't have to see Györfi without a shirt, he pulled off his own first. He gave Györfi the ball to start, and the man managed to dribble only two steps before he lost control. Alias swooped in, grabbed the ball, and went in for a layup.

Every time it was Györfi's turn with the ball, he'd lose it right away. Alias would snatch it and inevitably score. Each time, Györfi would shout, "Bro fist!" and hold up his hand until Alias returned the bump.

Györfi was beyond rusty. He showed no evidence that he'd ever been on a court or held a basketball, and Alias was mildly miffed about being misled. He was about to hang it up when he heard Györfi shout. "Give me your best shot!" He looked over and saw the man jumping with his hands over his head as though he was prepared to block.

Out of politeness, Alias gave him one more try, and he dribbled straight at him. Just as he was about to jump, Györfi swiped his leg and tripped him. Alias fell on his back, and his head bumped on the floor. A knock to the head was nothing to a fairy, but he did feel the crushing weight of his tutor who had fallen on top of him.

He blinked against the pressure, and then squirmed when he felt Györfi's hand awkwardly groping across his chest and his other hand sliding under the waistband of his shorts.

"Get off me!" he shouted and wiggled to get out from under him. But Györfi had planted his feet wide on the floor which kept him from being rolled over. Without using magic Alias was pinned. He tried pulling at Györfi's arms, but the man resisted.

"Come on, Alias. I know you like it," huffed the man. He shoved his hand further down Alias' shorts while he fumbled with his other hand to pinch a nipple.

Without considering the repercussions and in strict violation of the palace rules, Alias sent scalding heat to both of his tutor's hands. Györfi screeched and yanked them away. He rolled off onto his back and slapped his stinging hands against his thighs to ease the pain.

"You faggot! Don't tell me you don't want it. You didn't seem to mind when I touched your leg that afternoon in my room. Anyway, I see you two fairies playing footsie together every day. And when I use the word fairies, I think you know what I mean."

Alias stood up and quietly put on his shirt. "Thank you for keeping me company this afternoon, Mister Györfi. It was kind of fun, until just now." He motioned for his tutor to leave.

"Fuck you, and the rest of you fairies!" Györfi shouted, and he stumbled to the door.

"And I'm sorry for the pain I caused you." He snapped his fingers and the heat left Györfi's hands. He escorted him down the hall, and before he ushered him out of the restricted section, he added a final comment. "By the way, you do make an excellent martini. In the future, though, you should know that alcohol doesn't affect fairies. And by the word fairies, I think you know what I mean."

Alias expected to receive a written apology. Even a fake one that would have laid the blame on gin would have been better than nothing, but one never came. Nor did any mention of the incident, or that he called him by his first name. Because they never passed him in the halls, Alias assumed the man was using the back set of stairs that led to his rooms.

Alias took his own measures to avoid contact. Except for sleeping, eating, and sports, he'd spent most of his time during his alone period, the time he referred to as his 'lost month,' on the sofa in the library. He considered it their sofa, the Third King's and his. The odd little space where their passion was first ignited, and where it could be counted on to burn gloriously every day. Sometimes he had his staff serve his meals there.

But after the incident with Györfi, he gave it up. The sofa faced the fireplace shelves, and he didn't want to be there in case the man used his bookcase door. Considering that Györfi had started the ugliness, Alias was mad at himself for being the one to make the sacrifice and abandon the one place that gave him joy.

They didn't see each other either again until the Third King returned and classes resumed. Alias was dozing in his bed when he felt the Third King's breath against his cheek and then the gentle push to make room so that his friend could lay beside him. And then when his arm draped over Alias' shoulders and held him until it was time for dinner.

When their instruction resumed, the dynamics of the classroom were completely different. Questions and answers were suddenly stiff and brief, and discussions among all three of them lacked their former free-form banter. During private time with Alias, the Third King asked what was wrong.

"Why is Györfi acting so weird? Something must have

happened while I was away, because you two don't even make eye contact anymore. Are you going to tell me, or do I have to ask him?"

Alias shrugged. He didn't want to relate what had transpired, because he feared the Third King would tell his aunt, which would cause a scene. She'd ask why the tutor had been permitted in the private area, and there would be no end to the discussion. "Go ahead. Ask him. I'd be curious to hear what he'd say."

The next morning in class, the Third King did just that. He raised his hand and blurted out the question.

"I've noticed the vibe around here has changed one hundred and eighty degrees since I've been gone," he said. "Would you like to tell me what's going on between you and His Highness, the Prince? He won't tell me."

Györfi looked directly at Alias. "He won't, because there is nothing to tell. His Royal Highness and I only bumped into each other once, as I recall while your family was away. I suggest that any differences you feel may be Your Highness' imagination."

But it wasn't anyone's imagination that he stopped giving lectures in Latin and switched to French. Classes were shorter and the lectures less frequent, and when he wasn't involved with either, Györfi kept to himself.

Alias didn't mind. The less he saw of that man, the better. He figured they only had one more year with him before his contract was up, and he could tough out anything for that long. Besides, he'd absorbed all the knowledge he wanted from the man, and aside from the test Györfi had given him on the basketball court, he'd passed his other exams with flying colors.

"Did you know my birthday was coming up soon?" asked the Third King. They were lying together on the library sofa. Alias nodded. It was all anyone in the palace was talking about.

"Yes. If I got this right, when you turn eighteen, your aunt will lose her title as regent."

"Yes," said the Third King. "Finally! And you know what that means, don't you?"

"You'll be the big cheese. Lucky you. That's when you get all those new magic powers."

"Yeah, but on my birthday I want to give you a gift, too. Tell me what you'd want, but make it something that I could actually give you."

"I don't have to think. I know exactly what I'd want. To get rid of Györfi. You were right all along. He's creepy."

"Consider it done. I'll let him go tomorrow. I'm getting tired of studying, and I'd like to take a break for a while, anyway. So, that was easy." He looked at his shoes. "I have another wild idea to celebrate the day. And it also involves you."

"Your idea can't be crazier than what I've planned for you. I worked on it while you were gone, but I won't tell you, so don't ask. It's a surprise."

"Okay, well here's mine. Listen, since nobody will be able to tell me what I can and cannot do anymore, I was thinking that maybe you'd move in with me, at least for a while."

Alias was about to answer when they heard a click from the direction of the bookcase. "Was that the door?" Alias jerked up. "I thought I heard footsteps, too. Did you?"

"I think so, but I'm not sure. Do you think Györfi was listening?"

"I don't know. He's been keeping the door locked lately," said Alias. "But I hope not."

For being book-smart, Alias had to laugh at himself for the pathetic birthday cake that came out of the oven. He'd wanted to make it from scratch, so that his gift to the Third King would be special, and he'd been practicing late at night alone in the palace kitchen.

When he saw that all three layers were lopsided, it took a lot of willpower not to fix it with magic. But he stacked them together, instead, and slathered on twice as much frosting to fill in the gaps. Then he manifested eighteen candles in the true human tradition and waited until it was almost midnight.

He tapped lightly on the door before going in to surprise his friend. "*Felixnatalis!*" he said, in his best Latin. "I wanted to be the first to wish you happy birthday!"

The Third King beamed and threw back the covers on the other side. Still holding the cake Alias crawled in bed. "Since we can't grant each other real wishes, here's your chance to make a fun one. Go ahead. Blow out the candles."

The Third King looked at the grandfather clock. "Listen. In nine minutes, I'll be the full king and finally able to grant wishes," he said. "So, let's be patient." He winked. "I think you know what I'm going to wish for, anyway, so you know how much I want it to come true."

The candles were already burning down to their stubs.

"That's sweet, but please blow them out now, before they melt all over my masterpiece. You have no idea what went into baking this."

"You're right, I can't, being as that now I'm the only one in this room who hasn't cooked a day in his life. You made your point, though, and I love you for it. But in the interest of fire safety, let me help." He flicked at the candles, and they grew another inch. "But that doesn't mean we can't start on the cake."

He placed the lighted cake on the bedside table and manifested two slices. Shoulders touching and keeping their eyes on the ticking clock, they leaned back on their pillows, and Alias sang the birthday song in French through a mouthful of cake.

CHAPTER TWENTY-FOUR

At four minutes to twelve, Alias picked up the cake from the bedside table and moved it to their laps. Then he waved his hand to relight the candles. "I can't wait any longer! Ready to make your wish?" The Third King nodded and took a breath.

Suddenly, the door flung open, and someone snapped on the lights. "Not so fast!" shouted the aunt. "There will be no granting of wishes for you."

The boys bolted upright, and the cake went flying. When their eyes adjusted, they gulped. Glaring at them from the doorway was not only the aunt, but Uncle Györfi standing tall behind her.

"See? Caught in the act!" He walked to the bed. "As I was telling Your Royal Highness, I first saw them touching each other inappropriately several months ago. Who knows how long their naked debauchery had been going on before then?"

He grabbed a corner of the duvet. "Here's the proof!"

He ripped the blanket off the bed and exposed the boys lying next to each other.

The aunt peeked through her fingers and screamed, "Get out of my sight!"

Györfi's face flushed from disappointment at finding the young men fully clothed, but he was pleased that he'd convinced the aunt to take action, and he continued his charade.

"You heard what Her Royal Highness commanded. Leave at once!"

The aunt swiveled to him. "No. You!"

The smugness drained from his face. "What did I do?"

"For starters, you tried to rape the prince."

The Third King grabbed Alias' hand. "When?" Alias squeezed back.

Györfi growled at Alias. "You told her?"

"No," she said. "He didn't have to. You're as degenerate as they are, but I should banish you just for being stupid. How could you not realize that the palace has been watching your every move since the moment you arrived?" She shook her head. "And you were supposed to be this genius we hired to make the boys smart."

She clapped her hands, and three funnel clouds appeared on the floor. Then she flicked a finger, and the first engulfed the tutor. "Good riddance, Mr. Györfi."

She twirled her index finger, and his funnel started to spin. Through the force field, Alias could see him glaring back.

"This is your fault!" Györfi shouted above the whirlwind.

She waved at the funnel, and as it spun faster, his body

gradually faded away. When he disappeared completely, she flicked a finger. "Fstl Fstl," she commanded, and the cloud vanished. To where, Alias did not know, but he was sure Györfi would not have survived it anyway.

The aunt turned to Alias. "My nephew was not like you before you came, and I can't begin to imagine the elaborate web you spun to trap and then poison his mind. Since you are a prince of another kingdom, there are limitations to what I can do to punish you. But I can banish you from this kingdom and add a bit of misery to your already degenerate life." She clapped her hands, which transported him inside the second funnel.

As the clock began to chime midnight, she turned to her nephew. "You disgust and disappoint me. You are not fit to be part of this family, let alone be king." The third funnel bent toward the bed and sucked him in. "You will always be a fairy of this kingdom, but no one will remember your face. Furthermore, you will not remember your family or that you were ever the Third King." She spit on the floor. "It even makes me sick to mention you and that title in the same sentence."

From inside his own funnel cloud, the Third King stretched out his arms and shouted at his friend. "I love you, Alias."

Alias reached back. "I love you more." Tears streamed down both their cheeks.

Hearing the two boys express such tenderness sent her into a rage, causing the veins in her forehead to bulge and her face to flush. She faced them.

"Since you two have chosen this abnormal and abhorrent lifestyle and profess to love each other, I will give you the memory of your deviance. But it comes at a high price. I am clouding your minds, so that you will never remember each other's faces and will spend the remainder of your very long lives in eternal heartbreak."

Breathing became difficult for her and she leaned against the wall to steady herself as the clock chimed twelve. She summoned the strength to point at them. "Fstl, Fstl," she said, which started the clouds to spin.

Suddenly, she clutched her chest and fell to the floor. She looked up at the boys who were already beginning to fade from sight. "Help me," she choked.

Alias' funnel was nearer, and he shoved his arm through the force field. With the next rotation, he tried to grab her hand. "Come closer," he yelled. She crawled another few feet, and the next time around he reached for her hand again, but he missed.

"I tried, Your Royal Highness," he said, just before he faded away.

CHAPTER TWENTY-FIVE

A dozen or so flies buzzing in his face woke Györfi. His head banged with a fierce headache and as he slapped them away, an overwhelming stench of garbage made him turn to one side and puke.

He rolled over and let his head fall back to recover from his stomach spasms and get his bearings. It was dark around him and his mind was in a deep fog, but from the small slice of sky he could see looking straight up, he concluded that it was daytime.

He struggled to prop himself up on his hands, and as his eyes adjusted to the dim light, he realized that he was lying on top of a pile of trash surrounded by four metal walls. Something rustled at his feet. He heard the squeak first and then panicked when he saw the huge rat scurry across his feet.

Scrambling to stand made him sink deeper, and soon he was waist-high in the refuse. Lacking the upper body strength to pull himself over the top of whatever he was in, he managed to push cartons of rotted food and a broken table into a pile tall enough to stand on.

His stomach growled. He didn't know how long he'd been down there, but he was starving. He remembered seeing the remains of a felafel that was still wrapped in paper and didn't look too dirty, so he closed his eyes and shoved it into his mouth. Then he climbed on his newly created hill of garbage and lifted himself out, though not without a struggle.

As he brushed debris from his ripped and stained clothes, he read the printing on the container that had been his temporary lodging. *Dempster - For your worst trash.*

He was rubbing his stiff legs when he heard car horns. When he looked up from his end of the dank alley he saw a string of cars stalled in traffic at a cross street, and he shuffled to the corner. As he glanced around his eyes finally landed on something beautiful, the soaring magnificent art deco masterpiece, the Empire State Building.

He leaned against a stair stoop on the busy sidewalk. The scent of curry from the restaurant next door and the patchouli incense that billowed from a street vendor's table was a welcome switch from the putrid atmosphere of a few minutes earlier.

From the passersby who scowled at him and held their noses, he soon gathered that those powerful street aromas weren't as potent as the ones he was giving off. He held up an arm and took a whiff. While he didn't understand why or how he'd ended up in New York City, he was clear about a couple of things. He needed a shower, a change of clothing, and a drink.

A rail-thin bearded man with a guitar slung over his shoulder, who Györfi thought looked like a bum, tossed some change at his feet. When the man passed, Györfi bent down and picked it up. He spread the foreign sizes and denominations on his palm, and after studying both sides of the largest one, he dropped it in his pocket. It landed with a tinkle.

He patted the outside of his pants and felt a small bulge, and when he shoved his hand inside he was astonished to discover a pocketful of gold coins. The unexpected windfall confounded him as much as the other mysteries, but the small fortune meant he could easily acquire all three of his immediate needs.

He heard a scraping sound from across the street, and he looked up to see a young man dragging a male mannequin to the front of a store called *Second Time Around.* Not believing his incredible luck, he rushed over and tapped the kid on his shoulder as he was pulling a turtleneck over the model.

"Whoa! Get back!" shouted the boy. He covered his nose and mouth and backed away. "There's no homeless allowed in the store!"

Györfi held up his hand. "Please listen. You've got me all wrong. But to relate the complex string of circumstances that led to my uncharacteristic appearance would take up far too much of your valuable time. But if you would overlook my untidiness long enough to outfit me in your latest fashion, I will make it worth your while." He pulled out a gold coin, and holding it in the boy's face, he wiggled his eyebrows.

The clerk scrunched his face. "What am I supposed to do with that?"

"Can't you tell that it's gold?" He looked around at the used clothing. "This one coin alone is enough to buy everything in your store."

"Yeah, yeah. Whatever." He pointed to the pawnshop next door. "If it's real, they might give you something for it."

Even behind the plexiglass wall, the old man had to hold his nose against the stench. But he didn't seem to mind the insult to his nose once he saw the rare mint-condition antique coin Györfi was holding. He wrote down a number and shoved it through the slot.

"That's all? You can't be serious," stammered Györfi. "Have you no idea what this is and where it's from?"

"Take it or leave it," said the old man. Without looking up, he slid the coin back through the slot and went back to his business.

Györfi reached in his pocket. "How much for two?"

An hour later, he was admiring his new look in a floor-length mirror. As he turned slightly to get a view of the black jeans, the turtleneck straight from the mannequin, and a leather bomber jacket, he realized something was still off. The clerk did too, and suggested that a pair of Doc Martens would go better with his new look than the scuffed-up brown oxfords he was wearing when he walked in. He also recommended a visit to the bathhouse a few doors down.

Mr. Györfi found that the bathhouse offered much more than the name implied. After the first of many soapy showers, he followed an attractive younger man around, until the kid got tired of being stalked and told Györfi to buzz off. He walked through another door and ended up padding around in a dark labyrinth where for several hours he feasted from a distance on naked men, a couple of whom he imagined were what his former student Alias would have looked like. Chatting up men closer to his own age while soaking in the pool, he learned that he was in the East Village.

It was evening when he finally left the bathhouse. He'd let the day slip by without giving a thought to where he'd bunk for the night. But even after getting the lowballed figure for his coins, he had plenty of cash left for drinks, dinner, and a hotel room. He jingled the remaining gold coins in his pocket again, as a reminder that there was still a little more where that came from.

He crossed Washington Square Park into the West Village and was wandering the streets looking for the right bar when he heard a woman crooning *Are You Lonesome Tonight*. It was remarkable how closely the voice resembled Zsa Zsa Hajdu's, and as he no longer had possession of her out-of-print recordings, he was thrilled to find that at least one still existed.

For an instant, he believed the song came from an open window of a second-floor apartment, but the voice led him to a door that was slightly ajar in an alley just off Grove Street. Above it, a lighted sign glowed in red. *Gabriella's*. As he started in, a beefy man stopped him and pointed at a sign. *$10 Cover. 2 Drink minimum.*

His song was nearing the end. He knew every measure by heart. Whoever was singing had Zsa Zsa's vibrato down pat, and he was desperate to get in to see whose voice was so indistinguishable from the original he had on vinyl. He pulled out a wad of his new and still unfamiliar-looking paper money and glared at the bouncer for having to waste time to pick through it to find the right denomination. By the time he got in and sat at a table, she was finishing the last stanza, and as she took her bow, the announcer's voice booming over the sound system sent shivers through his body.

"Ladies and Gentlemen, give a hand for the incomparable Zsa Zsa Hajdu!"

Mr. Györfi ordered a martini and asked his waiter the name of the singer.

"Didn't you hear the man just now? Zsa Zsa Hajdu. She sings here every night." The waiter shook his head and started to walk away.

"Yes, I heard what he said, but I stand by my question. The real Zsa Zsa would be long dead by now, rest her soul, so I wondered who was pretending to be her."

"I don't know. Ask her. She owns the place."

"Aah, then her name must be Gabriella, right? The name of the bar?"

"You're asking these questions to the wrong person. All I know is that somebody named Célia something signs my checks."

Györfi finished his drink and waited for her next set. Another singer entertained for a while, and when she finished and a third singer appeared, he became irritated and flagged down his waiter to ask when Miss Hajdu would return to the stage.

"She won't," he said. "Miss Hajdu only does one set these nights."

Feeling depressed enough already, Györfi handed the waiter one of his gold coins with instructions to deliver it to the singer and to ask that she sing *Are You Lonesome Tonight* one more time.

The second singer returned for another set, and when she finished, the house lights came on and the bartender shouted his last call warning. Discouraged that his gratuity went unappreciated, Györfi signaled to his waiter and pointed to his empty glass. As the waiter returned with his last martini of the evening, suddenly the house lights went out, and the footlights flashed back on.

Györfi whirled around to see Zsa Zsa walk to the microphone. A stagehand brought her a stool, and she sat to face Györfi's table.

"It seems I have a secret admirer in the audience tonight." She shaded her eyes against the glare and pointed vaguely in his direction. "I don't know your name, sir, but I am happy to sing for you this one song."

The band began playing the intro and Györfi hummed along as he squirmed in his seat. The second most glamorous woman in the history of his world after the real Zsa Zsa was going to sing directly to him. Whoever she was, to his gin-fueled mind she had nailed his idol's look, and when he closed his eyes, he was astonished that her voice was indistinguishable from the one who'd captured his soul.

When she finished, she blew him a kiss and left the stage. The lights went on in the bar, and as other people straggled out to the street, Györfi lagged behind to savor the experience until the bouncer shooed him out.

The following night, he got to the bar early enough to snag the table closest to the stage. Well before the entertainment was to begin, he sent another coin to her dressing room with a message that it was from her same secret admirer.

She came out second that evening, and while she was singing some of her favorite sea shanties, he took care to study her face and hair. He compared her features to the face he knew so well from her album covers and in the other photos he'd memorized over the years. This woman was not only an identical lookalike, to his trained ear her voice sounded exactly the same. She especially nailed Zsa Zsa's long wobbly vibrato.

When she finished his song, she left the stage with a twinkle in her eye and a wink for him. Knowing she had finished her one and only set for the evening, he settled back in his chair and let the tingling sensation sink in for a few minutes. As he was preparing to leave, he felt a gentle hand on his shoulder and heard the unmistakable voice behind him.

"May I join you?"

He jumped to his feet and pulled out her chair. She asked what he was drinking, but before he could answer or sit down, a tray appeared on the table with a martini for him and something red in a stunning Waterford crystal goblet for her.

"Thank you," he said. "This is such an honor. I have been the real Zsa Zsa's biggest fan forever, probably ever." He cocked his head. "And you. You've got her look, and her voice, and that fabulous vibrato all down pat. I should know, because I'm kind of an expert on the woman. I have all her albums, and I used to listen to them every day."

"That's sweet of you to say, but what do you mean, 'used to listen'?"

Györfi coughed. "These days I'm doing a bit of travel-ing." He fluttered his hands in the air. "You know, seeing the world. And I'm, um, traveling light."

The singer took the two coins from her brassiere and placed them on the table. "I'm intrigued by the coins you sent me. I recognized them, of course. I guess we both know they're worth a fortune."

"Are they? The pawnbroker who gave me cash for a couple didn't seem to think so." He shot her words back to her. "But what do you mean, 'of course'?"

She leaned back and clicked her teeth. "Wait a minute. Here you just said you knew all about me. You don't need to be an expert to connect the Hungarian name Hajdu with a thousand-year-old coin from the reign of Stephen the First."

Györfi blinked at the woman's audacity, and wondered if she were one of these people that played a role so long they ended up believing they were that character. "Yes, I realize that. And Zsa Zsa would have indeed recognized them as such, but with all due respect, you are not she. The real one would have died decades ago."

She stared into her goblet for a moment. "Do you know this for a fact?"

He stammered. "No. Not actually, but even if she were still alive at the age of one hundred and twenty, she certainly wouldn't be singing or looking like you."

She returned his gaze. "Maybe. Maybe not." Then she finished her drink. "And now I must leave. Will you be staying?"

"Maybe for just one more drink," said Györfi. "Can I entice you to stay for one more?"

She laid her hand on his and shook her head. "Another time, perhaps. In the meantime, drink up." He helped her with her chair, and as she walked away, he thought he heard her snap her fingers. He sat back down at his table and was about to signal for the waiter when he noticed a full martini in front of him. He jerked his head around to thank her, but she was gone.

Eager to hear her sing again and maybe continue the conversation, he returned the next evening. After paying his cover he elbowed his way to a seat near the stage and sent her another coin. Then he ordered his usual drink and settled in for the show.

The singer from the night before sang to an appreciative audience, but enduring her two sets of jazz and a few standards was torture.. He crossed and uncrossed his legs and fidgeted all night. When Zsa Zsa still had not made an appearance shortly before closing, he asked the waiter if he'd given her his coin.

"Yes. But she only sings when she feels like it, so we never know if she will or not. If you come tomorrow, maybe you'll get lucky."

He returned the following night, and hoping to ensure her attention that time he sent her two coins. She disappointed him again, though, by not performing. On the third night, he sent another coin backstage. As closing time neared and she hadn't come on stage, he complained to the waiter.

"You told me she sang every night. I only come to hear her sing, not the other woman, and I've been paying your cover charges and two-drink minimums all week. Are you sure you've been giving her my coins, or have you been stealing them?"

The waiter glared back at the accusation. "Of course I've been passing them to Miss Hajdu. As a matter of fact, she asked me to give you an invitation to her apartment for a nightcap. May I tell her that you'll join her?"

Györfi used every ounce of willpower he could summon to assume a cool facade, and he bit his lip to keep his excitement from bursting through and saying something utterly foolish. Since he'd discovered Gabriella's bar, he'd been burning through a lot of cash. He had only one gold coin left, and until that moment he considered putting an end to his obsession with the singer. But suddenly, receiving her personal invitation seemed worth the investment.

The Third King shook his head and lifted himself up on his elbows. A brief look around told him that he was on the edge of a huge park on a busy street.

"Are you all right?" The question came in French from a twenty-something-year-old. Judging from his contorted face and the way he rocked on the grass holding his bleeding knee close to his chest, he appeared to be in pain himself.

The Third King nodded and responded in French. "What happened? And where am I?"

"Since we fell backward onto the grass here, technically I suppose that puts us both in the Bois de Bologne," said the guy who was still nursing his injury. "I'm really sorry. I was cruising down the sidewalk on my skate-board and ran into you. Actually, though, you kind of came out of nowhere, so we sort of knocked into each other."

The Third King rolled over to investigate the bleeding knee. "Ouch. You okay?"

"It's just a scrape," he said. "It stings like hell, but it's my wrist that really hurts. I must have landed on it. I hope it's not a fracture."

"May I?" The Third King waved his hand over the guy's arm. "No. It's not broken."

"How can you tell?" The Frenchman cocked his brow and brought his arm in front of him, and when he bent his hand and rotated his wrist without any pain, his skepticism turned to a smile. "Wow, you're right. It doesn't hurt anymore. What the hell did you do?"

"Nothing. I think you were overreacting. So skate-boarding, huh? You ride street?"

The Frenchman looked surprised. "Some. You?"

"Yeah, a lot. Mostly vert, though."

"Oh, man. Speaking of riding, where's my board?" He scanned the area and was visibly relieved when he saw it sticking out from under a bush. He limped over. "Oh crap! The deck broke!"

"What size do you ride?" asked the Third King. "From here it looks like about a 9, you know, in inches."

"Yeah, that's exactly right, but damn. I was on my way to practice at La Stade de la Muette, just down the street. I've got a competition in a couple days."

"No problem." The Third King reached behind his back and produced an identical skateboard. "Here, take this."

"What? No. How can I take your board? I don't even know your name."

The Third King realized he didn't either. He thought for a moment. A bus rumbled by, and he looked up to see a huge ad for the Christophe Café plastered on its side. "Christophe," he said. Then he looked behind him at the tree-lined entrance to the park. "Christophe DuBois."

The Frenchman held out his fist for a bump. "Gilles. Gilles Denfert."

"Okay. Now that we know each other, you can take the board," said Christophe. He reached behind him again and pulled out a second board, identical to the others. "Besides, I had two. Mind if I tag along?"

"That would be great," said Gilles. "But I don't think I can ride today. My knee's pretty banged up and I'm pretty sure it's still bleeding."

Christophe pulled a bandage out of his pocket and dangled it in his new friend's face. "Not for long." Gilles rolled up his pants and leaned his leg toward Christophe and let him tape it on. "How come you have just what I need?" He chuckled. "Are you some sort of magician?"

Christophe laughed back. "Not exactly. I just happened to be prepared, and you got lucky." When he finished he told Gilles to hop on his board and that he'd follow. "I'll bet by the time we get there your knee is going to feel a whole lot better."

They rode the two blocks to the bowl and spent a couple of hours showing each other what they could do. Gilles ran through the program he planned to use for his competition later in the week, and Christophe went through a long sequence of impromptu tricks. He ended with an advanced move Gilles had never seen.

"Where did you learn that last move? That's nbd, at least around here."

"So, never been done here, huh? Neat. I came up with it a year or so ago and had forgotten all about it."

"Well, you should name it. How about we call it the DuBois?" He laughed. "And then if you teach it to me, I'll buy you a sandwich."

They continued getting to know each other at a nearby brasserie, and the subject turned to where Christophe lived. When he replied that he'd only just arrived in Paris that day and hadn't figured out those logistics yet, Gilles offered his apartment. A housemate had just left to spend a month in the US, and his room was empty. He also convinced Christophe to enter the competition with him.

"It's an open entry kind of thing, and judging from what I saw, I think you'd have a good chance of winning."

CHAPTER TWENTY-SIX

A giant poster of Zsa Zsa Hajdu greeted Györfi when he stepped into the foyer of her apartment at One Fifth Avenue, only a few blocks away. The housekeeper led him to the elegant parlor where Zsa Zsa was waiting in a stunning black outfit and seated on a leopard print overstuffed chair.

"Daffodils. How did you know they were my favorites?" She placed the flowers he gave her on a coffee table and gestured to a chair that faced hers. On the same table, in a pile between his martini and her customary red drink, gleamed his gold coins. She raised her goblet and he toasted in return.

"Before we take our little relationship much further I must ask how you happened to come by so many of these priceless coins that you can toss them around as tips? Are you some titled aristocrat running around Greenwich Village?

"How rude of me not to introduce myself." He cleared

his throat to buy time while he chose a name more suitable than his own. "The name is Birnam." When her eyes didn't react with the recognition he anticipated, his brain scanned centuries of world literature for a name that was more impressive. "Birnam-Wood." Her eyes lit up at the hyphenation.

"Oh, like Shakespeare."

He was thrilled that she caught the literary allusion mashup. Still, he couldn't resist adding a flourish. "Lord Birnam-Wood, actually."

Well, it's lovely to make your acquaintance, your--" She stopped for a moment. "Is it Your *Highness*?"

He shivered at the word. "No, no. Not that. It's your lordship, but please call me Nigel." He laughed and waved his hand as if to dismiss any concern she may have for his elevated station. "Everyone does."

"Then I insist you call me by my real name. Célia. Célia Gabriella Hajdu. Zsa Zsa, of course, is the stage name I came up with when I started my singing career back in the nineteen twenties."

Györfi laughed. "Why do you keep trying to convince me that you are over one hundred twenty years old? Cheers, by the way." He took a sip.

She smiled. "Hmm. At least I'm being honest about who I am. Would you want to try telling me the truth...for a change?" He blanched. "The only thing you haven't lied about besides being one of my fans is that you're traveling light. For being lord whatever, I'm surprised you don't have a change of clothes. You've been wearing the same ones all week, or so my waiters tell me."

Györfi squirmed at being caught, and he was about to create a new fib to explain when she cut him off.

"I really don't care that you lie, so save yourself the bother of coming up with another. It's a skill that could benefit us both, which I'll explain in a moment. But in the meantime, I'd still like to call you Lord Birnam-Wood, because the name is hysterical and makes me laugh."

His face was still red when she pointed to the coins. "I asked you here because you intrigue me. Fans have tried to give me money and gifts for years to get my attention and prove their devotion, but you obviously don't have a clue about their value. The other night when I said they were worth a fortune, I was understating their market price."

She pointed at two chests in a corner. "And I should know. I'm a bit of a gold coin freak, myself. That first chest is half-full of Brasher Doubloons, if you know what they are. The other chest is full of something even more priceless."

Györfi sat up at how easily she shared where she kept valuables that he could steal with little effort. He glanced at the chests and then at the coins at the table, then back at the chests. "Why are you telling me this? Now that I know, I could easily overpower you and rob you blind."

"Impossible," she said. "Don't even try. But let's get back to these ones on the table. They bring back very unhappy memories for me, and you've still not told me how you came by them."

He stumbled with his words. "Honestly, I'm not entirely sure. I literally found them in my pocket the other day. I suspect they are my severance pay."

She grinned and called her housekeeper to bring a vase for the flowers. "Aah. The plot thickens. When I was a child, the only people I ever knew who had enough of those coins to use as money was a group of fairies." She reached for his hand. "May I?"

Györfi let her hold it, and he watched her eyes roll back into her head. While she remained quiet, he felt a buzzing in his head, as though his brain was a machine in a factory working overtime.

She released his hand and sat back. "I'm a fortune teller on the side, and I picked up a place called the Third King- dom. Does that ring a bell, by any chance, Mr. Györfi? It does to me."

His eyes bulged and he choked on his drink. "H-h- how…"

"I learned your real name and your recent past from touching your hand the night we met at my club. But after holding it longer just now, I picked up your desire for revenge. You see, I'm not just a very old singer. I can read minds. I can do a fair amount of magic, too. And so you don't waste any more of our time defending your under- standable skepticism, I'll prove it."

She snapped her fingers, and the daffodils he'd brought rose from the table and plopped into the vase. Then she pointed at his coins, which disappeared from the table and ended up in his pocket.

He fell back into his chair and gulped. "You're not a fairy, I hope. My experience with them has not been stellar."

"No. My encounter with them wasn't either. It's a long

story that began centuries ago, which I won't bore you by relating, but a bunch of them did a number on my family. I was only six years old at the time, and we were happy as clams. Then, one day we were dragged before the king, and poof! I woke up alone on a beach in the Caribbean with a pocket full of the same gold coins as yours. I never saw my family again. As you can imagine, I'm still rather pissed."

Győrfi's head spun from the coincidence, and as he wiped sweat from his forehead, he pointed with hopeful eyes at his empty glass.

"I'd be lying if I said I didn't want to get back at them, myself. But I'd rather become a fairy and use their own magic against them."

"Well, you're in luck, because that's where you come in. You proved your persistence these past nights at Gabriella's. What I am prepared to offer you is nothing short of a once-in-a-lifetime proposition. And when I say lifetime, I'm really talking about several lifetimes. I'll explain.

"An older local woman named HerSea found me on the beach. She was an original Arawak and one of the only women to evade capture by the Carib Indians when they invaded the island long before Columbus gave it the name St. Martin.

"She raised me and taught me everything she knew. As I grew older, she introduced me to the magic that came from rocks she found by chance in a nearby lagoon. Simply holding one gave a person immense powers. Cracking it open and mixing its red powder into a drink gives immortality of a sort."

Zsa Zsa pointed to her goblet. "I've been drinking this every day since she showed me, and it's obviously worked, for I'm going on four hundred. HerSea never knew the name of that rock, and I still don't, but that second chest over there is full of them, and there are plenty more where that came from.

"When I reached my late teens in the early eighteen hundreds, HerSea showed me how to pass as a boy. I was eager to leave the island and get on with my life when a ship stopped off one day to resupply. I talked my way onboard, thanks to my magic, I overpowered the others. Taking my adoptive mother's name, I went on to accumulate great wealth as the successful Pirate HerSea. Perhaps you've heard of me. I even commissioned a lighthouse in California and named it after me, although I understand they bungled the spelling.

"For decades, hell, centuries, I wanted to avenge the fairies of the Third Kingdom for what they did to my real family, but I confess that when I got to New York, my singing career seduced me and I never followed through.

"And now, in my four hundredth year, I feel that even this red drink cannot keep me alive much longer. But you can pick up where I left off and destroy the fairies for us both. All we need is a plan. I'll give you the wealth you need, and the immortality from the rocks will make it all possible."

Györfi rubbed his eyes at the odds that the singer he'd idolized all his life would be sitting across from him and dangling the opportunity for immortality in his face.

"I already know how," he said. "The key is their fairy dust. They all need it to survive, so the easiest way to kill them all is to contaminate the supply. I even know where to find it."

"Please, can you elaborate? I don't want to micromanage, but I'm going to press you for the names of all the players and where to find them. You can understand that I want to be convinced that our plan is airtight, you know, before I take the final and drastic step."

They spent the rest of the evening together. He began giving her the broad strokes, and she drilled for details. He gave her names and explained how the young Third King had been banished with his boyfriend, a prince, and that the new Third King was inexperienced and would be vulnerable to attack.

She placed her hand on his and winked. "This is so encouraging. I knew you had a brilliant head on your shoulders that first night I met you. I guess you've already figured out how to take down someone as powerful as a fairy king?"

He took another piece of paper and scribbled the basic shape of the fairy wing guillotine he'd spent weeks designing. "Yeah. I'd have to disable them first with some iron, but then when they run into this little baby, they'd never know what hit them."

"I love it. But how would you even get back into the palace?"

"Since I spent years there, I know the place inside and out, including the tunnels that run all through it. Here, let me sketch them out for you to prove I know what I'm talking about."

He drew floor plans and filled her in with what he'd learned from books in the palace library and from chatter he'd picked up from the servants. She pressed for more information about fairy dust, and he revealed that they made it not in the Third Kingdom but in the larger fairy kingdom not far away.

By dawn, they'd formulated the strategy, and he salivated at the prospect that she'd put his revenge within such easy reach.

CHAPTER TWENTY-SEVEN

Alias stared into space thinking how much better his quality of life in Myers Beach had been before the fairies came to town. He'd worked just as hard back then, but being free to goof off with Christophe and his friends had given his life balance. Now it had become desperately off-kilter.

He missed Greta and their coffee dates and heart-to-hearts that had helped them grow close over the past several months. He missed their weekly gossip sessions and movie nights, and her blunt approach to life and her assuredness. The ways she'd make him feel better about all his decisions. And even though communication with her these days was as easy as three fingers against his temples, it just wasn't the same as a face-to-face conversation.

He missed Julie, too. Her bubbly personality had drawn him in the moment they met. Because she wasn't one of his subjects or even a fairy like the rest of them, he could be himself and didn't feel like he had to be put together so much around her. Nor did he have to worry about damaging his family's reputation.

Desperate to make faster progress, he'd spent the morning overlaying the locations of the elements onto a map of Myers Beach. He felt strongly that finding six out of the nine in that sleepy little beach town wasn't a coincidence, and he hoped to discover a pattern that would help him find the last two. And fast.

Later, he filled Christophe in on his latest theory about the dust formula. "I've come to the conclusion that what's lacking is bulk. All the ingredients we have so far are super powerful, as we've found out the hard way, but they're very fine and need something in a large enough quantity to bind them together. I don't know what I'm looking for, but I'm pretty sure I'll know it when I see it."

Christophe walked to the edge of their infinity pool. "Look at those waves. One of them has your name on it. Come on. Let's go. You need a break."

"I can't afford one," Alias snapped. "I'm out of time and practically out of dust!"

Christophe crossed his arms and shook his head. He took a step back. "Don't you think I know that? But you're not getting anywhere staring at the same map, as though it's going to change if you look away. I know you are working hard to save the day, but sometimes you have to break the rules to trigger your brain into new ideas."

A chirp came from Christophe's back pocket. "When did you get a cellphone?" Alias eyed the screen and read the caller ID. It was Julie.

"I got it when she and I were in Florence," he explained. "We love to talk, so she convinced me to get one so we could stay in contact. Since she's not a fairy, this is the easiest way for us to communicate." He swiped his thumb over the green button to answer the call. "Hey Jules, you're on speaker. Alias is here with me."

"Christophe! Am I glad I made you get a phone," she said. "Hi, Alias. It's great to hear your voice, too."

"What's up?" Christophe leaned a hip against Alias.

"It's about that guy I met while we were abroad."

Alias didn't like the shaky sound of her voice. "Did he hurt you?" He asked. His shoulders automatically straightened as he fell into a protective brotherly role.

She sighed and they heard a rustle before her voice became more clear. "Turns out...he's married." Christophe's brows shot up to his hairline.

"Um...I—we don't know what to say."

"Say you'll come comfort me." While her voice had a cheery lilt, Alias recognized that she was trying to cover her pain. "I'm in St. Martin, you know the island, on the French side. Can you both come over and just...I dunno... make me feel better? We could eat a bunch of ice cream, drink a lot of French wine, watch romcoms, and talk shit about boys until I feel like I'm not dying. Please?"

Without consulting Alias, Christophe blurted out a response. "We'll be right there. Text me where you are. We'll bring the prosecco."

Though he could hear the smile in her voice when she thanked them, Alias' face pinched. Christophe had unfairly taken the decision out of his hands. "You *know* I can't leave the lab right now," he said.

Christophe frowned. "But she's our friend. And she's hurting."

Alias ran a hand through his hair. "Look, I love Julie like a sister. But I have a duty as prince to–"

"Yes, but you have a duty to her, too, as her friend."

"What would *you* know about duty?" He regretted making the hurtful comment as soon as it left his mouth. The way that Christophe's eyes widened and then watered cut him to the core. "I'm sorry," he said quickly. He reached for Christophe's arm to keep him from walking away. "I didn't mean that."

"The problem is, I think you did." He let Alias loop his arms around his neck in a loose hug and pull him back, so they could lean into each other. "You said you'd never use your social standing against me like that."

"I know. I'm so very sorry." Alias touched his forehead against Christophe's. "You were right. Being cooped up like this is driving me crazy. I'm saying things I don't mean."

Christophe rolled his eyes but smiled when Alias kissed his cheek. "I could get used to that," he said.

"My kisses?"

"No. You saying that I'm right. It's not often I get to pull one over on you, Doctor Doctor."

Alias laughed at the nickname Christophe had started using when he'd learned about his two PhDs.

"Boyfriends again?" Alias asked.

"Fine, but you have to make it up to me."

Alias took his hand. "Done. Lunch can wait. Let's go upstairs to the bedroom and relax. I have a feeling it may trigger a new idea or two."

Later that afternoon, they were sharing bits of a raspberry tart on their way back to the compound, when Christophe put the question to Alias. "You know, we never decided what we were going to do."

Alias licked the crumbs off his thumb. "In regard to what?"

"Visiting Julie." He looked toward the ocean, and after a pause, he said, "She needs us."

Alias sighed at the same old problem that kept him from doing all sorts of things he wanted to do. He shook his head. "You know I don't have time. I *literally* told you, right before she called."

"Come on. We're fairies. We can stop time," Christophe said.

"Yes, but to do that in a way that would be helpful to me, I'd have to use up the last of my dust."

Christophe eyed him and ate the last bit of the tart. "I could do it for you, so you wouldn't have to. How big of a time stop do you need?"

Alias laughed, "Oh, you know. Just enough to have the whole world stop turning, except for me."

Christophe nodded. "I hear your sarcasm, but still, your wish is my command."

He clapped his hands, and a whirlwind appeared on the ground. As he twirled his finger, the funnel moved across the boardwalk. Everything it touched stopped in its tracks. A seagull froze in mid-flight with a scrap of pretzel clutched in its beak. A group of small children froze mid-giggle as they were playing a game of tag. An old man in a wheelchair froze as he was flinging pieces of bread into the sand for the little birds to snatch up.

Alias watched in horror as he calculated how much dust Christophe had to be using. "Stop!"

Confused, Christophe dropped his hands. "Why? How is any of this wrong? I was just doing what you asked."

"I never asked you for this."

Christophe's eyes narrowed. "Oh, I forgot. You're the great Prince Alias. You never ask anyone for anything, because everything has always come so easily to you."

"That's not fair. You really think any of this is easy?"

"You said you needed the world to stop. I was just offering that to you."

"Yes, but you had to know I wasn't being serious." His chest heaved. "What if we need the dust to heal more people?"

Christophe crossed his arms. "Gosh. We just had incredible make-up sex, and already we're arguing again about the same old issue. I'll say this one last time. I've never touched your damn dust, and I'm really sick of you accusing me."

Incredulous, Alias shook his arms at the world around them that was silent since Christophe had stopped everything. "Then how is this possible?"

"I don't know. I just did it." Alias wished he hadn't been sharp with the man he loved, especially since Christophe had been spot-on about their recurring argument. "Listen, I think we need to take a break from each other for a while."

Alias reached for his arm. "Please don't. We love each other."

"I know. Just not enough, I guess. And I'm not blaming you, really. You've never gotten over your first infatuation enough to let me into your heart completely. I'm willing to give it a little longer, but in the meantime, this constant arguing and making up is getting old."

"Can we at least talk it over?"

"I'm done talking." He clapped and started the time again. "You stay here and think about it if you want. I'm going to St. Martin to comfort our friend." He rolled his shoulders and popped his wings, and Alias swallowed the lump in his throat as he watched his lover fly away.

Alias walked the rest of the way home, replaying who had said what, and kicking himself for letting their argument escalate out of control. He plopped down on their bed hoping to put the scene out of his mind when he got the message from Stefán, asking him to come to The Fairy Kingdom right away. And to bring some of his classic fairy dust with him.

He put his fingers to his temple and sent him a return message.

I really don't want to use any more today, Stefán. I hardly have any left. What is it? More fairies on edge?"

No. It's way beyond the jitters. Please come right away.

Alias got up and headed for the door and on his way he grabbed his last pouch of dust. When he noticed it felt full, he peeked inside. His heart sank. While he was glad he had enough dust to take care of whatever the current problem was, Christophe obviously hadn't touched any, and it killed him that he'd made the accusation.

He flew to The Fairy Kingdom and heard the yelling before he got to the dining room.

"Wow. They sound hyped up all right. But you know, if

you could just talk them into being a little patient, it'll wear off."

"Um. With all due respect, I'm afraid it will, and when it does, it won't be a pretty sight. During dinner, the fairies in the back dining hall started to levitate. They've been stuck to the ceiling for some time now, and I am worried about what will happen when they start dropping to the floor."

A dining room full of hundreds of fairies levitating out of control was not a situation Alias could ever have anticipated, and to reverse the force that stuck them to the ceiling took the whole pouch of dust. Their screams had turned to grumbles and dirty looks as he got them down safely one by one, but the complaints ringing in his ears didn't bother him as much as the pain in the pit of his stomach for not having trusted the man he loved.

As soon as he finished, he left for St. Martin to give the apology of a lifetime.

CHAPTER TWENTY-EIGHT

Christophe was lounging on a couch in Julie's St. Martin apartment when Alias showed up. He put down his magazine.

"What are you doing here? I thought you didn't have time."

Alias held up his hand. "First off, is Julie here? I don't want her to hear what I have to say."

"No. She went out for a new bathing suit." Christophe sighed and heaved himself up.

"Look, I feel really stupid." Alias leaned against the door jam. "I needed to use some of my dust after you left, and I noticed the pouch was full. I can't tell you how sorry I am for accusing you and saying those things."

"You have to stop lashing out at me," said Christophe. Alias wasn't used to seeing Christophe's usual happy features thrown in such stark, serious relief. "I'm not the reason you're stressed. You can't treat me like I am."

"I know that," Alias agreed. "But can I just say one more

thing about the dust?" Christophe rolled his eyes and then nodded. "It's just that I don't understand how you do all this advanced magic if you don't use fairy dust. I mean, where did you learn how?"

"I don't know. I just do it. Look. We've been living together for what, six months? Have you ever seen me use dust to do magic?" Alias was silent, as he searched his brain for evidence to the contrary. "Exactly. See? You haven't."

"Okay," said Alias. "Honestly, I think it's cool that you've got so much power. Really." He gave Christophe a poke. "As long as you don't try to use it against me."

"Then don't give me any more reasons." He gave Alias a hug. "By the way, Julie mentioned after she leaves here, she wants to spend some time with her parents." He wiggled his eyebrows. "So, I asked her if she'd mind if I put up a few friends in her building."

"I assume that when you say a few friends you're talking about the hundreds of fairies from the Third Kingdom?"

"Yeah. I mean, things are starting to get pretty intense in The Fairy Kingdom."

"And?"

"Of course she said yes. I figured I could remodel the place. You could help, if you felt like it, and if we put in extra-long nights, we could get it done in a weekend. And we can return it to normal before she gets back."

"Sure, I'll help. It'll be fun. But I'm wondering if we should clue her in. She must have some idea, doesn't she? I mean, you spent all that time together in Europe."

"She did ask a lot of questions, you know, about Lily

and Greta, but I played dumb. I'd love her to know about us, and I firmly believe we can trust her with the information. Nobody likes being transparent more than I do, so if you agree, then let's clue her in today, okay?" Alias nodded.

"Alias! Oh my god. You're here!" A gentle voice came from the front door. "And just in time for the beach, so I can try out this." Julie held up her teeny new bathing suit.

They headed straight to the beach, and she led them to her favorite beach club where they rented lounge chairs and umbrellas. They drank coconut milk from a beach vendor, and Alias picked up a sarong for Julie from another. Then they each took a hand and brought her to the water and made her go in. Julie took turns riding on their shoulders, and after a few minutes of screaming and laughter and horseplay and splashing, she stood still and touched a small spot on Christophe's back.

"Hey. After all our time together I've never noticed that little scar between your shoulders. Did you hurt yourself?" She waded around to Alias' back. "Wait. You've got one, too. Was that some sort of fraternity ritual, or something else you boys got into at school?"

"Yeah. Something like that," said Alias. "You know, crazy stuff from a long time ago."

When they dried off, Christophe suggested that he show Alias the nude beach, since it was his first time on the island.

Alias' eyes lit up. "Really? Can we surf naked, too?"

Julie grinned. "Yeah, okay. I can see where this is going. I'm guessing you two need some time to reconnect, so to speak. Meet up later for dinner?" She went back to the apartment to finish her romcom marathon.

The guys walked to the other end of the beach, and when they crossed over from the clothed section, they ditched their suits and blended in with the rest of the naked sunbathers. They found an abandoned part of the beach and sat on the sand next to each other to survey the gentle waves rolling in.

"Is this the part where you murder me?" Christophe joked as he sunk his toes into the warm sand.

"Only if you ask me to," Alias shot back with a mischievous grin. Then he pointed to the water. "I'm not exactly stoked by these shore breaks. Want to step things up?"

"Yeah. If you would make some epic swells, I'll work on the wind and conjure us up some boards."

Alias did his magic on the surf. With a wave of his hand, he increased the swell size to three meters, high enough to make it exciting for their skill level, but not so high as to frighten the sunbathers a bit farther away. Meanwhile, Christophe stopped the onshore winds that would have crumbled the lips of the high waves and made them close out faster.

They paddled out past the whitewater and gave each other a thumbs-up at how well they worked together. Then they spent the rest of the afternoon stark naked on their surfboards, racing along the perfect pockets they'd created. In a short time, others caught sight of the change in conditions and joined them. Alias extended the swell further down the beach to accommodate everyone and avoid dropping in on each other and ruining the waves.

As the sun began its descent and the other surfers and bathers had long gone, Christophe rode in first. He lounged on the sand and drank in Alias' amazing technique and how fearless he seemed at riding in the giant waves. When he finished, Alias rode the wave straight in and emerged about thirty feet from Christophe. His chiseled abs glistened in the waning light.

"Hi stranger," Christophe said when he got close. "You looked like a god out there. Even more so up close."

Alias bent down and caught him about the waist and swung him around. "Hello to you, too, hot stuff." He kissed him. "I missed you while you were gone."

His arms tightened around Christophe's shoulders. "Hey, we ditched our clothes. Why don't we ditch the boards, too, and fly around together for a while?"

"What about the ban?" Christophe asked.

"We both know that doesn't apply to me." He grinned. "Besides, if the fairy police give us a ticket, I know how to get it fixed."

Christophe looked at the sun that was just touching the horizon. "Okay, but we can't forget that we're meeting Julie."

Alias winked. "I haven't. We have all the time in the world, because this time I'm stopping it for us.

Christophe poked him. "But...what about the people? They might see us."

Alias looked around at the deserted beach. "What people?"

For their evening ride, Alias chose his everyday pink wings with pale blue streaks, and with a few quiet flaps, he lifted them silently straight up and glided out over the ocean. They'd been flying for over an hour when he noticed that his pendant was glowing, and he looked around to see what might be causing it.

The only thing that stood out against the gorgeous blue sky and the ocean was a long string of greenish-brown debris that was washing up on the shore. He pointed it out to Christophe and they flew closer. They set down gently on the sand, and as he bent to investigate the massive stretch of algae, the pendant pulsated faster.

"I guess it's not just seaweed, is it?" asked Christophe. "Your stone acts up every time we get near one of the elements."

Alias grabbed Christophe's hand. "Can you smell it? I think it's *urst*. Do you know it?"

Christophe brought a stringy handful to his nose. "I was never an expert in chemistry, but I do think you're right."

"I'll take it back and test it right away to know for sure. I was always under the impression that *urst* was the most elusive of the elements we needed, so I would never have thought to look for it in seaweed. But if that's what this is, can you imagine the luck of finding it in such a huge quantity?"

"*Fors favet animo paratis,*" Christophe mumbled.

"What did you say?"

"*Fors favet animo paratis.* I'm not sure what it means. It just came to me."

"Weird. I know it. It's an old quote by Louis Pasteur, and it means the better prepared you are, the more likely you'll be able to take advantage of chance events. I had a tutor who drilled it into me. He said it would be the most important lesson I would ever learn. If there is *urst* in this seaweed, I'll have him to thank."

Julie was already drinking prosecco at the restaurant and waved them over. "I ordered us an appetizer." She giggled and patted the seats next to her, indicating where they should sit. "God, I missed you guys. I couldn't ask for two better best friends."

She crossed her legs and glanced away. The waiter came by and poured them each a glass of wine she'd picked out. Alias saw her eyes water. "He was fun," she sighed. "But god I was stupid for thinking it could work. I should've seen the wife coming. But I'm done crying over that man."

"Not quite, I guess," said Alias. He handed her a handkerchief, and she dabbed at her eyes.

She sighed and folded her arms on the table, leaning forward so that her long bangs fell into her face. "I envy you guys. I'd love a relationship like yours. One that lasts." Christophe and Alias let her talk. "But now, I think I'm looking for something a little new. Different."

"How different is *different*?" Christophe asked.

She smirked. "Well. You know a girl doesn't like to kiss and tell."

"Want us to help set you up with someone?" asked Alias.

"Yeah, I have a few people in mind," Christophe's eyes sparkled. "Girls, guys, gays, and theys of every variety. You just say the word, Jules."

"You're the best. You have no idea how grateful I am that you guys came all this way. I've had a blast here, and nothing beats hanging out with the two of you. But I have to say I miss Myers Beach terribly." She shook herself and grinned. "And sleeping in my own bed. So maybe we can pick up on this matchmaking thing when we get back."

"Actually, Alias and I wanted to talk to you about something quite personal, those scars you noticed. You may want another drink before we do, because what we have to say is probably going to blow your mind."

CHAPTER TWENTY-NINE

Back at the compound after their customary early morning coffee and swim, he and Christophe headed to a meeting with Stefán at The Fairy Kingdom, his first appearance there since that catastrophic ceiling event. The first fairy to greet them bowed his head respectfully and then smiled and gave him two thumbs up.

Alias patted him on the shoulder. He never needed constant compliments to prop up his self-esteem, but he always enjoyed affable exchanges with his subjects. From that moment on, however, he felt The Fairy Kingdom was putting out a negative vibe.

The feeling started out small, with giggles among a group of women fairies who were taking tea in a corner. He smiled and turned to see what was funny, but when they saw him look they stopped talking and turned away, which gave him the impression that he might have been the subject of their joke.

He wondered if Christophe had gotten the same reaction, and when he leaned in close to ask him in a whisper, he heard gruff throat-clearing from a few older fairies behind them. He recognized them as three of the ones who'd been stuck to the ceiling, and as he passed he noticed them shaking their heads. When moments later another turned to the side as they walked by, he knew the odd behavior wasn't his imagination.

When they were in the privacy of Stefán's office, he asked the question. "Can you clue me in on what's going on? I feel like I'm being given the cold shoulder. Did I do something?"

Stefán rolled his eyes and pointed his thumb at Christophe. "Do you want to know the truth, or should I sugar-coat it?"

Christophe's face fell. "Why are you pointing at me?"

"Listen," said Stefán. "I didn't mean for you to think that you're the problem. There's been a lot of grumbling about the freak ceiling incident. Don't blow what I'm saying out of proportion, because as far as I can tell, the noise is only coming from a few."

Alias plopped down on the office sofa. "What is it that's making them so unhappy now?"

"They think that you've been making lots of serious mistakes and putting their lives in jeopardy because you've been spending too much time with your quote-unquote boyfriend. They believe you're more focused on him than getting the fairy dust formula right."

Alias sat up straight and blinked. "They know about us?" He collapsed against the cushions.

"Only recently. Someone saw you both shirtless and

holding hands at the parade and at another event. They felt you weren't just pretending. Anyway, a few of them started talking. I guess the ceiling snafu put everyone over the top, and they put two and two together."

In a sense, he knew they were right. He had been devoting a lot of energy and time to his relationship with Christophe. Truth be told, given the choice he'd rather enjoy time together than do anything else. But he didn't have the luxury of choosing. He'd been trying his best to balance his life-saving work in the lab with his personal life, and he rejected the insinuation that he was incapable of doing both.

"They really think that I care so little? Damn, they can be so fickle."

"At least they realize we're a couple," said Christophe. "That's progress, anyway." He reached to put his arm around him, but Alias saw Stefán looking and pulled away.

"Please, Alias. Don't worry about me," said Stefán. "I've known about you guys since Christophe came to town."

Alias stood. "Okay, look. This is too much. I'm going home."

Christophe shrugged and the three of them left the office. A hush fell over the dining room when they passed through, and Alias caught the side-eyes from some of the older fairies.

While the people who'd made his sexuality and chosen partner a problem for him had been replaced by a new, progressive generation including his brother and Zsombor, the disapproving looks were a stark reminder that old ideals were obviously still firm in the minds of some of his public.

He had no doubt that Stefán had heard right, and that the impetus for the sudden hostility was because of his relationship with Christophe. But addressing the prejudices of his people wasn't his place. That task belonged to the king, and Theos wasn't in the room. For the first time, too, he realized that the fairies were also dealing with a fear that had less to do with him and more for their safety, and he couldn't blame them.

They were nearly out of the room when someone made a loud smooching sound. He ignored it and kept walking until he heard it again. Alias stopped and faced the room. Though he didn't know what he was going to say, he was resigned to confront them.

"All right! Who did that?" Dame Gabor's voice filled the room before he got a chance. She pulled out her chair and climbed up on the table. "What's wrong with you people? Have you been cooped up here so long you've forgotten who you are? We're fairies, for pity's sake. Carefree, whimsical, devil may care. Why do any of you care about who other people love?"

Christophe whispered to Alias and tugged on his sleeve. "Come on. There are always a few jerks in every group. You know the vast majority think you're terrific. Ignore them. Let's go."

Alias started to leave, but she stepped in front of him. "Your Highness, with all due respect, I'd like you to stay. We've got something to work out with this crowd." She covered her eyes against the light from the chandeliers and surveyed the room. "Now who's got a beef with His Highness? Speak up or shut up."

A man raised his hand. "I'm sorry. I appreciate what His

Highness has done for us and all, but I am uncomfortable with fairies being homos. And I think I'm speaking for many of us." He looked around for support from the others. "It's just not, you know, normal."

"Well, well, well," said Dame Gabor. She jumped down and paced around the room. "Look who's concerned about what's normal all of a sudden. The one who made the kissy-kissy sound a second ago. Does everyone here know this guy?" She walked over to the man who'd made the comment. "I do, but I'll let him introduce himself to you. At the same time he can tell us about how he used to steal his sister's clothes and play dress up with his boyfriends." She raised her eyebrows. "Not that there's anything wrong with that, either."

The man sputtered his defense, but roaring laughter drowned him out. She continued talking as she strolled between the tables. "I'm older than any of you, and believe me, I know lots of your stories. Shall I continue around the room and maybe highlight a few more?" The room went silent, and many of them looked down at their food to avoid making eye contact with her.

"No? Okay, then here's an easy question for everyone," she shouted. "Show of hands. How many in here like Stefán and think he's doing a great job?" Every hand shot up, including hers, Alias', and Christophe's. And the crowd giggled when Stefán raised his own. "Great, so we at least agree on something. Now, would you keep your hands up if you learned that he was, I don't know, let's say...gay?"

Stefán blanched, and the dining room buzzed with muffled conversations as they checked to see how others were voting.

"But he's different. He can't be gay," said someone.

Dame Gabor slapped her forehead. "Are you all nuts? Not gay? Hello! He's in hospitality!" Stefán's face went from ashen to red, but he threw back his shoulders and stood tall, and the anxiety left his face when he saw that people's hands were still in the air.

"And now we have a second issue. The fairy dust. Dollars to donuts ninety-nine percent of you have no idea where the stuff comes from. Because we've always just thrown it around and had as much as we needed. Now, remember the dust he gave every last one of you when you were lucky enough to get to Myers Beach? Hundreds of you were on death's door. Remember how it brought all of us back to life?

"Did you know that he made that crucial, life-saving dust without a formula? Of course there will be glitches. I'd like to see one of you try. Our prince is a genius, and nobody has devoted more time to keeping our three kingdoms from extinction than His Highness. You should all be ashamed."

One by one, the fairies began to clap, and as the four made their way out between the tables, most of them were on their feet again in a standing ovation. When they were out on the boardwalk again, Alias hugged Dame Gabor. "You are one magnificent fairy," he said. "Thank you for sticking up for me."

"Ah, come on. I was past due to give a speech, anyway." She eyed him. "By the way, something about you looks different, Your H. Are you parting your hair on the other side, or something?"

Alias brought his hand to his chest. "Oh, it's probably

because I'm not wearing the pendant. It gets in my way when I'm in the lab, so I stopped wearing it. I'm not much of a jewelry kind of guy, either. Don't tell Greta. She gave it to me, and I wouldn't want her to think I didn't appreciate the gift."

CHAPTER THIRTY

They were lying in bed. Both were exhausted; Alias from testing the Sargassum in the lab, and Christophe from managing the fairies from the Third Kingdom.

"Want to hear something funny I heard on the boardwalk today?" asked Christophe. "The mayor has been saying how embarrassed he is that the town fell for the whole Big Tiny hoax. Apparently, he went on record to say that fairies weren't real. Never have been and never will be." Alias raised a brow and Christophe amended, "The magic kind, that is. Anyway, now it seems everyone is jumping on the bandwagon and denying that they ever believed in the story."

"Wow. Amazing that people have such short memories, isn't it? But that's terrific news for us. How are your new fairies adjusting to Julie's building?"

"They seem to love it. More than that, I feel they really like me. At least that's what Stefán said he's heard."

"That's terrific. At least fairies from your kingdom

aren't insane like ours. I still look over my shoulder whenever I walk in the teahouse, even after Dame Gabor's fiery speech."

"You've got to drop it. I'm hearing that the pendulum has swung back in your favor," Christophe said. "Everyone likes you again. And since they've heard I'm running things for the Third Kingdom, my status with your fairies has risen, too, and I'm not the evil person that seduced their prince."

"Speaking of royalty, is the Third King planning to make a visit?" asked Alias. "I would imagine she would want to check in."

"Why would she need to do that? I've been giving her regular updates."

"Oh, I don't doubt that she's on top of it. It's just, I don't know. Subjects want to know that their king cares, and a royal visit from her might elevate their spirits."

Christophe raised his voice. "What the hell are you talking about? I just got through telling you that they are very happy. You obviously know nothing about the king. She would never leave the palace. Nobody really knows her, since she keeps herself locked up all the time. She'd be the last person they'd want around to give them a lift."

"Gosh. We just had such a beautiful day together yesterday. Why are you trying to ruin it?"

"Me? You're the one who started it. And you know, I really don't believe you meant to. I think it's the same old problem. I know you love me, but it seems no matter how hard I try, I just don't ever measure up to Mr. Perfect from your past, your first and I guess the only true love you'll ever have."

Alias sighed at the replay of that ongoing issue. "Yeah, like you never remind me of yours. He set a pretty high bar for me to get over, too." They both rolled over with their backs to each other.

"Touché," said Christophe. "And by the way, I love you."

CHAPTER THIRTY-ONE

It was not widely known that the reigning Third King was a woman. She did her best to keep it that way, too. Not that a woman on the throne would have been difficult to accept, but her twisty and slightly unorthodox path to that position made her ascension rocky from the outset.

Besides having just turned eighteen, she had not anticipated taking the throne. That expectation belonged to her older brother, and he had been the one to receive all the training and education for the role.

They had been very young when their parents died in an accident, and because of that shared loss, they'd remained close. She had been thrilled when Alias came to stay. Not only was he handsome, but he made their games of tag hide-and-seek more fun.

Until the young Third King came of age, their aunt, the king's sister, acted as regent, and when she discovered that her nephew was homosexual, she'd banished him and his lover from the kingdom. In her rage, heart failure took her life, and with the brother exiled, his sister became king by default.

Because she had no trusted friends or relatives to call on for support, and was unprepared for the job, she chose to live as a recluse. Theos and Zsombor recognized her insecurity right away and the instability it conveyed. Unfortunately, the ones who chose to invade the palace recognized it, too.

Though the immediate threat had passed, she worried day and night that someone else would make another attempt. Theos called for a meeting with her, where he and Zsombor suggested that for the benefit of her subjects, she begin sending them to Myers Beach where their safety could be guaranteed. They suggested that she could trust their friend Christophe to take charge of the operation. He had, after all, already proved his loyalty by single-handedly quashing the invasion and saving her life.

Fairies from the Third Kingdom followed a different fairy dust tradition. They needed less than their counterparts in the other two kingdoms, and while they required yearly dustings, they rarely used it for magic. Because they had been resupplied just before the contamination, they hadn't received any poisoned dust, and there had been no casualties. And by instituting strict border controls, they didn't allow the pandemic to reach them, either.

In Myers Beach, the Third Kingdom fairies would no longer be able to live indoors at the human scale, but apart from that significant change to their lifestyle, Julie's building was ideal.

As promised, she had left to spend time with her

parents, so Christophe was able to get right on the project. He stopped time for a weekend so that he, Stefán, and Alias could put in long days to add the same number of floors to Julie's building as they had made in The Fairy Kingdom. Their new housing in Myers Beach didn't require a clinic, which simplified their work, but the Third Kingdom fairies had been used to a more lavish lifestyle, which added the need for more detailing.

Christophe turned out to be a natural leader. He greeted each new fairy, and he was overjoyed at how well-behaved and respectful they were. When the last of them arrived, he brought them together for a town hall orientation. After describing the nuts and bolts of the building and the schedule of meals and entertainment, he wanted to convey his personal enthusiasm for their new home. He broke them into small groups and personally took them on walking tours of Myers Beach.

The last stop was The Fairy Kingdom, where Stefán showed them how they could take advantage of the teahouse and spa.

"Let's celebrate!" said Alias, one morning. "I've put some thought into what you've been reminding me over and over, and it finally sank in. We've got one life. Ours may last a dozen centuries, but the concept is the same. Screw the rest of the day. Let's take some time for ourselves."

Christophe blinked. "Am I dreaming, or are you inviting me on a date?"

"You are not dreaming. What do you say you show me those gorgeous wings of yours, and we spend the afternoon in the air like we did in St. Martin. We could go back out to the sandbar Theos told me about, where he took Lily on one of their first real dates. It's supposed to be so romantic. He thought you and I would enjoy it."

"I would love that," said Christophe. "But no more talk about fairy dust for the rest of the day, okay?"

Alias nodded and took his hand. With a flap of their magnificent wings, they lifted up over their infinity pool and flew out over the ocean.

Sandbars were generally close to shore, so what made this one unique was that it was miles away from land, and therefore completely isolated. A second quality that made going there so appealing for Theos was its exclusivity. He and Lily often timed their visit to take advantage of the entire five-hour span when it was above water, which gave them time to relax, make love, and spend the rest of the time gazing at the profundity of the three-hundred-and-sixty-degree view of the ocean.

Theos and Lily had gone there to celebrate their good times, and he told Alias that they still went there when their relationship needed a bit of attention. Alias hoped to continue that tradition with Christophe.

From the air, he recognized the tiny stretch of pristine sand that his brother had described as just wide and long enough for two people to stretch out on. Still holding hands, they swooped down and stood on the barren sandbar for a moment to take in the rare view. Heat lightning flashed on the horizon, and when Christophe saw it, he gave Alias a poke.

"Gosh, heat lightning seems to follow you everywhere. What gives?"

"I've always had kind of a special relationship with it. I'll show you."

He reached out both hands, and in seconds, pinkish threads shot out across the water from the lightning and formed balls of electricity on his palms. He threw one in the air and then started juggling, what he told Christophe was a one up, two up. When he extended an empty palm, another ball appeared, and he launched into a new series of tricks.

"This is called a half shower, and this is a cascade." He juggled the balls in the other direction. "Yup. This is a reverse cascade. And here's another cute one. If you keep your eyes on the one on top, it's supposed to resemble a tennis ball going back and forth over another tennis game that I'm playing with the other two below it. And yup, it's called Juggler's Tennis."

"Can I try?" asked Christophe. He got closer and held out his hands. When he was ready, he nodded, and Alias tossed him a ball with an under-the-leg throw. The moment Christophe caught it, his hair stood on end, and Alias laughed so hard, he dropped one of the balls. Christophe picked up on the technique right away, and soon they were juggling all three together.

When the fiery balls fizzled out, they retracted their wings and dropped down on the sand. Alias gave Christophe a devilish look, and soon they were taking advantage of the sandbar's other appeal, its privacy. They stayed until the last possible inch of sand remained uncovered, and then flew off again, making a miles-long loop around on their way back to Myers Beach.

Christophe wanted to stop at the skatepark to show

Alias a new move he'd been working on, so to avoid being noticed, they waited until dusk before landing in the small grove of trees to one side of the park. The track was lit, and after he manifested a board, Christophe joined the other skateboarders already zipping around the bowl.

CHAPTER THIRTY-TWO

"Hey, would you take a look at my wings?" asked Christophe when he finished his routine. "I feel like I've still got some sand in them from the sandbar, and you know how annoying that can feel."

They walked behind a tree, and he popped his wings. Alias began to run his hands over them when he stopped. "Hey, you pushed out the wrong set. These are silver and gold and kind of formal looking. The ones you used earlier were plain silver."

"Gosh. Beats me. I didn't realize I had two different ones," said Christophe. "Let me see if I can switch." He rolled his shoulders and the silver and gold ones retracted and the silver ones popped out.

"Found some." He showed Christophe two tiny white grains and laughed. "Wow, I didn't realize you were so sensitive."

"Yeah, I always have been. Anyway, they hurt like hell. Thanks." He turned around and stopped. "Whoa! What's this?" He pointed to the ground. "Looks like somebody dug a hole in about the same spot where we found the chests."

They walked over and Alias used visual coordinates to double check the location. "No. It's not about the same spot. It's *exactly* the same spot." They peered over the edge. "I wonder why?"

"Only one way to find out," said Christophe. He laughed just before he jumped in. "I hope I don't find anything dangerous down there like a snake."

Alias would never forget the sound of the razor-thin iron blades that sliced through Christophe's wings, or his agonized wail that pierced the still night. He waved his hand, and when light illuminated the hole, he saw Christophe reaching up for him. Alias grabbed at his arms, but they were covered with a liquid that made them slick, and it took immense strength to pull him out.

His wings had been sheared close to his back, and Alias gagged when he saw the fairy blood spewing from the two enormous gashes between his shoulder blades. As he stopped the bleeding, he stared into the dark hole and saw the trap someone had set, a guillotine-like device that was clearly designed for no other reason than to clip a fairy's wings.

CHAPTER THIRTY-THREE

Alias hadn't left Christophe's bed or let go of his hand since he'd rushed him to The Fairy Kingdom medical facility to recover the day before. Stefán tried to encourage him to at least grab a tea, but he'd been unable to eat or drink, from seeing the man he loved suffer the worst pain a fairy could endure.

Shearing off a fairy's wings was to maim them for life. Centuries ago, the horrible practice had been a punishment for the worst of fairy criminals until the kings had finally agreed the practice was too cruel and unusual to continue.

A weak grip against his hand brought him back to the present, and he blinked down to see that Christophe had managed to intertwine their fingers.

"Hey, you're back." He smoothed Christophe's bangs away from his face. "You gave us quite the scare, buddy. But don't worry, I'm going to fix this." When Christophe's eyes finally opened, the dam broke on Alias' carefully controlled emotions, and tears flooded down his cheeks.

"I'll fix this for you. For us. I promise. In a little while, I have an audience with the Third King. She'll be able to help. I know it."

Christophe blinked slowly. "You're going there?"

"No. She's here. Came to check up on the rest of her people as they settle in at Julie's."

"Why?" Christophe said with a frown. "I told her everything was fine."

Alias shushed him and kissed the back of his hand. "Don't worry about that now. I'll make sure she's taken care of properly. Just focus on resting."

Christophe raised his head. "But this doesn't make sense. She specifically said she wasn't going to come." He tried to sit up, but the pain was too great, and he screamed in agony.

Stefán appeared with a syringe, and Christophe's eyes grew wide. "No. Alias! Don't go to her. There's something wrong–"

Stefán pressed the needle into Christophe's arm and Alias' voice matched the soothing effects of the sedative. "I'll take care of everything." Christophe's eyelids became heavy, and he drifted off.

As he faced Julie's building, or the Second Third Kingdom, as they'd started calling it, he stood back to admire the remarkable job Christophe had done to spruce up the facade. For centuries, the Third Kingdom fairies had been used to the lavish and refined elegance of the palace, and he knew the casual atmosphere of a beach town would be a tough transition for many. So he did everything he could visually to make them feel at home.

While he knew they were free to renovate the inside in any way they wanted, the challenge was to convey a sense of royal grandeur to the exterior without drawing attention to what was actually going on inside on the upper levels. Mindful of the town's prescriptive building code, he needed to keep the exterior in the same beachfront style as the other buildings on the boardwalk.

The independent bookstore that occupied the ground level was charming and popular with the town, and he knew that opulence was the wrong vibe, so he pretty much left it as it was and simply replaced the older windows and added better lighting.

He directed his focus to the nondescript door to the right of the store. That was the door to the upper levels, and his opportunity to create a proper entrance. He replaced the plain weathered six-panel door with a heavy, richly carved one that he had flown over from the palace, and he paired it with equally ornate framing. Above the door, carved into the transom, gleamed their new kingdom logo, 2 III K.

To throw off anyone wondering what was behind that fancy door, he installed a simple push-button doorbell with Julie's name on the tag.

Alias took a breath and threw back his shoulders. He hadn't been to the building since he'd installed the security system, and he hadn't seen Christophe's finished product. As he climbed the stairs to the floor that Christophe referred to as the Palace Level, he wondered if it, too, would be finished for the new Third King's tastes, but when he reached the top he found an exact, though slightly scaled-back, replica of the Third Kingdom palace. The furniture, artwork, and carpets all were the same. Elements that Alias recognized so well from his many years at the palace. He wondered how Christophe had been able to memorize those same details given the brief time he'd recently spent there.

He walked down the central hall, past the reception rooms and the library and through the open doors to the solarium. Not only was the king not waiting for him, but the throne was missing.

He giggled at the oversight. To Christophe's credit, he hadn't expected a visit from the king, and Alias considered the possibility that Christophe had more urgent fish to fry. A servant entered and whispered that the Third King was waiting for him in the throne room.

To prepare for his audience, he'd asked Theos what to expect and for any last-minute advice or tips on his approach for the request. Theos had described her as not having changed much from the young girl Alias knew from his days in the palace.

"I think your meeting should go well," he said. "You'll notice that while your old friend is still adorable, she's very insecure in her new position. When we met with her, she admitted to feeling over her head, and she thanked Zsombor and me over and over for our help."

Alias took a breath and nodded to the throne room guards, who flung open the door. He strode in and blinked. Her face looked very much like an older version of the girl he knew from the old days, but the way she was spread out on the beanbag chair that served as her throne was not how he would have expected her to act. With both legs draped over one side and her head lolled back on the other, she did not give the impression of an insecure woman, as Theos had suggested.

"Alias," she said, her voice unusually husky. "To what do I owe this pleasure?"

"Highness. It's been a long time, so first of all, congratulations." He gave a slight bow, and while he raised his head, his eyes stayed glued to her feet. The king was barefoot, and the ruby toenail polish was at odds with the kingdom's centuries-old image.

"We're surprised to hear that you were in town, since you gave us no notice," he said. "Naturally, we, especially Christophe, would have preferred to be more prepared." He waved his hands at the opulence and gave her a smile. "I trust, however, that you find the Second Third Kingdom suitable for your needs. Maybe good enough for a game of tag hide-and-seek?"

He waited for the snicker that never came. They had always gotten along well as childhood friends, and he was in no mood to waste further time with the formalities of court protocol. As he opened his mouth to get to the point, his eyes caught the way the light glinted off the front clasps of her black lace corset, and the visual distracted his train of thought.

He never recalled the Third King caring much about fashion when she was younger. To the chagrin of her aunt, she'd always been something of a tomboy. Now well into her twenties, and given the wealth at her disposal, he expected her to have acquired some new level of sophistication. He wasn't expecting those elevated tastes to include couture.

Though half hidden by the corset, the comfortable-looking white mesh lace dress in a knitted rose pattern with a plunging v-neckline looked vaguely familiar. The long sleeves and asymmetrical hem tapped at the back of his memory and reminded him of one of Greta's Habib outfits but in the reverse colors. The coincidence made him look away from her to regain his composure.

He took her clicking her extra-long red fingernails against the golden throne as impatience for him to continue, and as he collected himself he searched for a time when she'd acted like this. He couldn't even remember a time when she had cared about her nails, let alone worn them in that manner, and he wondered why Theos hadn't mentioned her radical style change.

"And?" She waved her arm. The deep umber of her skin looked almost black in the shadows cast by the spotlights above the replica throne.

"Right, well, it's about Christophe." He closed his eyes against the horrible nightmare of a memory—Christophe's pained screams. The oozing wing ports he'd been forced to sew up in the aftermath of that horrible accident. "His wings have been sheared off."

"He...what?" She let out a deep laugh that Alias wasn't expecting and tossed her long legs over the chair so she could sit straight up. She leaned forward, elbows on her knees, which caused a ruby red pendant that Alias hadn't noticed upon his arrival to hang down low from her neck. That too, tugged at his memory, but he pushed it aside to examine later. "Surely you're joking. Our wings are indestructible." She looked at him for corroboration. "Or so I thought."

"I'm very serious, Highness." He hung his head and crossed his arms to stave off the chill that had settled into his bones since the accident. "It was done by a device that clearly had been designed for the sole purpose of cutting off a fairy's wings," he said. "After Christophe is made whole, we must focus on finding whoever did this and bring them to justice."

He looked up to see the king's extra-long eyelashes blink rapidly like she was still trying to digest the news. After a moment she said, "I'm sorry. But I fail to see how I can be helpful in this matter."

"Easy. By restoring his wings."

She leaned back in her chair so that she could look down at him. "And why would I do that?"

His heart sank at her lack of empathy. "Because he saved your life? And he's a hero to your kingdom?" He squinted at her. "We could fix them ourselves with fairy dust. But because we don't have any more, it would take the power of his king...you."

Suddenly her features softened. "Look, I'd love to help, Alias. I really would. But like you, I don't have any dust to spare. Our kingdom had so little to begin with."

"But I just said, as his king, you don't need dust to restore them."

"I don't?" She quickly looked away. "You're just like your brother and Zsombor, presuming to tell me how to run my kingdom. They've been acting like bullies ever since I took over."

He scrunched his face. He'd remembered Theos mentioning that she'd been grateful for their support.

"Then I *ask* you, as your friend for so many years. Please help him."

"I'm truly sorry, Alias," she ran a hand through her hair, and suddenly she looked just like the little girl he'd once known. Unsure and a little confused. "I would still need dust."

"Maybe it's because you are new at this and don't know how powerful you are yet. Christophe is a mere fairy of your kingdom, and yet he can manipulate the wind with a snap of his fingers. How could he be more powerful than his king?"

Her eyes glinted, and Alias couldn't place her expression beyond the intrigue he saw reflected there. "Where is Christophe? Perhaps I could at least see him."

"He's recovering at The Fairy Kingdom. I'll take you there myself. Just say the word."

"Thank you. Now, though I can't help you with his wings, I can solve your other dilemma. Only one person is smart enough and evil enough to have created the device you describe—Györfi, the same man who contaminated the fairy dust. I tried to convince your brother and Zsombor, but they chose not to believe me. Considering that he lived at the palace for so long, I believe that I'm in a position to know."

Alias held up his hand. "Well, I was there, too, and I don't agree. There's no way he lived through that. Besides, why would he want to mess with the fairy dust?"

"If you don't believe me, you're just as foolish as they were." She laughed, but the sound was utterly devoid of humor. "Obviously, the pompous old man managed to stay alive somehow."

"Where would someone like him find such a power? I saw what happened to him."

"You'd be surprised, especially given how intent he was on revenge."

"Revenge for what?"

She shook her head. "Not for *what. For whom.*" She jerked around to face him. "You obviously still haven't figured it out, so I'll spell it out for you." She pointed at Alias. "You! You're the reason we're all where we are. Out of dust across the kingdoms, with fairies dead and dying. You apparently did something unforgivable to him, and this is his revenge. I found the proof in his room."

Alias blanched. "Then he meant to cut *my* wings?"

"I can't think of a reason why he'd want to harm Christophe." She dismissed his question. "You all are missing the point. Györfi told me he'd do anything it took to become king of the fairies. I laughed him off and reminded him that he'd need to be a fairy first. He laughed back in my face and told me that wouldn't be a problem. The man is wretched and will stop at nothing, but he's smart. I'm still surprised at how you and the others fail to see that."

Alias sighed. He wanted to go home, curl around Christophe, and pretend the nightmare never happened. Duty and tradition had him bowing and gritting out, "Thank you for the audience, Your Majesty."

He walked woodenly out of Julie's building as the king's words about Györfi being behind everything echoed in his head. His mind began connecting the dots. Györfi's pursuit and clumsy attempt at seduction, and his anger when Alias rejected him. His threat when the aunt banished him. Alias should never have just assumed the man was dead.

Bile rose in his throat and he had just enough time to duck into an alley before he was spewing the contents of his stomach onto the asphalt. He'd been responsible for all the darkness. All of his subjects, whole kingdoms, had been affected because of that one interaction. It all made sense.

His next stop was to Györfi's room to find the proof she said she'd found. With that corroboration in hand, he'd go to Theos and Zsombor to convince them to look for Györfi and stop him from carrying out his madness any further.

He leaned his head against the brick building and fought away a fairy migraine.

CHAPTER THIRTY-FOUR

At the very least, Alias thought he might run across something in Györfi's room that would give them an advantage so they could put a stop to his reign of terror. This time he'd have to sneak in. Unless the culture had changed, the loyal palace guards would be sure to alert the Third King if they found him, and he couldn't risk that. Catching Alias breaking and entering could cause a political nightmare for Theos.

Getting in without being detected would not be a problem. He was familiar with the tunnels under the palace, because the sister had taken him and the Third King through them herself. The three young royals had spent his first weekend exploring the many secret passageways and hidden stairs tucked here and there inside the old palace. At the end of a memorable game that had mashed together hide-and-seek and tag, they'd discovered the tunnel that he would now use to gain entry.

They'd enlisted one of the butlers to play "It," and in escaping from him, she had pulled Alias and her brother down a hallway that had looked like a dead end. Alias thought they would be caught, but suddenly the Third King poked the spot right next to an ornate bust of a previous king.

The wall slid open and revealed a passageway covered in cobwebs. All three had scampered in, and as the butler rounded the corner, she pushed a lever that caused the wall to slide shut. She showed them that the tunnel connected their rooms, the kitchen, the garden, and even up to the study that would later be their tutor's. That was the way he went in.

Though he couldn't put his finger on it, Alias could tell that there was something off about the grown-up version of the sister who was now king. She hadn't reacted to his comment about hide-and-seek. She'd dodged questions and had been adamant that she couldn't help Christophe, when he knew very well that she should have had the power.

Alias shook off the memories when he reached the plain wooden door to Györfi's room, and he swallowed the rush of bile that threatened to spill at the thought of that horrible man. He pushed past his hesitation and opened the door.

He'd only made one visit to his tutor's rooms before, and while he hadn't bothered to notice how they were set up then, he had been surprised that someone whose mind was as organized as Györfi lived in such a mess. Like the young Third King and himself, their tutor had been banished without notice, so he hadn't been able to take anything with him.

His books sat in dusty, precarious piles on the low

nightstand, and scribbled half-thoughts and notes in his sprawling cursive filled a whole chalkboard on one wall. His unstylish clothing littered the floor. When Alias plopped on the unmade bed, a cloud of dust swirled around him. He coughed and as he reached to open the small window above the head of the bed, he felt something shift under his leg.

He shoved his hand between the mattress and box spring and hoped that the book his fingers found was of value, and not a gross porn magazine from the thirties. A leather-bound book with Alias and Theos' family crest embossed across the front was not what he was expecting. There was a handwritten inscription on the inside front cover.

This journal is the property of the Keeper of the Dust. If found, please return to Perseus Puck immediately.

He turned the page and thanked the stars that Perseus Puck had a type-A personality and enough excellent organizational skills to add a Table of Contents. But reading the title of the first section made his jaw drop.

The Eight Elements

They'd always assumed there were nine. He scanned the list and quickly learned that *Fstl Fstl* was not one of them. Having to locate one fewer ingredient was terrific news, particularly since he'd been unfamiliar with an element by that name and had no idea where to look.

Instead, *Fstl Fstl* were the magic words needed to bind everything
together.

*Say one Fstl as it begins to swirl, and then repeat it when the
whirlwind settles.*
The material will dry, and you can collect the dust.

It was then that Alias remembered that the Third King's
aunt had said those same words when she banished the three
of them. He'd remembered never hearing them before, but he
had been so emotionally wrought at the time that he hadn't
given them another thought. He did wonder, however, why
the other kingdoms didn't use the powerful phrase.

Next, his fingers found a listing for the order of
elements, and when he turned to that page and read the
answer that had eluded him for so long, he wanted to bang
his head against the nearest wall. The order was the same
as the song.

He scanned the different sections and was thrilled
when he ran across educated guesses he'd gotten right.
Using the Sargassum algae in the same manner as oil was
used as the base in cosmetics was one. He'd also been right
to recognize that *arbara* was the most powerful of the
eight, but he shuddered when he read that he'd been using
it all wrong and that he'd been extremely lucky that the
side effects hadn't been lethal to the fairies.

Arbara was supposed to be used as the filler, the way
talc was used in lipstick to make it spread smoother. He
scanned the next several pages with a glee he hadn't felt in

a long while, as he discovered more instances where he'd made good choices and explanations for why some of his trials had gone haywire.

Overjoyed at his discovery and eager to get started making real fairy dust the correct way, he was about to shove the book into his shoulder bag and leave when he glanced at the cover again. Since Györfi had managed to find and steal the Keeper of the Dust's journal, he wondered how many other secrets the man had squirreled away in his room.

On his way to take a closer look at the chalkboard, his foot caught the leg of the nightstand, which sent all the books stacked on top of it crashing to the floor. Among the scattered books, he noticed a sketch pad.

Worried that a servant might have heard the noise, he stood and twirled his index finger like Christophe had done and rewound the action. The books went back to their places on the table, and then the action stopped. When he started it again, he stepped more carefully and avoided catching his leg.

He opened the pad. Detailed pen and ink still-lifes filled the first pages. He was impressed with the level of detail and perspective and surprised to learn that his egghead tutor had an artistic side.

The next sketch was a realistic portrait of a brooding, dark-haired woman. Her profile reminded him a little of Zsa Zsa Hajdu, the evil witch that had terrorized Greta and Zsombor, the woman they'd defeated at the top of Hersey Lighthouse. He sat down on the bed to let the coincidence sink in. When he flipped the page and saw dozens more portraits of the same woman from different angles, he giggled at his tutor's secret obsession.

Guessing the inspiration was his singing idol, he glanced around the room for her infamous record album, which he found leaning in a place of honor on top of his bureau. Alias instantly paired his portrait with the sexy woman dressed in black on the cover. *Zsa Zsa Hajdu Sings!* He closed his eyes and pictured the Zsa Zsa they'd encountered in Myers Beach dressed to the nines in her sexy black Habib couture. Both shared Zsa Zsa's striking physical features, and though the singer had lived over a century earlier, she was clearly wearing the latest fashion of her time.

It wasn't difficult to imagine that their Zsa Zsa had stolen the name and look from the singer. He had to admit that the name was catchy, and he gave her points in retrospect for staying on brand. But he squinted and recalled the image of the pirate captain he and Christophe had watched burying the chests and how exactly she looked like the Myers Beach witch. That, too, had to be a coincidence. They were now talking about a difference of over four hundred years.

He flipped the page and swallowed when he saw his portrait next. It appeared Györfi had sketched him almost as many times as he'd drawn his singer idol. The style was different, too. He'd depicted Alias in classical poses as though he'd been the model in a life-drawing class. Alias holding a discus, Alias in a thong with a bow and arrow, Alias sunning on the chaise in a skimpy bathing suit by the pool. Alias nude.

His heart pounded. Györfi had seen him shirtless, but

he wondered on what occasion the man could have seen him naked, unless he'd been spying on him. He looked closer and saw that the drawings had details of his privates wrong, and he was relieved to learn that he was looking at an artist's conception, and not a sketch from memory. Artist's conceptions, plural. Györfi had drawn easily fifty more nudes of him.

The next few pages were blank, which helped bring Alias' breathing back to normal. But then he choked at the change in subject matter and style represented on the last page. Györfi had made a finished and detailed mechanical drawing of the diabolical apparatus that severed Christophe's wings, complete with dimensions and precise specifications for the operation of the blade mechanism.

Given that he'd drawn it when he was living at the palace, and given Györfi's out-of-control obsession with Alias, he concluded that his tutor may have intended to use the contraption to maim him. Furthermore, as far-fetched as it seemed, he had to admit that the Third King had been right. Györfi must have discovered a means to give him some type of immortality, and more importantly, that he'd been responsible for the contamination.

He would also have been the one to set the trap in the skatepark, and Alias' body shuddered at the image of his vengeful tutor not only alive, but currently in Myers Beach. Setting it in the precise location as the buried chests could not have been coincidental. In his quick scan of the elements in the book, he'd read that *arbara* contributed to the fairies' longevity, and he surmised that Györfi had also learned about the rocks, which could have accounted for his extended lifespan. Perhaps he was looking for more of it.

He may have guessed that whoever had dug them up would be a fairy who needed it too, who would be curious at seeing the new hole and might jump in. The scenario was a long shot. As he was leaving, he stepped on a crumpled piece of paper that stuck to his shoe.

He pulled it off and he recognized Györfi's handwriting again.

May 22–Midnight

That bastard prince doesn't know what he's done or who he's messed with. Alias wants to reject me after all his teasing? Fine.

I'll tell the regent that she has a queer nephew, and she'll banish both of them. In the meantime, I'll have made my own fairy dust and can overpower them, so I can rule. With me in charge, Alias won't be able to refuse my advances.

Alias' heart sank. Györfi wouldn't have been the one to destroy the kingdoms he wanted to rule. There was no need to create a truth table to solve the logic behind this problem. Everything was upside down again, but it was clear.

CHAPTER THIRTY-FIVE

Alias gathered his team for an emergency session in the lab. His worried expression matched the top priority designation he'd given the meeting, and while they waited for him to speak, they stared at the leather-bound book with the curious logo in the middle of the table.

He looked each one of them in the eye. "I want us all to throw what we've learned about making fairy dust so far out the window. That means forgetting D1 through D6." He held up the book. "We now possess all the knowledge we need to make perfect dust every time. This is the absolute authority, straight from the official kingdom Dust Keeper. Inside you'll find everything there is to know about each element, how to prepare them, and most importantly, the order in which to mix them together. We have access to all his notes, as well." The team applauded his discovery.

"The book gives us other good news, too. That we've been searching for nine elements, when there are actually only eight. *Fstl, Fstl* which we thought was an ingredient, turns out to be magic words instead, but equally critical to making the formulation come together." He set down the book. "Now, here's what I want us to do."

The first task he presented was easy. To begin from scratch and make a brand-new dust following the instructions in the book and using the seven elements they had on hand. He pointed to the passage in the book in a section that described the value of dust made from incomplete elements. According to the journal, the dust they would be making was considered ninety percent effective and could be put to enormous use. Better yet, the product would be safe for use on all fairies with no possible side effects.

"But we're still not out of the woods. The book goes on to say that without the *yano*, it won't be effective for regular quarterly dustings, so the kingdom doomsday clocks are still ticking."

His eyes misted. "But now I must get to the second and equally important part of the project, Christophe. From what I can gather from the Dust Keeper's notes, this new iteration with the seven elements should be strong enough to give him complete and instant recovery from the wounds. So, we're all going to stop time and make the first lot. Since we won't need to conduct testing on it like we did before, I'll take some from that first batch to heal him immediately." He swallowed hard. "But beyond healing, what I'm hoping is that it will also be powerful enough to restore his wings."

They were amazed at how quickly and easily they could refine the elements using the techniques laid out so comprehensively in the journal. Other tips cut their time in half, too, and when they had everything ready to mix, they gave Alias the honors.

"*Fstl, Fstl*," he incanted, as they added the *igdia* to the *arbara*. Adding the *redach* caused the mixture to swirl on its own.

"This is encouraging," said Dr. Anderson. "We've not seen this before."

The addition of *danog* caused a type of steam to rise, but the *urst* induced calm again, and the *sudf* gave the concoction texture. When they added *tepa*, the final ingredient, Dr. Anderson nodded to Alias.

"*Fstl, Fstl*" he pronounced again, and the swirl in the large vat grew stronger and spun faster, producing what looked like cotton candy.

Christophe was sitting up in bed next to Alias in a conversation with the Third King and Dame Gabor.

"It was nice to see you doing so well, Christophe," the king said as she stood to leave. "May I visit again tomorrow?"

"Certainly, Highness," Christophe winced when the movement from his bow pulled at the stitches on his back.

The Third King extended her hand. "Dame Gabor, a pleasure, as always."

As soon as she left, Alias pulled out his pouch of new dust. "I've got a surprise for you," he said with a grin. "You're going to love this. Let's see your back."

Dame Gabor helped roll him over, and Alias took in the ghastly sight of his lover's mutilated wing port one final time. He took a breath and sprinkled a generous amount of dust over the stitches. Then he made Dame Gabor turn away, so he could sprinkle the rest of Christophe's body.

"I can't tell you how fantastic it feels to use as much fairy dust as I want," he said. "It's like the old days. Look!"

The ugly stitches melted away, and as Alias gently massaged the spot, Christophe's olive skin glowed as it smoothed and tightened. When they rolled him back over, he was smiling. His eyes had lost their dullness, too, and their sparkle had returned.

"Hey handsome," Alias said, with a smile of his own so wide that he thought it would crack his face. Christophe reached around behind to feel his back.

"You did it!"

"It was a group effort, but yes. It looks like your wounds are completely healed."

Dame Gabor touched Alias' wrist. "Hey, Your H. I've got a little pain in my hip. Got any more of that?"

"We've got as much as we need! We're celebrating!" He held the pouch open, and Dame Gabor reached in and doused herself.

"Oh. That feels good," she said. "Real good."

Alias called for Stefán, and when he came in she flicked some at him, which transformed him into a lifeguard. His face reddened and he looked puzzled at his skimpy bathing suit and flip-flops. "I've never dared to wear a Speedo before."

She giggled. "Well, I've always wanted to see you in one."

He took a pinch from the pouch and flicked it back at her, which manifested a bouquet of daffodils. "Thanks,

Dame Gabor. I love looking buff and bronze, but now change me back. I feel silly."

She turned his red suit back into business attire but kept the flip-flops. Then she flicked some against the wall, which changed color to a warm dark brown.

"No offense, guys, but I've always thought that the battleship gray color in here was depressing. And this burnt umber matches Christophe's beautiful eyes."

"With all this great dust we're making now, you can change the color every day if you want," said Alias.

"Then let's pull out all the stops," she said. Instantly, a silver tray appeared on Christophe's bed with four champagne flutes and a bottle of prosecco.

As she and Stefán guzzled the bubbly, Alias sat next to Christophe. "I'm really surprised the king came to visit you."

"So am I. Because during the last conversation we had, she specifically told me she wasn't coming, and it wasn't that long ago. There's something very wrong about her being here." He hooked a thumb to Stefán. "I was trying to tell you when he put me under."

"So, did you ask her why she came?"

"You can't ask that question to the Third King. I was about to anyway, but she cut me off."

"Then what did you guys talk about?"

Christophe shrugged, "She wanted to see how I was doing."

"Better than my audience with her, then?"

"I wouldn't know. She didn't mention it. And of course I couldn't ask. Kings don't discuss their private conversations."

"Well, I can tell you that she was utterly unhelpful when I asked her to restore your wings."

Christophe drained his glass and swung his legs over the bed. "No need for her anyway, now you've given me my wings back. Can I pop them out now?"

Alias wanted to project a positive air, and he worried if the wings didn't work, Christophe would become depressed again.

"Hey, let's not rush. What we just made is close to what we need to bring them back, but we can't be sure. How about we give it a few days to see how you feel before you try?"

Christophe's face fell. "I get the feeling you're telling me that I'll never fly again."

"No. Of course not. But you do remember that we're still short the *yano*, don't you?"

Christophe nodded and snapped his fingers to create a three-sided full-length mirror. Before he took off his hospital gown he asked Dame Gabor to avert her eyes again. Then he turned slowly around so he could see himself from every angle. Then he stretched out his arms and pulled Alias to him. "You did a magnificent job. How can I ever thank you?"

"I'm not done, yet. I won't rest until you get them back, I promise."

Christophe's eyes misted. "But do you still think I'm hot, without them?"

Alias buried his face in Christophe's hair. "You'll always be the sexiest man alive to me."

Dame Gabor poured them each another glass. "Weird that the Third King was wearing a dress, didn't you think? My contacts tell me that nobody's ever seen her in one."

Christophe chimed in. "I know this is gonna sound weird, but Alias…I don't think she's really the Third King."

Alias blinked. "Look. I agree that she's not acting like herself, and she's far from adorable, which is how Theos described her only this morning. And she certainly didn't treat me like we were friends, and now that I think of it, she didn't show any recollection when I mentioned playing tag hide-and-seek." He took Christophe's hand. "But she's been under tremendous stress, which I can certainly relate to, so I wonder if we can really jump to such a drastic conclusion?"

Christophe let out a frustrated breath and pulled his hand away. "I didn't think you'd believe me." He sighed and looked down where his hands hung limp in his lap. "Look, I can't explain it. But it's not her. I know it."

"I'd have to agree with Christophe," said Dame Gabor. "Something is very wrong. I've met her many times, and I was surprised that she didn't remember any of my anecdotes."

Alias scratched his head. "All she wanted to talk to me about was Györfi, and how he was the one behind the contamination. She told me that he had a plan to take over all three kingdoms, and had a way to do it, and she insisted there was proof. She said he was even behind the recent attempt to kidnap her."

"Wait, wait. You're going too fast. Who's Györfi?" Christophe asked.

"Oh. Sorry. He was my tutor when I was at the palace. I thought I'd mentioned him."

"You've talked about your tutor a lot, but I guess you never mentioned his name. Why on earth would your tutor destroy all our fairy dust?"

"According to her, to get back at me. I thought she was blowing smoke out her ears. She tried to convince Theos and Zsombor that the guy was behind it, too, and they didn't believe it either. I mean Györfi was a human, and I have a really hard time believing he survived what the King's aunt did to him. Not saying he couldn't have done it. It just seems very unlikely."

Christophe, Dame Gabor, and Stefán sat with their mouths gaping as Alias told them the Third King's reasoning and suggestions that the man had found the secret to immortality.

"Anyway, to find out if she was right, I snuck back into the palace to look for the proof she said was all around. And you know, she was right. I found tons of evidence in his room to support her theory, as crazy as it sounds."

"How'd you get in without them seeing you? Did you use the tunnel?"

"Yeah. How did you know about it?"

"It's how those thugs tried to get in. There are all kinds of secret passages around the palace, and they tried them all."

"Hmm. I wonder how they learned about it? Maybe Györfi. Anyway, I got to his room, and that's where I found the Keeper of the Dust's book, which is pretty damning evidence. He was obviously using the fairy dust manual to figure out how to destroy it."

"Some tutor," said Dame Gabor. "This is getting interesting. Would anyone care for something stronger than prosecco? I was thinking of switching to a Cosmo." Stefán raised his hand, and she created two.

"So, that was the biggest prize I took away from his room, um, next to these." He handed Christophe the nude sketches.

Christophe's eyes bulged. "Well, well, well. You never told me you'd been a nude model. They're good." He pulled the first one closer. "Not entirely accurate, but you look very handsome."

"Hey, can I see?" Dame Gabor leaned over.

Christophe laughed and covered them with his blanket. "No! So, what were your nudes doing in his room?"

"They're his, silly. He drew them. And no, I didn't pose for them."

Christophe looked at the rest and chuckled. "Hmm. From the looks of all these, I'd have to guess that you were the teacher's pet."

"Funny. Someone else accused me of that once. No, I'm afraid I was more like his obsession. Did I tell you that he came on to me once?" Christophe jerked his head around. "I pushed him away, and that's the reason for his revenge, at least according to the Third King."

Christophe chuckled. "Wow. The face that launched a thousand ships. I've been hooking up with a celebrity."

"You're not going to laugh at this. Look what else he drew."

Christophe gagged when he saw the sketch of the guil-lotine. "That was his?"

"I'm afraid so, which is why I've been feeling so guilty about your wings. I think his trap was meant for me."

Christophe ran his hand through his hair. "Then either

I'm really confused, or this doesn't actually make sense. I can see why this messed-up Györfi character might want to target you, but if he wanted to take over the fairy kingdoms, like the Third King said, why would he want to kill all the fairies by poisoning the dust? He wouldn't have anyone to rule over."

Alias shuddered. "Exactly what I was wondering. We've got a lot of pieces to this puzzle, but something's still not adding up." He shook his head. "And whether she's the real king or not, I don't think we can trust her to tell us the truth. I wish I knew how they were all connected."

Christophe let out a small laugh. "Ah, there you go, yet again wishing for things."

Alias pressed his fingers to his temple and the other three turned to learn what he'd heard. He grabbed Christophe's wrist.

"It was Zsombor. He was finally able to wrangle information out of those goons who attacked the palace. The ones you captured. They've never heard of anyone by the name of Györfi."

"Then who the hell hired them?" Christophe asked.

"A woman named HerSea."

"Her Sea…as in Captain Hersey?" Dame Gabor asked. " Of lighthouse fame?"

"Oh, man. Her again." Christophe said.

"My head is spinning, guys," said Dame Gabor. "You have to catch me up."

Alias patted her knee. Then he stood and paced. "Okay, let's recap. Here's what we know. Hersey, or HerSea, is probably the same person. Somewhere along the line, she must have changed her name. And yes, she was the pirate captain. By the way, she looks a lot like Zsa Zsa Hajdu, a singer from the nineteen twenties, and one of Mister Györfi's other obsessions.

"She also was the one who buried the *arbara* back in eighteen sixteen. Christophe and I watched her do it from my Time Cube, so we know that for a fact. Another Zsa Zsa lookalike terrorized Greta and tried to suck the life out of Zsombor, but we destroyed her. But then just days ago, someone, maybe Györfi, dug a hole right in the same place as the original trunks and boobytrapped it. On top of that, the Third King is acting strange. Did I leave out anything?"

Christophe tapped his finger against his lips. "We never did find Zsa Zsa's body...."

Alias stopped pacing. "You think–"

"That the Third King is being controlled by this Her Sea woman? Yes. Maybe."

"Maybe HerSea is Zsa Zsa's alias." Gabor poked Alias in the ribs and laughed at her own joke.

"If she's managed to assume all those identities over hundreds of years, is it really so hard to believe that she is still out there?" Christophe asked.

"But then, how does Alias' pervy tutor factor into it?" Dame Gabor asked.

"That's what we need to find out," said Alias. "Now, Christophe, are you ready to come home with me?" As they left, he turned to the others. "Nobody is to know that Christophe has left, okay?"

CHAPTER THIRTY-SIX

Christophe hosted a pool party the next afternoon to thank the scientists who'd worked on the dust project. To make his gift more personal, he chose to cook the old-fashioned way, with his hands. He spent the morning making his signature peasant pasta and homemade biscuits, and he talked Dame Gabor into tending the bar.

After lunch, Alias acknowledged his trusted team leader, Lydia Anderson, and announced that Theos had made her the new Keeper of the Dust. He agreed with the centuries-old policy that only select individuals should know the contents, but he never understood relegating that precious information to only one person. So, in this case, she would share the responsibility with Christophe. As long as a handful of people knew how to recreate fairy dust, the knowledge would never die, and they'd never find themselves in those dire straits again.

When the team went home after the party, Alias announced that he, Christophe, and Dame Gabor were going down into the Time Cube. They'd been so successful using the cube to go back to when Captain Hersey buried the treasure in the early eighteen hundreds, they hoped to have just as much luck by scanning the time periods before and after. Watching her life play out for hundreds of years would take several grueling hours of tedious scanning, so he gave the team and the household staff strict instructions not to interrupt them.

Since being thrown off-kilter by its contact with the *arbara*, the Time Cube had been recalibrated and was back in balance thanks to a timely application of the new fairy dust. Inside the isolated safety of the cube, Alias allowed his brain a moment to process as they discussed what they hoped to accomplish. He'd come around to the opinions of Dame Gabor and Christophe that someone was controlling the Third King, possibly even possessing her. But the question remained: Was it Zsa Zsa or Györfi?

The king's mannerisms, dress, and speech reminded him of the Zsa Zsa he'd encountered in Myers Beach. She'd been stylish, too, but malicious. She'd demonstrated plenty of magic. She could snap her fingers like a fairy and make things happen. He also remembered that she could throw out a wicked force field. If she'd taken over the Third King's body, at least he knew what they were up against.

Since she'd hidden chests full of *arbara* rocks deep in the ground, it was evident that she'd discovered its power to extend life, and that the string of lookalikes they discovered that spanned hundreds of years were actually the same woman. And since they hadn't found her body after the battle on Hersey Lighthouse, as Christophe reminded them, she was a likely candidate for the most recent incarnation as the Third King.

But they hadn't figured out a motive for her to strike against any of the fairy kingdoms. Györfi had one, at least that's what the Third King said. He sought revenge, and to live as long as he had, he'd obviously learned the powers of *arbara*, too, most likely from Zsa Zsa.

They agreed there was compelling evidence to suggest that he was controlling her. In addition to the drawings and the stolen dust manual, his obsession with Alias and subsequent humiliation at being romantically rejected was a strong motive for revenge. But none could jibe with the contradiction of committing genocide on the population he wanted to rule.

He tapped a panel, and they went back in time to Captain Hersey's shipwreck. On another panel, he typed in a long mathematical sequence that would have his tech comb history for all of the same biomarkers of her throughout history, adjusting for aging, potential hair changes, and fashion styles.

Single images or a large collection of existing images, his tech would scan time before and afterward, until they discovered where she came from and when she died. If she hadn't, they'd know they could find her at the Second Third Kingdom.

The panels of the cube flashed in a dizzying rewind of images going backward from the shipwreck to a girl in her late teens going in and out of a house with an older woman on a Caribbean island. Alias stopped the action and zeroed in on the woman. He flicked at the screen to get information, and all three gulped at the readout: *HerSea - native Arawak.*

He continued going backward in history a few years

and settled on the image of a little girl lying alone on a beach with tear tracks on her face.

"That's her!" shouted Dame Gabor. "No question. Look at the cheekbones!"

"Okay," said Alias. "So we've got a little girl on an island in the Lesser Antilles growing up with a woman named HerSea. The readout says we're looking at a time around sixteen hundred and fifteen. Those cheekbones don't look like those of an Arawak. Let's go back a little more and see where she really came from."

He waved at the screen and switched the play to slow motion, and they watched a funnel cloud hover over the shore and drop her to the sand. They zeroed in on the spinning cloud next and traced it back through space from where it emerged like a belch of smoke from a castle tower in a remote countryside.

"Holy crap!" yelled Dame Gabor. "I recognize that tower. It was the old palace of the Third Kingdom. I played a couple of shows there for the old king, but it burned to the ground a couple centuries ago." She clicked her teeth. "Terrible acoustics."

Alias checked the coordinates. "You're right. That's exactly where it is. They built the new palace on the same spot."

"Can you zero in?" Christophe studied it from every angle. "It looks vaguely familiar, but I can't be sure."

"Geesh!" said Dame Gabor. "Didn't they teach the non-royals anything back then? It should have been part of your history class."

Alias cut them off. "Never mind all that. Why did Captain

Hersey, or whoever she was called back then, get expelled from the palace of the Third King as a ten-year-old? This is getting very complicated, and a little close to home for me."

"Well, she must have been a bad girl," said Dame Gabor. "Because that's how the old king punished people back then. Threw up a funnel cloud and sent them off. Poof! Just like that." She turned to Christophe. "Kind of like that trick you taught Alias."

"I wish the Time Cube could take us inside the castle," said Alias. "But for some reason, we're blocked out. I'll have to put that on my bug report for the next update. At least we've found a connection. Now, let's go forward from the shipwreck."

"You can jump straight to New York City. Remember? I already traced her to an apartment at Sixteen West Eleventh Street. The name on the buzzer was Célia Gabriella Hajdu, if that helps."

With that tip from Christophe, they quickly found Célia Hajdu and easily tracked her as the owner and principal entertainer at Gabriella's bar, and then moved later to an apartment at One Fifth Avenue. He wanted to find something more current, so he kept the Fifth Avenue location but changed the time to the present and rewound from there. He heard snoring and turned to see Dame Gabor leaning back on her chair with her eyes closed and her mouth open.

He also noticed Christophe's blurry eyes. "I think we're ready for a break. We still have to find Györfi and follow him around."

Christophe elbowed Dame Gabor and she jerked

upright. "I wasn't sleeping," she cried. "I was just resting my eyes. I'm one hundred percent paying attention."

While the picture continued behind them in slow motion, Alias and Christophe shared notes. It was impossible to know anything further about what happened to her in the Third Kingdom, but they agreed that she must have taken the mother's name HerSea, which had been anglicized to Hersey.

The monogram on Hersey's chests consisted of the letters CGH, so they surmised she was born Célia Gabriella Hajdu, which made sense, since the name was Hungarian. But the monogram could work using either surname. The *arbara* in the chests was obviously how she'd come to extend her life. The Keeper of the Dust had discussed that aspect of the element in his journal.

At some time during her life in New York, she became a singer. Alias could verify from the record album he'd seen in Györfi's room, she'd performed under another Hungarian name, Zsa Zsa. What they couldn't figure out was why she had been after Zsombor and Greta, and what she was doing controlling the Third King.

"Would you guys come and take over?" asked Dame Gabor. "I've been staring at this while you were yammering away, and it's worse than watching paint dry, though of course, I've never done that. I'll bring you up to date. Your lady friend has a gentleman caller, and all he's been doing is writing on paper she keeps giving him. Page after page of something I can't get close enough to read. He's been drawing diagrams and stuff too. Worst date ever."

Alias looked up and his jaw dropped. "Györfi!" He kept his eyes glued to the scene. It appeared Györfi and Zsa Zsa were having a heated discussion, and not for the first time, Alias wished the tech had an audio feature.

Györfi reached for her goblet and finished her drink. She bristled and flicked a finger, which slammed Györfi back down on his chair. He brushed all the papers off the table and glared back. Then she walked up to him and pointed her finger in his face. He grabbed at her throat with both hands as if he was trying to choke her, and when she pulled away the chain of her necklace broke and he ended up with her red pendant in his hand.

She flicked her finger at him again, but nothing happened. He held out the pendant and grinned, and she sat back down. He waved his hand in the air and the lights went out.

Alias fast-forwarded, but the living room was empty from then up to and including the present day. He switched perspectives to the skate park on the day of Christophe's accident. While Christophe was skateboarding in the background, they watched Györfi or Célia Gabrielle HerSea Zsa Zsa Hajdu, or whoever was masquerading as the Third King arrive at the skatepark.

That person checked visual coordinates to find the exact spot and snapped her fingers to create the hole. She jumped in and stayed below for close to a minute before she came out and rechecked her location. She peered back down and shook her head. Then she planted the fairy wing guillotine.

CHAPTER THIRTY-SEVEN

"So do we agree that it could be either of them controlling the Third King?"

"At this point, I don't see a clear pick. Györfi certainly seemed to have the upper hand when we left them in Zsa Zsa's apartment, but I would never underestimate the woman. We've seen the tables quickly turn for her before. Besides, I'm sure she was wearing the red pendant when I met with her."

Gabor asked a follow-up question. "But who do we think the Third King will come after next? Alias, out of revenge? Or Christophe, for some other reason?"

She, Alias, Christophe, and Stefán were huddled in the living room of Alias' compound planning their next move. Their first had been removing Christophe from The Fairy Kingdom and bringing him to the safety of the compound.

"I don't think she was after either of us. I could see me maybe being a threat, though she'd have to be quite para- noid to believe that. And no offense to Christophe, but why would she have been after him? He's one of their own, one of their heroes, etcetera, etcetera."

He rubbed his chin. "I believe she was running out of *arbara* and came here to get more." He turned to Christophe. "How many chests of rocks did we find? Nine, wasn't it? That's the same number they buried, which means they hadn't been touched until we found them. We watched them unload thirteen from the ship, and we saw her take four with her, so those numbers add up."

"I see where you're going, Alias. Let me help," said Christophe. "Based on the amount of *arbara* in each rock, I'd say conservatively she could get fifty-plus years per chest. So, yeah, she'd be running low."

"And when she didn't find any, she put the guillotine at the bottom in case whoever dug them would notice the new hole she dug," said Dame Gabor. "Hey, I'm getting good at this."

"Györfi may have hoped I'd jump in, to get even, but I believe she's changed her target. You should've seen the look on her face when I told her how easily Christophe could control the wind and conjure up funnel clouds. If whoever is in the Third King's body believes they are king, then why would they fear the power of a lesser fairy?"

Stefán walked to the windows overlooking the pool. "I'd like to take that question one step further. I'm obviously not from the Third Kingdom, so maybe I'm missing something, but why do you suppose she can't do the things Christophe can do? You know, if she's really the king?"

Christophe threw his hands in the air. "So you're telling me that she's really after me, now? Geez. As if she hadn't done enough."

"So what do we do now?" asked Dame Gabor. "We need a plan."

"What we need to do is rescue the real Third King and draw out whoever has taken control," said Alias.

"Do you think we can even save her? Zsa Zsa or whoever has probably been sucking out her soul the whole time, and I wonder if there would be anything left," said Stefán.

"I'd like to set a boobytrap of our own," said Christophe.

Alias paced the living room floor. "Let's stay on that idea. What if we lure her in with a Christophe lookalike and get her cornered? I'm stronger than she is, and with Christophe and Stefán with me, she wouldn't stand a chance."

"What about me? I want a job." Dame Gabor cocked her head toward Christophe. "Something besides a barmaid."

They brainstormed for the next hour, and when they were satisfied with their strategy, Dame Gabor gave them all hugs. "We better survive this crazy plan," she said. "I won't forgive any of you if you die on me."

"Are you worried about tomorrow?" Christophe asked after the others had left.

"No," said Alias. "Not when I have you by my side. Hey? How about we go out and feel the wind on our faces for a bit?"

"I could never say no to that, but it's going to be weird being carried."

Alias lifted him up in a bridal style. Then he popped his wings and carried him out over the ocean. They'd been enjoying the wind on their faces for a while when Christophe spotted a strike of pink heat lightning.

"There's your heat lighting, right on time. It really does seem to know when you're out and about."

"Yeah. Feeling the electricity all over is such a rush. I wish I could take you directly into it."

"There you go wishing again. You don't have to remind me it's only for Highnesses."

They flew back toward shore, but just before they got to the compound, Alias dropped down on the small beach beneath their house at the bottom of the cliff. After he helped him stand, Alias positioned Christophe to face him.

"I want to get something off my chest," he said. Even in the dark he could see Christophe's face turn ashen.

"W-what?"

"This." Alias unclasped his pendant and slipped it around Christophe's neck. "It brought me closer to you, and it found us two more elements. So I want you to have just as much good luck." He kissed Christophe. "You came into my life and made it more beautiful than I could ever have imagined." He got down on one knee. "And I want it to last forever. Will you marry me?"

Christophe blushed and looked out at the heat lightning. "You are such a charmer."

"Is that how they say *yes* in the Third Kingdom?"

"No. This is how we say it." He leaned in and kissed him. "Of course, I'll marry you. We make one of the great romantic tropes: mundane, average Joe falls for a superstar upper-class guy."

"Don't be ridiculous. There's nothing mundane about my skateboard champion!" They laughed and held each other. "Want to do it now?" Christophe nodded, and they held each other's hands and repeated the fairy marriage vows.

Christophe ran his hand through Alias' hair. "Now that I'm married, am I a prince? I don't feel any different."

"I suppose so. Why not? You've got the magic of one." Alias changed the subject. "Hey, let's go skinny dipping. I'll throw up a wall so no one can see us."

"Works for me," said Christophe. "But I hope wearing my pendant doesn't count as clothing, because I'm never taking it off."

When they finished swimming, Alias lay down on the beach, panting. "Let's rest for a minute, okay?" He closed his eyes.

Christophe joined him on the sand but lay in the opposite direction. He was still for a while, and after his breathing returned to normal, he gently nudged Alias' foot with his toe.

Alias brushed back with his. When Christophe curled his toes and caressed the bottoms of Alias' feet, Alias could feel his heart beating faster. He thought he could hear Christophe's beating harder as well. Soon, the bottoms of their feet found each other, and they pressed them together at the same time.

They kept their eyes closed too, and didn't see the white light that oozed like a liquid from the pendant stone. The light saturated Christophe's head and neck and traveled down through his legs to his feet where it seamlessly passed into Alias' and flowed up and made a circle around his head.

Their breathing became shallow, and their heads sank

into the sand from the sensation of complete bliss. Out of the blue, Christophe began to hum a melody.

"Oh man, you're giving me goosebumps," murmured Alias. He hummed along with the melody too, until they got to the chorus and Christophe's quiet humming segued to quiet singing.

"Are you lonesome tonight," he crooned.

Alias joined in the tune. "Do you miss me, tonight?"

With their feet still together, they sat up and belted out the next line. "Are you sorry we drifted apart?" They snickered at Christophe's funny and exaggerated vibrato.

"How did you know that song?" asked Christophe.

"Györfi used to play it all the time. How do you know it?"

A crackling sound came from the bottoms of their feet, and they opened their eyes at the same time. Moonlight illuminated the astonishment on their faces, as the shock of recognition turned to joy at their reunion.

"Alias. You're *that* Alias! My first crush." Christophe's eyes misted.

Alias let his tears flow. "And you are mine, Your Royal Highness." He bowed, and when his gaze landed on the pendant he'd given him as a wedding gift he smiled. "Looks like I married a king."

Christophe stood and rubbed his hands over his face and chest. "You know. You're absolutely right. Not only am I a king. I'm the Third King."

Alias laughed. "You sure are, and by the way, you're naked on the beach. Let's get dressed and go home."

CHAPTER THIRTY-EIGHT

Célia Gabriella Hajdu never imagined that she'd find herself commanding an entire fairy kingdom from a beanbag throne, but plenty of unpredictable things had happened in her long, long life.

She could've done plenty of damage by possessing any number of fairies, but she was greedy. Ordinary fairies didn't have the same power-boost as the royals, she'd come to learn. If she was going to tear down the entire species and cause them to go extinct, she needed as much power as she could get her hands on. And after spending four centuries getting her way, she'd developed high standards. She wanted to be a king.

It's why she had gone after Zsombor when he was a prince. She'd learned his father was very ill and that he'd soon take the throne. She also learned that he was enamored with Greta, whom she made a target, and whose willpower she'd underestimated. When Greta, Alias, and Zsombor humiliated her at the top of Hersey Lighthouse, a tower that she had built and named after her mother, she vowed to get even.

She knew that Theos and Zsombor were too strong, and her chances of winning against either were slim. When Györfi had told her that the new Third King was vulnerable, Célia was thrilled. It meant skipping over lower levels and going straight to the top. And taking over the Third Kingdom meant she'd come full circle, considering a former Third King had been the one who'd banished her and her family.

Györfi sketched out a psychological profile of the king that made clouding the girl's mind easy. If Célia played her cards right, revenge, power, status, and a head start on taking over the other two kingdoms were within reach. She'd have it all. Including the wings! For the first time, she would have her own gorgeous set.

She'd considered herself lucky that the Third King was reclusive. Not having to make public appearances made her transition easier. She was able to take over the girl's mind and test drive her body for a while, without the scrutiny of the public eye.

Célia reveled in her new power, but she could tell almost immediately that the Third King didn't have as many abilities as Theos or Zsombor. She'd chalked it up to a difference in biology or some other type of gender bias that put female fairies at a disadvantage, even the royal ones. She wondered where the power had gone when the girl's father died, though.

It burned her that Alias was only a prince, and he was far more powerful than she. Winning against him required something she had more of than he had: wiles.

When Alias made the mistake of mentioning that his floppy-haired friend, Christophe, could do things she couldn't do, she became suspicious that somehow the power of the Third King had been transferred to him.

And that meant either getting it back or eliminating him.

At five p.m., Stefán rolled Christophe on a wheelchair down the boardwalk to the door of the Second Third Kingdom. Dame Gabor walked at his side, carrying a medical bag. Thanks to the unlimited quantity of new fairy dust, they were able to levitate the chair up the long flight of stairs to the Palace Floor.

"My goodness. This does look exactly like the real palace," said Dame Gabor when they entered the grand foyer. "Christophe, you did all this? Wow! You've got quite the eye for interior design, wink wink." She shot Stefán a wry glance and poked Christophe in the shoulder.

Christophe yelped. "Of course I got it right. I spent half my life in that palace. And by the way, you're not supposed to touch me there, remember?"

"I wonder where they have you set up?" she asked. "As I recall, the library is off to the left and the reception rooms are on the right. The solarium is all the way at the end. I'll bet that's where she's going to put you."

A member of the palace staff approached to inform them that her Highness had made modifications to the library and that they were to take Christophe there. She would join them presently.

The library was an exact replica. The sofas, the walls lined with bookshelves, the clock on one of them that chimed the quarter hour, everything was identical to the library in the Third Kingdom palace.

What was different was that the two high-backed leather chairs that flanked the fireplace had been moved apart slightly to accommodate the hospital bed. They elbowed each other at the proliferation of unnecessary equipment. Surrounding the bed were monitors and intravenous feeding bags, and the types of tables and other equipment one would expect to find in a standard human hospital room.

Stefán and Dame Gabor were helping Christophe settle into the bed when the king entered. Her beautiful curls had been flat ironed straight, and someone had helped twist it up into a witchy looking, half-up bouffant.

She spoke directly to Stefán. "I trust that our setup here is more than satisfactory. As you can see, we went to great pains to ensure that Christophe would lack for nothing during his convalescence."

Stefán stepped forward and gestured to the equipment. "Then with all due respect, Highness, rather than set up all this, wouldn't it have been easier just to restore his wings? As his king, you could do that with a mere snap of your fingers."

The king glared. "And how do you presume to tell me what I can and cannot do?"

Stefán bowed his head. "Hmm. The power of the fairy kings is well-known among all the fairies. King Theos and King Zsombor demonstrate their abilities frequently in front of us all."

"Please, Stefán, show respect," Dame Gabor said. "Surely the Third King's magic would be as puissant as theirs."

The Third King clenched her fists. "Such disrespect to the sovereign would never be tolerated at my real palace. Theos and Zsombor have nothing over me. My magic is unsurpassed."

Stefán smirked. "Then perhaps you'd like to show us what you can do."

"I've had enough of your insolence." The Third King flicked a nail, and Stefán went flying across the room. When he slammed into the wall, books fell from the shelves onto his head.

Christophe held up his hand. "Stop. These hostilities are creating a negative environment for my recovery. Stefán, please apologize to Her Majesty."

Stefán stood tall. "I will not. I am not convinced she really is the Third King. Furthermore, Christophe, you have no right to give me orders."

Dame Gabor covered her mouth to muffle her gasp at his behavior. Her eyes darted between Christophe and the king to see who would make the next move.

"You're quite right, I don't. But I can evict you from my room," Christophe replied. He twirled his finger and a funnel cloud appeared around Stefán. "*Fstl, Fstl!*" he shouted, and the cloud disappeared. He slapped his hands together. "Okay. That takes care of him." He turned to the Third King. "Now, I'd like to get some rest, if you don't mind."

Dame Gabor caught the king blinking at the spectacle. "Pardon me, Your Highness, but judging from the face you made when Christophe sent Stefán packing, it looked to me like you'd never seen one of those little cyclone clouds before. Can this be true?"

"What I've never seen before is such rudeness." She looked over at Stefán and then to Dame Gabor. "How did I get surrounded by persnickety gay fairies and has-been actresses?" She flicked a finger and sent Dame Gabor sailing across the floor in the other direction.

Gabor stood and readjusted her cap. "That's all you've got? From where I stand, I'd say the Third King is kind of a one-trick pony. It looks like even Christophe, who is confined to a bed over there in critical condition, has more magic up his sleeve than you. Oh...and fun fact: Stefán may be a bit persnickety, but he's not gay."

Christophe rolled over on his side. "Your Majesty, I apologize for her behavior. This little one has been a thorn in our sides since she got here. But I'm too tired and in too much pain to deal with her right now. I fear that I upstaged you by dispensing with Stefán." He pointed at Dame Gabor who was standing defiantly with her hands on her hips. "So, would you do us the honor of conjuring up a cloud and sending her away, now?"

The Third King held up her finger, and as she twirled it, she noticed Christophe and Dame Gabor were watching her. When nothing happened, Gabor stuck out her tongue, and the king slammed her against the wall again. Then she pointed at a marble bust of King Stefán the First. It rose from the library table and fell on Gabor's head.

Christophe leaned on one elbow. "Look, I can't stand to see the old goat take such a big hit." He gave an exaggerated sigh. "Here, I'll do it myself." This time, he used his little finger to conjure a cloud and he did it lying down. The cloud engulfed Gabor, and after saying the magic words, he laid his head back and closed his eyes.

The Third King waited until he was snoring before she crept to Christophe's side and clamped iron leg cuffs on his ankles.

"I wonder why you were gifted with such power. Now, it's clear. You're the one." She sprinkled *arbara* on his forehead and then slowly brought her face toward him and pressed her lips against his. As his skin absorbed the red from the dust, red light filtered from his mouth into hers. She inhaled and took long, deep pulls of the red light like it was water and she was dying of dehydration.

Christophe moaned as though he was carrying on a conversation in a dream, but he didn't budge. When the red light began to flow on its own, she pulled her mouth away and let it find its way to her pendant which pulsated in sync with his breathing. Convinced of the steady transfer of his spirit, she lay next to him, smiled, and closed her eyes, knowing it wouldn't be long.

"Did you enjoy French-kissing my husband?"

She bolted up and saw Alias standing a few feet away. She looked back at the bed and saw that Christophe was still pumping out red. A quick check of her pendant brought a smirk to her face. She sneered.

"Yes. He was much more delicious than I guessed." She eyed his crown. "Look at you, all dressed up and pompous in your crown and all, Mr. Prince."

"Where are your manners, Célia Gabriella HerSea Zsa Zsa Hajdu? I'm waiting for you to bow."

"You should be bowing to me. I am a king." She flung another set of cuffs at Alias' feet, and when they snapped together, he crumpled to the floor. She laughed and kicked his ribs with her stiletto. "I'm so glad I thought to bring two sets."

Alias groaned and raised himself on his elbow. "You're so stupid. You've been wasting your time with the girl. Christophe is the real Third King." He gagged and collapsed on the floor.

She clicked her teeth. "Thanks for telling me what I already figured out. Geez! That idiot Györfi convinced me you guys were smart. If I had known that you were all benchwarmers, I'd have been king ages ago." She held up her pendant. "See? All done. There's barely anything left of him, now."

Alias' voice was barely audible. "You'll never get away with it, I tell you."

Zsa Zsa rolled her eyes and stood to leave.

"Not so fast!"

She looked up and blinked. Standing tall and fierce in the doorway was someone who looked like Alias. "And who the hell are you?" The new Alias smiled, and she walked back to the man in leg cuffs on the floor who she thought was Alias and kicked him again. "Then, who is that?"

The person on the floor stood and rubbed the spot

where her stiletto had punched him. Alias snapped his fingers and the fake Alias facade melted and Dame Gabor stood in his place. She smiled and took a bow.

Zsa Zsa yelled for the guards, and they came immediately but blocked her path out. "Get out of my way," she commanded.

"I don't think so," boomed a voice from behind the guards. She turned to see a person who looked like Christophe.

"This is getting ridiculous." Zsa Zsa shoved him aside. "I don't know why you think you can trick me, but you're too late to the party, and this is my palace now." She hooked her thumb to the bed. "I already sucked the Third King out of that sad excuse for a body, so, I really am the Third King." She chuckled. "You could say he passed the title on to me."

"The title perhaps, but not the power," said Alias. The man on the bed she'd thought was Christophe jumped up. Alias snapped his fingers again, and the Christophe character dissolved, revealing that Stefán had been playing his part. He glared at Zsa Zsa, and on his way to stand next to Dame Gabor he wiped the red from his mouth on his sleeve.

"You shouldn't be standing. I put iron cuffs on you."

"If you'd bothered to read the Keeper of the Dust's journal like I did," said Alias. "You'd understand how *sudf* counters the effects of *arbara* and iron."

"Yeah. Stefán and I drank *sudf* Cosmos earlier tonight in preparation for our roles, so the iron didn't faze us," Dame Gabor said.

Alias turned to Zsa Zsa and laughed. "And, in the right

amounts, the mixture can cause a bit of mischief. You'll see in a few minutes. In the meantime, let's give our two actors a big hand for making a fool of you."

While they bowed and Christophe clapped, Alias pointed at the cuffs on Stefán. "Speaking of iron." He snapped his fingers and they left Stefán's ankles. When they hopped over and clamped around Zsa Zsa's, they heard a blood-curdling scream and stood gaping when a young woman with curly hair peeled away from Zsa Zsa's body and fell to the floor in a clump behind her. Christophe recognized his sister's face and rushed over.

When she didn't respond to his shouts, he bent to check her pulse, and though it was very weak, he announced that he could feel it flutter against his fingers. He motioned to Stefán, who raced over and brought her to the hospital bed where he and Dame Gabor used the new fairy dust to revive her from the iron poisoning.

Zsa Zsa scoffed. "Good riddance, you twat! At least you were inside me long enough to turn me into a fairy, so thanks for that." She popped out red wings trimmed in a black lace pattern and made a runway strut toward the door. "I hope you're impressed. I think I wear them well."

Alias stepped forward and pushed out his massive, multicolored royal wings. Christophe stood next to him, and their two crowns sparkled under the lights of the chandeliers. "It took a while to track down all your aliases, Zsa Zsa, but we finally connected them, and here we all are."

She smirked. "Coming from a man whose name is Alias, I hope you see the irony in your insult."

"Touché," he said. "But now, sadly we must do away

with you, and please take these parting gifts from us." He tossed fairy dust in her face, and she choked. Then she lost control of one leg and stumbled.

Christophe leaned closer and threw more dust at her. She gagged and hobbled backward in retreat. As he was about to toss another handful, she slipped on a glove. Then she reached into her bag and flung a handful of iron filings at Christophe. "I've got some dust of my own to share." She cackled.

The layer of fine iron that covered his body sparkled and pricked his skin like a thousand bee stings. He fell to the floor and writhed in agony. Alias held up his hand and sent a force field that shoved Zsa Zsa through the doors and out into the hallway. Next, he pointed to a switch on a wall panel that activated a palace-wide grid of powerful electromagnets that he'd built into the ceiling along with the security system.

Stefán watched the filings lift away from Christophe's skin and up to collection points in the ceiling. Then he scooped him up and brought him to the sofa where he and Dame Gabor doused him with the new fairy dust.

Since the powerful magnets were designed to attract anything made of iron that may have been introduced into the palace, they also drew Zsa Zsa's leg cuffs, and the force pulled her feet to the ceiling, where she hung upside down and wriggled to get herself free.

But using her newfound fairy magic, she snapped her fingers and the shackles sprung apart. Then, as she dropped to the floor, she flapped her new wings and flew out of the library into the hall. Alias followed her and produced another force field that pushed her tumbling down the hall toward the solarium. She staggered to her feet and ran inside. With a snap of her fingers, she shut the doors behind her.

When Alias flung them open again, the room was empty.

CHAPTER THIRTY-NINE

Theos

So, Zsombor and I got taken for a ride. We'd both been suspicious that the new Third King kept trying to push the theory that Györfi was to blame for everything, but now we know that it was Zsa Zsa Hajdu talking, and trying to distract everyone from her own scheme.

What we didn't count on was that they were both in on it. Still are, as far as we know. That's going to make retribution twice as hard. At least we know who they are now, and what we're up against. Complicating things, though, is learning that at least one of them has become a fairy.

But that fairy is going to have to show its face one of these days. It'll need fairy dust for its regular therapeutic dustings, and by now all the high-test dust is regulated, and we know where every bit of it is.

Thank goodness for Alias' newest dust. It has improved the situation of fairies everywhere in countless ways by bringing back basic magic to everyday life. But it won't keep us alive. We still need to add yano, and we've only got thirty days left to find it.

CHAPTER FORTY

"How's my sister," asked Christophe. They'd moved her to The Fairy Kingdom several days earlier, and the staff was monitoring her coma-like condition. Stefán stopped by the pool, to give them an update.

"I'm sure you know I'm giving her my full and personal attention. Her vital signs remain steady, but I can only guess that the trauma of having someone else navigate her body did a number on her mind." Stefán reported. "So, we'll just have to wait until she decides to wake up. How are you guys?"

Christophe reached for Alias' hand. "Being together with your soul mate and one true love is the most amazing feeling on earth. By now, we both remember pretty much everything about our beautiful relationship that started as teenagers in the palace."

"But we're still mystified at his aunt's cruelty," added Alias.

"Yeah. My mother was the complete opposite," said Christophe. "And I'm grateful I inherited her genes, and not the heartless ones." His eyes focused on the snake cleaner that wiggled through the water in the pool. "But without wings, I have to say that I still feel like half a fairy."

"You've not been able to reproduce them? I assumed that as the king, you'd have the power."

Christophe shook his head. "Believe me, I've tried."

As Stefán was leaving, Dame Gabor came through the gate. "Sit back down, Stefán. I brought us each a Queen Greta Fairy Frappuccino."

"Whoa! You're patronizing Joe's again?" asked Alias. "I thought you were the one who always said we had to 'walk our talk.'"

"I still believe that. I also believe in redemption." She passed the cups out. "You'll never guess who made these for me." Nobody spoke. "All right, I'll tell you. Derek."

"Who's Derek?" asked Stefán.

"Derek is a wonderful young gay man who had the misfortune of being born Joe's grandson," said Christophe. "It's hard to believe that Joe even let him in his shop."

Dame Gabor popped the lid on hers. "I admit I did a double take myself when I went in and saw him behind the counter."

"But what possessed you to go in?" asked Alias.

"I was walking past the joint when I noticed a rainbow flag decal in the window and did a double take. Naturally, I stopped to see if I was mistaken. But there it was. And next to it was the sign that designates Joe's Java Joint as a 'safe place.' Can you believe it?"

"So, are there new owners, or something?"

"No. Derek told me that he couldn't stand keeping his friend Michael a secret, and he was also tired of his grandpa trying to pander to gays to get votes. So one day he just came out to him. He said Joe was flabbergasted at first, but he loved Derek so much that he accepted him. He even bought him a lavender apron and let him work the counter."

"Well, what do you know? Maybe it's time we started going back." Alias took a long gulp. "These are still fantastic."

———

They were in bed when Alias woke Christophe with a slow, soft kiss. Christophe looked out the window and pushed him away. "It's not even dawn," he groaned. "Lemme sleep."

"No, c'mon, birthday boy." Alias slid out of bed and tugged on his hand. "I made you a cake...from scratch." He led Christophe to the pool deck where a three-layer cake was ablaze with candles. "Make a wish," he said.

"Ugh. We don't have to go over that again, do we?"

"You're a king now. You can wish for things."

Christophe smiled and thought for a moment. Then he blew out the candles. "Now what?"

"Now, I'm going to grant that wish."

"How do you know what it was?"

"Trust me. I do." He scooped him up and popped out his wings. "Don't worry about eating the cake," he said as they flew away. "I guarantee you're not missing anything."

"Where are we going?" asked Christophe.

Alias snickered. "To the palace of my husband, the Third King."

They'd been flying for over an hour when the barest

hint of light pink peeked over the horizon. He flapped his wings and they soared higher, and when he saw heat lightning streak across the sky, he made a sharp course correction.

"We're making a slight detour," Alias said. "To pick up your birthday present. I think you'll like it."

He squeezed Christophe to his chest and straight toward the chaotic band of electricity. His nostrils flared from the increase in ozone as they got closer. Another swoosh of his wings took them right up to it, and he hovered in front of the gigantic, crisscrossing network of flashing reds. "It's time to grant your wish, Your Highness. Are you ready?"

Christophe was smiling like a schoolboy at the entrance to an amusement park. He held up his pendant, which had started shooting out laser-like beams of light. "This thing is going bonkers. Let's do it."

Alias turned and flew them in a wide circle to pick up speed. Then he gave one final exertion, and they shot forward and let the blinding light take them. The first lightning bolt streaked inches from their faces, and the deafening crack that exploded over their heads rocked Alias backward. He screamed when he felt his hands let Christophe go, and he had to shield his eyes from the massive pops and blazing bursts of light that followed.

Alias had made hundreds of trips into heat lightning, and though he struggled a bit this time, he was in his element and knew how to maintain his position in the air. A small strike of electricity slashed the sky, and the momentary flash of light allowed him to catch a glimpse of Christophe suspended in the air nearby, buoyed by wild winds that lifted and tossed him around. When the prolonged thunder boomed, he watched Christophe's body jerk from the pounding vibrations that pummeled him from every direction.

A single streak of pink lightning struck his pendant, and the stone responded with a brilliant burst of dazzling kaleidoscopic colors that spun around and enveloped him with such an intensity that Alias was forced to squeeze his eyes shut again.

He felt fingers interlacing with his, and when he opened his eyes he saw Christophe hovering next to him under the power of colossal new wings the color of monarch butterflies. Alias took his other hand.

"Follow me," he said. "Your birthday party isn't over. And I see you're dressed for it."

They touched down at the palace of the Third Kingdom, where the entire staff was waiting to give them the full royal ceremonial welcome. They had prepared an elegant banquet along with an enormous birthday cake, which Alias assured him had been baked by the palace chefs and would taste far better than his. Following the feast, he led Christophe to the library and kicked off his shoes.

"I thought we might pick up where we left off," he teased.

Christophe was about to lie down on the side of the sofa that had always been his, when the clock chimes striking the hour drew his attention to the bookcase. He walked over and opened the door to Györfi's old rooms and motioned for Alias to follow him up.

He laughed. "I want to be sure we're alone."

The man's clothing had been folded and stacked on the dresser top, and his books and papers had been organized into neatly stacked piles on his desk. They searched the other rooms in the suite, and when they found them all empty, they gave each other a thumbs-up and went back down.

Christophe grinned when he closed the door and heard the latch click shut, and then they hopped back on the sofa to resume a highly anticipated toe wrestling championship. After a few intense minutes with no clear winner, the exertions of the day got the best of them and they stopped wrestling. Content to be together again with their first loves, they pressed their feet together and drifted off into a half-sleep.

Alias heard the quiet click of the door latch first. He jerked up and cupped his ears to listen. Then he poked Christophe and raced to the bookcase.

"It's open!" he shouted.

He yanked the door the rest of the way, and they raced up the steps. Györfi's clothing and items from the desk were gone, but they gulped when they saw Zsa Zsa Hajdu's album cover on the floor. Someone had scribbled over her face with a black magic marker, and her vinyl records lay broken in pieces and scattered on the carpet.

THE STORY CONTINUES

The story continues with book four, *Summer Cyclone,* coming soon to Amazon and Kindle Unlimited.

AUTHOR NOTES

MAY 27, 2023

From characters, to locations, to plot points, to playing footsie, much of what I've written in *Summer Lightning* is very personal, beginning with the main character, Alias.

Some have suggested that he's autobiographical. If they're referring to his personality and his longtime struggle with sexual identity and adjacent insecurities, I'll plead 'guilty.'

Descriptions of his good hair and buffness, though I'm afraid, fall under the category of aspiration. Alias, the beautiful will probably always be my alter-ego.

If you are an author of fiction, somewhere along the line someone will give you a mug or a t-shirt inscribed with a warning that goes something like this: *If you're not careful, you'll end up in my novel.* Call them gag gifts if you like, but I'm here to say that my books are filled with characters from my past who weren't careful.

One of them was my high school chemistry teacher. If you sat through his class with me in the sixties, you couldn't ignore the resemblance between our teacher and this book's villain, Mr. Györfi. Both were smart and terrifying and egomaniacs, but they forced us to think. And, like the young boys' tutor, our chemistry teacher often flailed his arms to make his points more memorable, which is why that after all these years, I'm confident that I could pass his final exam.

One day he departed from speaking about valences and carbon chains and gave us a lecture on the subject of <u>Louis Pasteur's famous quote</u>, "Chance favors the prepared mind." We'd never seen him so animated, as he danced around the room promising that we would never hear a more valuable lecture from anyone in our lifetimes. The young royals react the same way when Györfi presents that same lecture to the boys and makes that same guarantee.

And my teacher and Györfi were both right. Despite rolling my eyes from the back row at his nutty behavior, my teacher's over-the-top presentation had secretly been searing Pasteur's words into my hippocampus. In fact, I drew on that nugget of wisdom throughout my life and found that adhering to the aphorism was responsible for many of my successes.

Giving credit where it's due, I honor my teacher by making his lecture a recurring theme in *Summer Lightning*.

So then why did I cast such a memorable teacher to whom I owe so much as the villain?

Easy. Revenge. He gave me the one and only detention I ever received in high school–for forgetting to lock my lab drawer after class...once, and I never forgave him.

Incidentally, the name Györfi served as payback to another person from my past, and Christophe was the name of a French photographer's assistant on a fashion shoot I led in Haiti. Feel free to speculate all you want about those relationships.

While many people consider obsessions to be negative attributes to one's personality, I consider all of mine a blessing, and this book is jammed with examples. Among them, secret stairways and hidden passages.

I encountered my first in a _Hardy Boys Mystery,_ perhaps my earliest obsession. It was fictional of course, but as my literary tastes evolved and I learned that the <u>secret stairway behind the fireplace</u> in _The House of the Seven Gables_ was real and open to the public, I was ecstatic enough to talk my parents into taking a family trip to Salem, Massachusetts, just so I could see and touch it firsthand.

Given that Mr. Györfi was the boys' tutor, entering his through a secret door in the palace library bookcase seemed appropriate.

Fun fact: My university German professor also had a secret door in his home library's bookcase.

Locked and unmarked doors that one passes by while touring monuments and castles have fascinated me every bit as much. You may recall in the previous book, _Summer Storm,_ that Greta was equally curious about what went behind some of those unmarked doors she passed on her way down the winding stairways below Alias' mansion at the top of the cliff.

Spoiler alert: I'm not done with them. You'll see a different take on secret entrances in _Summer Cyclone,_ the fourth and final book in the Magic at Myers Beach series, as well as in nearly all my upcoming thrillers.

The Sargassum algae situation in the world's oceans is

very real. As a lifetime beach nut and a former boater, I'd first encountered the prolific algae years ago in the Yucatan Peninsula. It was only on my recent trip to St. Martin in the French West Indies that I witnessed the extent to which the growth has gotten out of hand.

Unlike seaweed, which finds its way into food and cosmetics, scientists have yet been unable to find a use for Sargassum. So, by turning it into a key element of fairy dust, I feel I am doing my part in saving the planet. Click on this link. You'll be amazed, and possibly sickened by the economic and environmental consequences.

A few days after researching my books in St. Martin's Orient Bay, I travelled to Paris, where I found the perfect spot near a skatepark on the edge of the Bois de Bologne for the Third King to materialize after being banished by his evil aunt. Location, location, location.

You may have guessed that I'm also obsessed with nobility. That began by reading wondrous tales about kings and queens in fairy tales and mythology, well before I was exposed to the Hardy Boys. It later came in handy in college, where peeking through the lenses of kings and queens was my secret weapon for nailing world history.

Oddly enough, instead of tiring from those fantasies, my fascination has grown, because as I write this, I'm experiencing royalty every day, firsthand.

A few more fun facts:

- Despite everyone else drinking martinis in the book, I don't. Not an obsession of mine.
- I've never been on a skateboard.

- If you try hard enough, you'll find the solution to the fairy dust formula everyone missed in the book.
- I named Hersey Lighthouse and the fierce pirate Captain Gabrielle Hersey for my talented assistant by the same name.
- I listened to 20's crooner Vaughn De Leath's recording of "<u>Are You Lonesome Tonight</u>" nearly every day while I was writing *Summer Lightning*.
- <u>Elizabeth Taylor</u> and I dined together at <u>Dominique's</u> in Washington, DC in the 90s. Her <u>White Diamonds</u> perfume ad has kept me in stitches for years.
- I've been a fan of the <u>Gabor sisters</u> since I was a child, and I was lucky enough to have dinner with Zsa Zsa and her mother <u>Jolie</u> in Washington, DC.

The saga continues with *Summer Cyclone*, the fourth book in the *Magic at Myers Beach* series, with a new and unlikely romance, the return of a favorite villain or two, and plenty of fairy dust. To learn more about what goes into writing my novels, subscribe to <u>my blog</u>.

ACKNOWLEDGMENTS

Thanks always to my publisher, Robin Cutler, for keeping my nose to the grindstone. To Gabrielle Hersey for carrying me over the finish line. To <u>Elias Black</u> and crooner, <u>Vaughn De Leath</u> for inspiration. To <u>Sean Daniel Giampietro</u> for his skateboarding expertise. And a nod to <u>Elizabeth Taylor</u>.

CONNECT WITH ALAN

Website: http://alanbgibson.com/

Instagram: https://www.instagram.com/alanbgibson/

Twitter: https://twitter.com/abgibson1

Facebook: https://www.facebook.com/alan.gibson1/

IMBD: https://www.imdb.com/name/nm6561512/

YouTube: https://www.youtube.com/channel/
UCYkZ6C1sv3Ha_bSfViw7Tzw

Amazon author page: https://www.amazon.com/stores/
author/B018UG2AS0

Summer Thunder, Magic at Myers Beach, Book 1

They call him Theos, the King, the handsome and charismatic reigning kite-surfing Champion of the World. But he keeps his real identity and his other title a secret... Crown Prince of a fairy kingdom.

While at a competition in Myers Beach he learns from his father that in an act of revenge, someone contaminated the kingdom's fairy dust supply and set off a pandemic. His father gives him the monumental task of making new dust, which includes finding new sources of its nine elements.

Lily makes and sells fairy figurines in her shop on the Boardwalk called The Fairy Kingdom. Though every day she assures her customers that, "Fairies sweep away bad dreams, make worries disappear, and grant wishes," she doesn't believe in fairies herself. Theos seems an unlikely customer for a fairy figurine, but when he buys one, he takes on a second mission–to convince her that they do.

She gives him a good luck pendant, which sets in motions a series of magical happenings that bring them together and reveal that the small California beach holds the keys to the fairies' survival.

Summer Storm, Magic at Myers Beach, Book 2
The clock is ticking as Theos' kingdom suffers increasing casualties from the contaminated fairy dust and the quest to find the additional ingredients to make a new supply becomes more urgent.

Greta the Witch, the shopkeeper next door to the Fairy Kingdom, longs for fame and fortune and a fairytale romance like her best friend Lily. She meets Dos, an attractive man who is not the royalty she was seeking, but his kindness and a mystical quality in his voice win her over.

But Zsa Zsa Hadju, a rival witch with look-a-like features complicates her budding love relationship and skyrocketing popularity.

Summer Cyclone, Magic at Myers Beach, Book 4
With only one month of fairy dust remaining and one more ingredient left to find, Theos, Lily, Zsombor, Greta, Alias, and Christophe must join forces to fight the ones who sabotaged their fairy dust and who continues to threaten the fairies who have relocated to Myers Beach.

Will the fairy dust Alias finally creates from all the elements be strong enough to succeed, or will it take a force even greater?

OTHER FLORID ROMANCE BOOKS

To be notified of new releases and special promotions from Florid Romance, please join our email list:

https://floridromance.lmbpn.com/about/sign-up-for-our-newsletter/

For a complete list of books published by Florid Romance please visit our website:

https://floridromance.lmbpn.com/